THE GULL CRY HOTEL

By Catherine G. Lurid

All rights reserved.
No part of this book may be reproduced or used in any manner without the prior written permission of the author, except for the use of brief quotations in a book review.

This is a work of fiction. Any resemblance to person living or deceased is purely coincidental.

Introduction

My favorite genre has always been detective fiction, especially the mystical kind. I've always dreamt of writing a murder mystery with a twisted plot and an unpredictable ending—one where the killer is anyone but the gardener. To say that I was apprehensive about starting this journey would be an understatement. But after three years of being a writer, the idea for this novel came to me naturally. It began with a title that just stuck with me and refused to let go. Friends and family would often sigh in exasperation: "Another story set in a hotel! The only thing more clichéd would be a hotel murder!" But the story wouldn't let me go. One day it settled inside me and started living its own life.

First came the gloomy atmosphere of the place where the events would unfold, aided by a relentlessly rainy autumn. Honestly, autumn in England is nothing but rain and fog. The morning starts with a white veil that lifts to the sky by noon, only to pour down again by evening. And it's like this every day. Northern Ireland is even more somber, so, slightly exaggerated, I found the perfect mood for my novel.

Then came the idea for the murder. The motives, the clues. However, soon enough I realized I'd have to write it almost backward, as I needed to investigate the murder first and then scatter the clues throughout the story. This part turned out to be the most challenging, and the more I complicated it, the more tangled it became. Like an inept spider, I spun a web only to get caught in it myself. At that moment, it felt like I was learning to write all over again, just like when I started my first book. That was when I understood that I was on the right path, as I am now the author of ten novels. Skill comes with practice; it builds up, and what seemed impossible eventually becomes easy and enjoyable.

Once the drafts of the main part were finished, I rushed to start my story. Honestly, I love starting novels. But I dread finishing them. It feels like the story drains you completely, like an insatiable vampire sucking your strength until the last drop. And it happens every time. Each time, it's exhausting. So much so that you unintentionally think, "God, this must be my last work!"

But time passes, and a new novel starts brewing in your mind. And it all begins anew!

In our novel, it all starts at Heathrow Airport. My first impression of it left an indelible mark on me, because that's where I first got to know England. Although the main events take place in Northern Ireland, the book is filled with England: descriptions of the country, its customs, and that specific mysterious atmosphere unique to the British Isles. There's a lot of my beloved London and a lot of me in it. I don't even know how it happened, but for some reason I endowed the main character with my habits, my phobias, and stories from my life. I wonder if you can guess which parts of it actually happened to me?

Well, I won't keep you waiting any longer. Enjoy your reading, and try to savor this novel for at least three days. Remember: it took me almost a year to write it.

THE GULL CRY HOTEL

Prologue

She sat in my office, waiting for her discharge papers. Her strong hands traced the stitches along the edge of her pajamas, and her eyes calmly scrutinized the report.

"How are your voices? Do you still talk to them?" I asked, peering at her with curiosity.

"I won't make up stories, Doctor. I still hear them," she replied quietly.

"So, how are we going to discharge you?" I placed a ballpoint pen demonstratively on the desk.

"I've learned to negotiate with them," she replied quickly and decisively. "Although I must admit, it would be inappropriate to call one voice a multitude."

"My dear Eleanora, what do you mean by that?"

"Before, there were five of them, now there's only one," she mumbled, avoiding eye contact.

"This is undeniable progress," I said, unable to hide my joy. "But what we're interested in is whether the most aggressive one is still there. Do you understand?"

"Absolutely. And I can confidently say that the most rational and logical one is the one that remains."

"How does that manifest?" I squinted.

"He doesn't like being cooped up, and we've agreed to have our conversations late at night. During the day, he doesn't show up at all." Eleanora's voice trembled, revealing her agitation.

"What do you talk about late at night, if you don't mind me asking?" I inquired without changing my tone. Eleanora's eyes were no longer darting around. Even though she couldn't withstand my gaze for more than a few seconds, she seemed focused on the even stitches, a reproduction of a Bosch painting on the wall to the right, and the pattern on the carpet.

"We talk about life and death, good and evil, eternal human values," she replied.

"Really?" I couldn't hide my surprise. "Who talks more in your nocturnal dialogues?"

It was evident that Eleanora hesitated with her response. However, she soon stated quite reasonably, "I talk more. But when I ask him to tell me something, he speaks quite a lot, recounting remarkable stories."

"What are these stories about?" I asked, closing the medical history folder, already almost certain about her discharge. We can't keep all schizophrenic patients; there are too many of them. Therefore, patients with a sluggish form of the illness can leave the hospital at the request of their relatives. We usually think that the mentally ill are primarily dangerous to society, but that's not true. More often they harm themselves and very rarely others.

"These are stories of humanity." Eleanora fixed her tea-colored eyes on my white clothes longer than usual.

"I'm sorry?"

"Stories from the history of nations. About wars, betrayal, death, violence ... About the horrors of the past."

I opened the pale lilac folder again. Both parents were historians, both associate professors in the history department.

"And how do you feel listening to these stories? Do they sadden you? Anger you, perhaps? Offend you?"

"They don't evoke any of those feelings in me. I'm a historian, just like my parents, and knowing the truth is important to me. So I simply write them down."

It seemed like the truth.

"May I take a look at your notes?"

My patient had been seeing another doctor before she was transferred to me just a couple of months ago. Eleanora pulled out a stack of notebooks from her cloth bag. The handwriting in the first one looked quite round, which was encouraging. The letters leaned correctly to the right, with hardly any sharp angles. The overall lettering didn't strain the eyes, except for the absence of sentence divisions. I couldn't find any full stops in the text and consequently not a single capital letter except for names. The most common punctuation mark was the dash, coming to the rescue in any attempt to complete a thought and structure it.

It was clear that Eleanora had done well in school and had written a lot in her life. The other peculiarities were quite natural for someone suffering from schizophrenia, as the literal translation of the illness is *splitting of consciousness*. This is why the patient futilely attempts to unite everything, avoiding the use of separating punctuation marks. In the struggle not to lose the integrity of perception, the patient's brain might even combine several words into one incredibly long one. My eyes caught a few isolated prepositions combined into words, but even this was more than normal for Ms. Maze. Overall, it was the text of someone afflicted with schizophrenia, showing no tendency toward aggression or violence, which was what I was trying to determine.

Suddenly, at the very bottom, in the middle of a word, a Cyrillic 'Ш' appeared more and more frequently as I flipped through the pages. It multiplied, and words that included this foreign letter were written in more sweeping and impulsive handwriting.

"Do you have notebooks from when all five of them were talking to you?" I inquired.

It was important for me to see the difference in her internal state between "back then" and "today."

When fragile Eleanora was first brought to us, she would switch between voices and threaten the staff with violence. She used to endlessly argue and contradict herself. Covering her ears, she would scream for all four of them to speak one by one and not enrage the fifth. An hour earlier, she had attacked her father with a knife, accusing him of spreading lies. But now, for the past four months, the patient hadn't shown any signs of aggression; she had behaved rationally and only spoken in her own voice.

"This one—maroon. It's a bit messy; I'll have to rewrite it. They were all yelling, interrupting each other," Eleanora shyly admitted, placing a cherry-colored notebook with crumpled corners in front of me.

My right hand trembled. The Latin script, which had become so familiar to my eye, now featured letters from various linguistic groups. There were o's crowned with umlauts, s's with cedillas and a's adorned with accents. Hieroglyphs and cuneiform script appeared less frequently.

"Are you sure you'll be able to decipher this text without assistance?" I inquired, feeling somewhat embarrassed.

"Of course. I'm a historian!" Eleanora repeated with a forced smile.

Well, in my opinion, progress was evident. In six months of treatment, it seemed that our mentally ill patient had managed to reconcile with herself. Moreover, her parents had been writing letters to the consul for two months, pleading for assistance in getting Eleanora back home. Nobody wanted to oppose it. It seemed that if she left these walls, it would only make things easier for everyone. I marked the date and signed the discharge form.

Pressing one of the buttons under the desk, I called for an orderly to escort her. Soon the door opened and a tall young man walked into the room. In the corridor, a white head appeared—the next patient was waiting there. As she passed him, Eleanora briefly looked into his eyes and immediately lowered her gaze, clutching the bag full of unique knowledge tightly to her chest.

"She, she … Haven't you seen?" exclaimed the man. He was in a straitjacket, which he began to struggle against as soon as they lined up at the door. The patient spat after Eleanora and, the next moment, began to chant a monotonous prayer, spraying saliva around his mouth. His gray, disheveled hair made him look much older than the thirty-six years indicated by his medical history.

"Untie me!" he almost ordered.

"Please, have a seat," I said calmly, ignoring his request, and gestured to offer him a chair.

"Then at least wipe my beard," he asked in a calmer tone, looking at the orderly. The sturdy guy removed a towel from his neck and wiped the patient's face. "Don't tell me you've discharged her!" Victor stared at me.

"What surprises you about that? She, by the way, has been behaving much better than you for a long time." I pointed my finger at him as if talking to a child.

"Really? You didn't see anything?"

"What exactly do I need to see?"

"How her face distorted!" He furrowed his brow genuinely.

"No, I didn't see anything. Next time you see something, you can tell me?"

"Simpletons!" The man exhaled with exasperation. "How can you be so blind?"

"If you could continue without insulting me, I would greatly appreciate it."

"But there's a demon inside her! What's wrong with you people? She needs to be tied to the bed and have a priest summoned, not discharged."

THE GULL CRY HOTEL

Chapter 1

The scent of slicked-back hair struck Anna and she turned towards the airplane window, grimacing at the rainy grayness outside.

Due to the storm, their takeoff had been delayed, forcing her to endure three long hours at Heathrow. In a futile attempt to make notes for a new chapter on her Android notepad, the first ninety minutes had already passed. Anna still couldn't hear any information about boarding, but she could clearly hear the lyrics from her neighbor's headphones, the playful shouts of an energetic little boy, and the angry protests of his father, all interspersed with announcements of delays and cancellations. She learned about who had lost whom and how much longer she would have to wait for the flight to Belfast—her flight.

Next came coffee in a cardboard cup, followed by another, until the machine was sealed with yellow tape when the coffee had run out. But after two servings of the less-than-appetizing drink, she had an urgent need to visit the restroom.

Anna slung her voluminous bag made of worn brown leather over her shoulder, adjusted her checkered travel blazer, and headed towards the restroom, following the signs. Having flown from Heathrow too often, she knew well that if the signs ever disappeared one day, the airport would become a labyrinth with no way out, as without arrows, symbols, and labels, no one would ever find their way.

"Damn Heathrow!" she exclaimed as she stopped in front of the never-ending queue for the ladies.

Anna Walker, the screenwriter of box office hits and the author of top-rated detective novels, leaned against the plastered wall and once again checked her notes on her phone.

The dim light flickered unpleasantly, instilling an odd unease in Beth's heart ...

"An odd unease," Anna murmured disapprovingly. *An odd unease ... Damn, that's just not right!*

The woman next to her shoulder loudly blew into a handkerchief, folded it to hide its substantial contents, and used a relatively clean edge to wipe her nose.

Slicky ...

Slicky unease, Anna typed quickly.

Waiting in line took nearly twenty minutes, and it enriched her notes with a couple more repulsive associations.

Returning to her seat, Anna found a sleeping man occupying the narrow plastic chairs. He lay sprawled across four of them, legs pulled up, his dark socks not faring well under the pressure of his big toes, which had poked through. Long, light hair covered the tattooed forearms serving as his makeshift pillow. There were various stains on his joggers, and the only neat thing about him was the rows of loops on his sweater.

Perfect for a murderer's disguise. Anna froze over the sleeping man. *Although it's better suited to describing a body tormented by a maniac ...*

"Would you like to sit?"

Anna was momentarily perplexed as the body she had just discovered tried to speak.

"Excuse me?" she said, not quite grasping the fact that the man she had just found was talking to her.

"Would you like to sit?" he repeated, replacing his legs and vacating the chair where he had just rested his feet, still in their tattered socks.

"Me? No, no. Don't worry." Anna gestured to dismiss the guy's notion that she wanted to sit next to him.

"No, please!" He seemed to have fully come to life and sat down, still hugging the backrests of the neighboring chairs.

"No, really ..." Anna hesitated. "I think my boarding time is coming up soon."

"Don't make things up." The stranger smiled. "There's no boarding! We're all stuck here."

His confidence left Anna dumbfounded and she, finding no valid excuse to leave, carefully settled onto the last remaining seat.

"Eddie." He extended a surprisingly clean hand.

"Anna." She paused for a moment but eventually shook it.

"Where are you headed?"

"Rathlin …"

"Rathlin?" Eddie frowned.

"It's an island off the coast of Northern Ireland."

"I know—the northernmost island off the coast of Northern Ireland." Eddie's light eyebrows rose to meet his hairline. "You can't find a more depressing place on this planet."

Anna forced a tight smile as her interlocutor bent his head, gathered his hair, and tied it into a messy knot.

"Flight 1418? To Belfast?" Eddie grinned.

Just what I needed! The company I have always dreamed of, Anna thought, but instead of voicing her thoughts, she simply nodded in agreement.

"What's your seat?" Eddie immediately went into action, extracting a folded boarding pass from his bag pocket.

"I don't remember—" Anna started to say when he blurted out, "28B!"

"3A." She breathed out in relief.

Eddie grinned again when a stern voice suddenly came over the intercom. Heathrow fell silent. Those who had been wearing headphones took them off, the ones scrolling through their phones glanced up, and even the crying babies ceased their monotonous wailing.

Without waiting for the announcement to finish, Eddie slipped his feet into his sneakers and started tying his shoelaces. Anna got up and slung her broad leather bag over her shoulder.

"It was nice—" she began to say, but Eddie interrupted her once again.

"If you get too bored, come join me in the back." He fixed his cunningly narrowed blue eyes on her.

This time her smile didn't quite come out as she'd hoped.

Anna managed to get ahead of the never-ending line, and after traversing the telescopic tunnel, she stepped across the threshold of the airplane.

3A—I'm in place! she exclaimed to herself, tossing her bag onto the overhead luggage rack before settling into her seat. She wasn't expecting anyone, so she gazed out of the window at the colorless rainy landscape. But the first to arrive wasn't even a passenger; it was his scent.

THE GULL CRY HOTEL

Anna couldn't stand the aroma of scented hair product mixed with pretty strong parfum. Without turning her head, she already knew—the man who had just taken the seat next to her was either a true trendsetter or had limited sensitivity to smells.

She reluctantly greeted her fellow passenger and then turned away to look out the window once more.

"Headed to Belfast for business?" Mr. Fashionista inquired.

"Yes." She nodded and resumed her previous posture.

Pheromones—the language our DNA speaks in hopes of finding something in common. Today, Anna's genetic code refused to converse with anyone, and she tried to cover her nose discreetly as she stared at her electronic notepad.

Outside, the wind was howling, crying out for justice, but the storm's efforts were in vain—Georges plunged a knife into his victim's lifeless body ...

Lifeless ... Anna sighed. *This is awful!*

"Is it still raining outside?" her seatmate asked, moving closer and peering out of the window. Anna froze, trying not to move and, most importantly, not to breathe.

Georges plunged the knife into his victim's paralyzed body. Anna corrected her notes.

Eddie greeted her cheerfully as he passed by, immediately assisting someone with their carry-on bag. Anna, for some reason, found herself staring at him, but Mr. Strong Perfume swiftly motioned for her to return her attention to the dreary landscape.

Passengers seated themselves, the rain eased, and the plane slowly taxied onto the runway. The Boeing gained speed and took off. It became stuffy during the ascent, and her seatmate's distinctive fragrance intensified. His hair, slicked with either gel or natural hair oils, emitted an overpowering almond scent. It enveloped Anna, entered her lungs, and made her feel nauseated. Her forehead grew damp, and the coffee she had drunk earlier began to creep up her throat.

As soon as the prohibition signs turned off, she quickly unfastened her seat belt, squeezed past the other passengers, and rushed to the nearest lavatory. However, it was already occupied. So she headed toward the back of the plane and soon unlocked the flimsy restroom door.

The cold water helped. It smelled like lemon essence in the tiny cabin. Not lemons, but their essence. For Anna, these were entirely different things. While lemons refreshed, their essence clung to the air and persisted until dispelled by a long walk in the open air.

She returned to the aisle, hesitantly approaching her earlier interrogator.

THE GULL CRY HOTEL

"Anna!" came a call on her right. It was Eddie. He was sitting like a king between two empty seats.

She waved warmly, surveying the available spots. Were there others somewhere else? But no, the faded plush seats encircled only this young man—all the others were already taken.

"Are you alone?" she asked assertively.

"There was a guy here, but he moved somewhere else. Would you like to sit with me?"

"What?" The wording left Anna momentarily speechless. "Although sure! Why not?" She gazed at her neighbor varnished hair, almost mirror-like in the artificial light.

"Window? Or by the aisle?"

"Window …"

And it wouldn't hurt if you, Eddie, moved to the aisle, she thought.

After taking a seat, Anna froze. Despite her new acquaintance's visual untidiness, he didn't smell of anything. Absolutely nothing. It pleasantly surprised and, given recent events, even impressed her. Actually, she was so impressed that she forgot about his tattered socks.

"Intrusive neighbors?" Eddie smiled, nudging her with his elbow for some reason.

"What?" This was already her second foolish *what*, with the potential to become a habit. "No, no … It's not about the neighbors."

"Not about the neighbors?" Eddie stood up and looked with interest at seat 3B.

"Sorry. I guess without some revelation, our conversation won't go anywhere."

"I'm all ears," he said, his eyebrows forming an ironic arch.

"Smells … I run away from smells."

"Mmm," Eddie muttered, looking like a psychoanalyst. "Osmophobia?"

"What?"

If she said that cursed "what" one more time, he'd think she was hard of hearing in addition to everything else.

"Fear, dislike of smell or odors," Eddie explained obligingly.

"Hmm, perhaps …" Anna blushed. "And what about you?"

"Me?"

"Yes. Do you have any phobias?"

"Plenty," Eddie asserted with absolute confidence.

"I'm burning with curiosity." Anna folded her arms.

"For example, hypengyophobia."

"What's that?"

"Fear of taking on responsibility," Eddie said matter-of-factly.

"Hmm, expected." Anna smiled.

"Expected?" Now Eddie folded his arms in protest. "What about papaphobia?"

"And what's that?"

"Fear of the Pope."

"All right." Anna chuckled. "Is there anything else besides the Pope?"

"Um …" Eddie pondered. "How about hippopotomonstrosesquippedaliophobia?"

"My goodness, what on earth is that phobia?"

"Fear of long words!"

Anna laughed heartily. "I think if you can't avoid the Pope, you're perfectly capable of avoiding long words in your life."

"Not always. In my work, they come up quite often."

"In your work?" *Does our Eddie have a job?*

"I'm a writer," he stated calmly.

"What?"

Another "what," Anna, and nobody in the whole world will believe you're a novelist!

"I travel and write for the *National Geographic*."

"What?" Anna covered her mouth, as she had just said it again. *You've written eight darn bestsellers and you still can't recognize someone from your own profession! Bravo, Anna! Simply bravo!*

"Actually, I never thought I'd become a writer. But after I ended my career as a professional traveler, I found a passion for telling stories about the remote corners of the planet, where the vast majority of people have never set foot, but where I have been. I still miss those places, but when I tell those stories, it's like going there all over again."

"But why did you quit?"

The answer to that question was one word: *Everest*. Eddie wasn't ready to tackle that story. He had started writing in an attempt to describe everything that had happened at the base of the highest mountain in the world. Five years had passed, but he hadn't written a single word about that fateful night.

THE GULL CRY HOTEL

Chapter 2

Eddie remembered that evening as if it were yesterday. How he had held the hot mug in his palms. He brought his wind-chapped face close to the steam and inhaled the aroma of black tea. The small ice crystals on his gloves were melting relentlessly, in the same way as the icicles in his thick beard and the snow in the folds of his knit hat. For lunch and even dinner there was pea soup from a tube, but how Eddie Farrel longed for a fried egg …

The orange of the tent was fading as a storm approached from the mountain. At noon, the bright sun still shone, and climbers held on to the hope of reaching Camp 2. It was dangerous to stay the night at C-1. This was where the Khumbu Icefall ended—the most treacherous section on the way to the highest point on Earth: Everest. But there was no other choice. That's how it goes with the eight-thousanders. Either you conquer them or they conquer you, and the latter happens far more often. Fortune favors those who turn back in time, calming their ambition and ego. Less fortunate are those who return with frostbitten limbs, not to mention those who never return at all.

***

THE GULL CRY HOTEL

"Can I have an experienced Sherpa?" Eddie, who had just arrived from Nepal, leaned on the counter of the information window.

"For which date?" the young Mongolian girl asked.

"Second of November," the mountaineer stated confidently.

She stopped typing and finally tore her gaze away from the monitor. "Second of November?" she repeated, seeking confirmation in Eddie's eyes.

"That's correct. Any issues?" he inquired.

Of course Eddie was aware of the local superstition. After the global madness known as Halloween, the Asian Night of the Dead begins. *Absurdity*, that was Eddie's opinion, and he had no intention of altering his schedule because of this.

"I'll make an inquiry, but as far as I know, no Sherpas will go up the mountain on that night."

"Why not?" He was definitely pushing boundaries.

"Because of all the dead …"

"Let's not dwell on that," interrupted Eddie, a sarcastic smile on his face.

The Mongolian girl said no more. She quickly filled out the form and sent it to the camp. Eddie waited for two hours, but none of the Sherpas responded to the request.

Well, if I have to go alone, then so be it. I'm quite used to it. Eddie got up from the wooden chair and hurried to catch the departing bus.

A day later, he ascended the folding ladder connecting the two peaks of the glacier flowing down the southern slope of Everest. They were named *peaks* out of respect for the Khumbu, but they were more like a thick layer of broken ice spanning fourteen miles, with giant crevasses and seracs reaching up to 100 feet deep. Even now, as he savored his tea, Eddie Farrel could still hear the clanking of carabiners, the scraping of crampons on metal, and his own heavy breathing. Every step was a choice between life and death. However, that choice was no longer his to make. He had made his when he had come to the base camp and begun climbing the mountain.

At sixty-five feet the white ice turned to celestial blue, while at the bottom of crevasses darkened the frozen bodies of mountaineers—those who were unlucky at the very beginning of their journey. Those who are left remain as a warning to madmen. Especially ones like Eddie Farrel.

He was the one who had conquered twelve mountain peaks over 26,000 feet in height. But it wasn't that which made him a madman; it was the fact that he had conquered nine of them alone and without supplemental oxygen. By the time he had reached the world's highest summit, he had lost the tip of his ear, and he could still feel the fused fractures on his ribs, which throbbed relentlessly during every storm.

The bodies at the bottom of the Khumbu were far from the last living monuments of Mount Everest. At different altitudes, frozen daredevils served as grim landmarks for climbers. For instance, at 27,800 feet above sea level, an Indian named Tsewang Samanla, known as Green Boots, was frozen solid to the rock. Wearing green boots on Everest is considered a bad omen, because if such a fashionista was to fall ill at this altitude and get stuck in the snow, no one would come to their aid. Everyone would mistake the poor soul for a corpse without noticing the difference. Next door to Tsewang for the past fifty years, on one of the slopes just 2,000 feet from the summit, Hannelore Schmatz has been sitting. The German woman conquered the peak but remained there forever. For several years her gray hair streamed in the wind and the glassy gaze of her lifeless eyes sent shivers down one's spine. Relentless storms had done their work, leaving behind Hannelore's bare skull, her body frozen in an unnatural pose.

Needless to say, it isn't without reason that the altitude above 26,000 feet is labeled the Death Zone—the zone where you're basically dying. At that height the air is so thin that even with supplemental oxygen, every minute you spend there is killing you. The brain becomes confused, and even small movements require Herculean efforts.

As a mad addition, every climber carries an astonishing amount of equipment. It's important, no doubt, to stay in touch with their families and loved ones, but most of all with the television crews to secure their moment of fame. Many perish due to the weight of their gadget-filled backpacks, but they can't be blamed for it. Fame is a normal desire for human beings. It's the driving force that pushes people towards the capricious slopes of Jomolungma, the power that makes them risk their own lives.

This would be true for the vast majority of peak conquerors, but not for Eddie Farrel. He enjoys being where no human foot has trodden. And he prefers that few people know about it. That was why no one had no idea where he was or what he was doing at that very moment. To some extent, Eddie did it to spare others unnecessary worry. On the other hand, he simply didn't care about the accompanying benefits of personal achievements.

The merciless Everest has claimed the lives of 304 daredevils. However, the official statistics hardly reflect reality. If Eddie never returned to the base camp, he wouldn't become the 305th victim. He hadn't registered his route, hadn't informed any journalists of his intentions, and hadn't managed to hire a Sherpa. If he was destined to get lost there, no one would go looking for him.

THE GULL CRY HOTEL

The tingling sensation on his skin had a calming effect. It was like acupuncture administered by the snow-laden winds. The tent tarp darkened and sagged. After hastily consuming the warm soup, a pleasant heat spread throughout his body, lulling him to sleep. His eyelids grew heavy, and his hands fumbled with the zipper of his sleeping bag. With a little more effort, Eddie would immerse himself in his down-filled kingdom. Fatigue triumphed over his remaining senses, and he closed his inflamed eyes.

The wind outside grew stronger, but it didn't disturb his slumber. Was there any point in worrying about the storm when it had already begun? Nothing could be changed. The tent might be buried in snow; an avalanche could sweep down from the slopes; the glacier could crack and rupture. In four out of five unlikely scenarios, Eddie Farrel would be a dead man. It was always better to fall asleep and never wake up than to die in agony, waiting for help in this place that had been visited by no more than 10,000 people in the entire history of mountaineering.

Slowly, Eddie's consciousness returned after a brief sleep. He had trained himself to wake at three-hour intervals, which meant that after assessing the situation, he would be able to sleep again for the coveted 180 minutes. Without opening his eyes, he could clearly hear that the storm persisted. The green glow of the night lamp seeped through his eyelids, while gusts of wind continued to tug at the left side of the tent. What did it mean? He wasn't drowsy; there was a chance he could tackle the thirty-minute task of clearing the debris in the morning. Suddenly, amidst the monotonous howling of the wind, a prolonged moan reached his ears.

"Wolves!" Eddie opened his eyes and freed his hand from the sleeping bag.

He twisted the dial of the camping lamp and hunkered down. The mountain gathered strength and unleashed a new gust, depositing an extraordinary amount of snow onto the tent. The howling wind gave way to a guttural groan that seemed to emanate from somewhere very close by. Eddie knew what animal sounds were like—the bark of a dog, the howl of a wolf, even the growl of a bear. But the sound that approached his fragile tent couldn't easily be attributed to any of them.

Steps. The crunch of snow as someone slowly made their way through the storm. Eddie was momentarily paralyzed. His body lost its tone, while his heart, on the contrary, beat like a wound-up toy. Someone stopped right at the entrance and shuffled in place.

"Is anyone alive?" came a voice from outside.

Eddie let out an audible exhale. He leaned forward and switched on the nightlight.

"Yes, yes! I'll open it now!" He bent down and pulled up the zipper.

THE GULL CRY HOTEL

The tent tarp fluttered helplessly in the wind, and in the green glow of the lamp, a smiling bearded face appeared. "Greetings! Can I come in?" The stranger raised an icy mitten into the air.

"Of course!" The mountaineer squirmed in his sleeping bag like a caterpillar inching away.

The giant squeezed himself beneath the low roof. His hefty frame occupied no less than half of the space. For a moment Eddie recoiled, regretting his act of hospitality. But someday it could be him asking for shelter, so it was better not to provoke fate.

"Boris." The burly man extended his hand, still concealed in a glove.

"Eddie." Farrel shook the firm, ice-cold hand and glanced at the camping stove. "Would you like some tea?"

"Only if it's from the thermos." Boris smirked. "Haven't you heard about the poisoning? Everyone at the 20,000-foot camp fell ill. Every single person!"

"Poisoning?" Eddie furrowed his brow. "What could you possibly get poisoned with up here?"

"Snow, my friend; plain old snow! First we noticed a strange smell as we melted it, and then there was an ammonia taste in the water."

"Ammonia?" Eddie's eyebrows shot up beneath the edge of his knit hat.

"Feces, dear colleague. Those masses don't just disappear. Tons of excrement flows down the slopes during the thaw. Well, we have nothing to be proud of. Humanity has poisoned even the most remote corner of the planet with its own excrement."

Numb with disbelief, Eddie could only swallow loudly. If this was true, he would have to turn back. The preparations, the training, and most importantly, the journey through the Khumbu—all would be in vain.

"So you came down seeking help?" He broke the silence, suddenly noticing that his companion had shrunk in size.

Eddie blinked. What a strange mirage. Just a couple of minutes ago, Boris had barely fit in the corner where he sat, and now ... now he was deflating like a balloon. Moreover, a puddle had formed beneath the man, and a droplet fell from his beard with a resounding thud. However odd it all seemed, the visitor was thawing, sitting there at Eddie's feet.

"Are you all right?" Eddie asked, observing the limp gloves and the withered trousers.

Boris's stomach gurgled. He didn't turn around. Now he sat completely still, seemingly lost in thought.

"Boris!" Eddie leaned forward, but his voice was drowned out by a dreadful gurgling sound emanating from beneath the visitor's jacket.

"You know, everything fades away: pain, sadness, misunderstanding. But this … this remains forever." At last he spoke.

"What?" Eddie rubbed his eyes.

"Cold! This infernal cold. It stays with you forever …" Boris's voice came out in a raspy whisper, barely audible over the howling wind.

"What are you talking about?" The mountaineer touched Boris on the shoulder, causing him to jerk and turn around.

The first thing Eddie Farrel noticed was the foolish smile on the bluish lips.

"Are you al—" He suddenly fell silent, noticing the vivid corpse-like patches on the man's face.

"I'm fine, really." Boris revealed his bloody gums.

His eyes had slightly clouded over, and strips of thin skin detached from his cheeks. He wiped his damp nose, the tip of which promptly fell off. It didn't seem to bother the visitor at all—he continued to wear his horrifying smile and stared at Eddie with lifeless eyes. New rumblings erupted in his abdomen, and he recoiled, releasing a putrid fluid from his body.

Ask anyone what smell is the most unbearable, and every living person will answer: nothing compares to the stench of death. There is nothing more repulsive than the rotting flesh of a human being.

In a daze, Eddie scrambled out of his sleeping bag and bolted out of the tent. The storm was subsiding, only sporadically tossing remnants of snow. But in his terrified state, Eddie failed to notice any of this. He ran blindly away from the walking dead that had dropped by for a visit in the middle of the night. The snow quickly clung to his woolen socks, slowing his pace. Before long, gasping for breath, Eddie found himself mired in a snowdrift. From behind, he heard a familiar haunting moan. It was a cry that did not belong to an animal but to a human. And this time, the traveler realized, the screaming figure was one of the risen dead, just like Boris.

The bloodcurdling cries grew louder, and Eddie felt the urge to break free, but a strong grip held him back. Someone long buried in the snowdrifts had come alive. They drew nearer, converging upon the unfortunate soul trapped in the snow. Stripped bare by merciless winds, frozen solid, forever trapped here—the undead. They did not speak like Boris. They seemed to have long departed from the realm of the living, completely losing their human form. Their moans still conveyed the suffering of a past that, once a year, became the present.

THE GULL CRY HOTEL

Rising from hell, they leaned over Eddie. Their long lifeless hair brushed against his inflamed face. The cold, bone-chilling fingertips scraped against his living flesh. It was only a moment before he snapped out of his daze and, letting out a wild scream, wrenched himself away from their grip. He ran again. Back towards the tent. It resembled a snowdrift, with the canvas triangle ominously glowing green. It was the only flicker of light in the unending darkness of this relentless nightmare.

The fugitive hesitantly approached and pulled back the flap. Inside, there was no one—only his crumpled jacket and a stuffed backpack. No corpse, no putrid liquid. Eddie dove headfirst inside and hastily zipped up the entrance. He dragged his hefty backpack to the door and twisted the lantern's flame shut. Darkness engulfed everything.

He exhaled into his trembling palms as the scratching on the tarp reached his ears. And then came the faint whisper, the indistinct plea of "let us in," and the wild howl that summoned all the surrounding undead. They continued to call out, all those who had once sacrificed their lives to forever remain a part of Everest's history. To forever remain prisoners of this mountain.

"Lord, save and protect." The atheist crossed himself, his sweating palms covering his face. "I have caused no harm to anyone. But even if unknowingly, forgive me for everything. Lord, save and protect. Lord, please, I'm begging you to save and protect my sinful soul."

With his face shielded in his hands, Eddie prayed as best he could. Perhaps in moments like these, his heart spoke more eloquently than ever before.

"Our Father, who art in heaven ..." slipped from his lips, a prayer he had memorized as a young boy. Not by choice, of course. It was his strong-willed grandmother who had insisted on it. Arguing with her was futile, and Farrel junior had surrendered.

"Lead us not into temptation and deliver us from evil. Amen!"

He repeated the words again and again. He didn't open his eyes and didn't fall silent even when the dead tore through the tent—when they surrounded him and began whispering incoherent words into his ear. He didn't cease his prayers even when slimy saliva touched his hand, accompanied by a putrid tongue and rotting teeth. Eddie didn't know what they wanted—perhaps to take his clothes or warm themselves with his blood. He screamed and prepared to die, but suddenly everything fell silent.

Through his fingers, a soft light seeped in. Instead of whispers, he heard the crackle of snow and the sound of oil sizzling on a cast iron skillet. A tantalizing aroma of scrambled eggs wafted through the air. Cautiously, Eddie opened his eyes. There was no trace of the storm. The tent remained intact, but the zipper was open. Its flaps swayed in the wind, welcoming the rosy haze of dawn.

THE GULL CRY HOTEL

Eddie swallowed hard and straightened up. Outside, someone was bustling around, crunching through the snow. The guest did not keep him waiting, and soon he beheld a lovely maiden's face. He screamed and huddled against the floor. Tremors racked his body. He was chilled to the bone, consumed by primal fear.

The stranger stood frozen, hesitating at the entrance. Dark strands of long hair fell over her turquoise jumpsuit, while a rosy blush adorned her cheeks. She smiled broadly and handed the bewildered man a plate of hot scrambled eggs and a slice of black bread.

"Who are you?" Eddie croaked and immediately coughed.

"Jacquie." The girl took off her glove and extended her hand for a handshake. "Jacqueline."

He didn't rush to accept the eggs or respond to the gesture.

"How did you end up here?" He glanced at the snow, searching for the walking dead.

"I'm descending from the summit!" Jacqueline declared proudly.

"Descending? Alone?" Eddie's tongue struggled to move.

"I got left behind at C-2. So I'm making my way down to base camp alone." The woman sighed in frustration.

"But you can't cross the Khumbu alone." Eddie continued the conversation, attempting to reassure himself that Jacquie wasn't a figment of his imagination—that she was truly here, preparing food for him, and most importantly, that she was a living human being.

"But you crossed somehow, didn't you?" She pierced him with a cunning gaze.

Eddie held his breath, captivated by her immense blue eyes.

"I crossed Greenland, Antarctica, and the Gobi Desert all alone," he mumbled and began examining the scrambled eggs.

Jacqueline laughed and placed the plate at his feet. "I'm really scared," she whispered. "I was hoping you were also descending. Would you escort this girl to the camp?" She blushed even more than before.

Eddie wanted to give a coherent response, but after sitting for a moment with his mouth agape, he involuntarily averted his gaze.

"I understand. We all come here with one purpose—to conquer Everest." A sad smile flickered across her face. She extended her hand to Eddie once again and added, "While the weather is good, I must go. Perhaps we'll meet again down below."

THE GULL CRY HOTEL

"It was a pleasure ..." Embarrassed, he couldn't find the right words. "Thank you for the egg. I've been dreaming about it since base camp."

"You're welcome! If you don't start to eat, they'll turn into a block of ice, just like everything around here." Jacqueline winked.

"Thank you, but how did you manage to cook them?" Eddie gave her a surprised look.

At the same time, she turned towards the exit. The turquoise jumpsuit was torn on the back. Through the cut he could see a wound that extended from her neck to her middle, exposing shattered vertebrae, bloody cartilage, and ligaments hanging by threads.

Eddie suddenly felt unwell. His stomach started to pulsate, and a flush spread across his face. The young woman disappeared, along with the plate of scrambled egg. Eddie was hardly able to catch his breath. He hesitated for a long time before getting up. He rubbed his weakened knees, massaged his temples, and slapped his cheeks.

"What was that?" Eddie tried to dispel the horror from his face. "Could it have been an illusion? Hallucinations usually start much later, at a higher altitude."

However, the horrifyingly realistic vision wouldn't release its grip. Eddie could swear that all of this had happened to him—Boris, the resurrected dead, and the tragically deceased Jacqueline.

He stepped out of the tent. The smooth expanse of snow shimmered with the pre-dawn blue. There was no trace of a campfire or stove. Eddie Farrel turned towards the glacier and froze, foolishly scanning the vast expanse, searching for a lone figure on its surface. He cleared the snow from the tarpaulin, gathered his belongings, and set off. However, he wasn't heading for the summit of Everest; he was heading back to base camp through the Khumbu Icefall.

With disappointment he distanced himself from his lifelong dream. He wasn't in the best condition for the ascent. He was tired and freezing. But above all, he was frightened. Did it seem to him that he was going mad? Oh yes! It seemed so more than ever.

By evening, he was back at base, where news had arrived of a fatal poisoning at C-3. The ascent route on the southern slope had been closed. A search and rescue team was evacuating survivors. The memorial board of the deceased was being updated daily, and as Eddie examined the photographs, he suddenly saw a smiling girl in a turquoise jumpsuit.

Jacqueline Smith, the caption read.

She looked at him from the photograph with her huge blue eyes. The girl who had conquered Everest just a month ago. She had only to cross the Khumbu Icefall, which she never did.

Chapter 3

"I'm just tired of risking my life," Eddie replied formally, rubbing his palms as if they were once again gripped by the icy chill of death. "What about you? So, what's your line of work?"

"I'm a writer too, but I specialize in fiction."

"No way!" Eddie exclaimed. "How did you start writing?"

"Well, I've always loved reading. I started to read even before school. During that wonderful period, so many stories resonated in my imagination, inspiring me to start creating my own. Once I learned to write, I started crafting small paperbacks, stitching notebook pages into makeshift books and filling them with thrilling detective stories. The books were a hit, first among my classmates and then with the whole school."

"Amazing! So you're a born writer!" exclaimed Eddie.

"Well …" Anna hesitated. "I'm really counting on it."

"Come on, stop being modest! I'm burning with curiosity to read one of your earliest books," urged Eddie.

"No, not that one! The very first book started like this: Once upon a time, there was a girl who lived on the fifth floor of a three-story mansion."

Eddie burst into laughter, wiped away a solitary tear from the corner of his eye, and looked at Anna with an entirely different expression. He genuinely liked her. With all her deliberate writerly mannerisms and introverted aura, there was still a little girl inside.

"All right, all right! Where can I find your books? Something contemporary if possible." Eddie smiled.

"Just look for Anna Walker's books."

"No way!" It was the second *no way*, and it was Anna's turn to surprise Eddie. His thoughts raced. "I read it! *The Mysterious Tale of Eleanor Maze*."

Anna shuddered. It was more than just a story. It was her first book—the sensational tale of how a mentally unstable girl one night brutally murdered her parents. Perhaps Anna would have been less frightened by this novel if it hadn't been based on real events recounted to her by a doctor at a psychiatric clinic on the outskirts of London. On that rainy day, her first mystical detective was born, and the book later became a bestseller—a ladder to the sky in which a star named Anna Walker lit up.

"To write something like that is the height of professionalism. For a moment I thought it was simply impossible to come up with a story like that." Eddie continued to admire her as Anna became more and more uncomfortable. "It's based on a true story, isn't it?"

"Well, we may say inspired by ..." Her mind traveled back to that time. She could clearly hear the heavy raindrops drumming on the windowsills, echoing in the long corridors of the old building. She followed the orderly up to the first floor, walking beneath the lofty Victorian arches. It might have felt like she was strolling through a museum or admiring ancient architecture if it weren't for the window grilles and the distant cries of the mentally ill. Listening to their incoherent pleas, Anna didn't notice when the orderly stopped at a door painted white. It creaked open, startling her.

Anna stepped into the dimly lit room. There was a colorful patterned rug and a shelf full of medical books. By the window stood a writing desk, and opposite was a medical couch equipped with sturdy leather straps. She swallowed hard, taking a few determined steps toward a vacant armchair to avoid looking at the couch, which resembled more of a torture device than anything else.

"Good evening, Miss Walker. How are you?" A tall woman in a medical gown rose from her armchair and extended her hand.

Anna returned the handshake. "Good, thank you."

"You look frightened."

"Well ..." Lowering her gaze, Anna sat down and concentrated on finding a comfortable position in the plush armchair.

"And it's better to be," Dr. Judy Richter continued, taking her previous seat. "That which I agreed to meet you about is information that has never left these walls." Dr. Richter pressed her crimson lips together and adjusted her short blond hair. "If you ever mention me in press releases or interviews, I will deny any involvement. Is that clear?"

Anna nodded.

"I apologize for my rudeness." The doctor softened. Anna was far from behaving like a reporter. "I've survived one scandal. I don't need another. I promise to tell you the whole truth, but in return, I ask for a promise—you won't mention any real names, and you'll always refer to it as a product of your imagination. I've never given you an interview. You've relied on newspaper clippings and archives exclusively."

"Of course. I'm a fiction writer."

"Good, good ..." The psychiatrist let out a heavy sigh and nervously shuffled a stack of papers on her lap. "Once you step into it, you'll never come back," she said. Her eyes appeared genuinely concerned. "Going insane is truly terrifying. Moreover, you'll never realize that it has already happened to you. That's the cunning part of madness. People around will seem strange, their actions devoid of logic, their behavior unjustifiable. But in reality, it will be you who has gone insane, not them. That's why I agreed to this interview. Perhaps I can share this burden with someone else."

"I understand. It's as terrifying as death," Anna blurted out inadvertently.

"As death?" Dr. Richter exclaimed. "I assure you, madness is worse than death." She pulled out a pack of cigarettes from the drawer and lit one without asking for permission. "At least because your madness can bring death to others," she said, this time more calmly, exhaling a cloud of smoke. "Losing yourself is much worse than death. Why do you think the clinic, much like a prison, is surrounded by bars? The mentally ill cannot escape through the window on the fourth floor, but they can jump from it because they are no longer capable of living in a world they cannot share with their family and loved ones. Their reality differs from the reality of society, and they can no longer step back across that threshold."

"I understand." The words slipped from Anna's lips.

"Do you?" the doctor shot back with an eagle-eyed squint. "They really see what they're talking about. This should be as clear to you as it is to me, otherwise our conversation will hit a dead end sooner or later."

This time Anna was afraid to answer and simply nodded.

THE GULL CRY HOTEL

"I'd like to clarify right away that in psychiatry, there is much more that remains unexplored than what has been studied. We cannot be certain what exists and what doesn't. Similarly, the nature of schizophrenia remains incompletely understood. Essentially, schizophrenia cannot be cured, but it can be managed for a while. The voices quiet down. They transition from malicious commands to a quiet whisper, which can be controlled. And that's all we can do for our patients. In rare cases they can negotiate with the voices. Personally, I know only a few with this illness who managed to banish the whispers forever."

At such a beginning, a shiver ran down Anna's arms. She had thought she had full control over her body, but as it turned out, she had been completely mistaken.

Chapter 4

She sat in my office, waiting for her discharge papers. Her strong hands traced the stitches along the edge of her pajamas, and her eyes calmly scrutinized the report.

"How are your voices? Do you still talk to them?" I asked, peering at her with curiosity.

"I won't make up stories, Doctor. I still hear them," she replied quietly.

"So, how are we going to discharge you?" I placed a ballpoint pen demonstratively on the desk.

"I've learned to negotiate with them," she replied quickly and decisively. "Although I must admit, it would be inappropriate to call one voice a multitude."

"My dear Eleanora, what do you mean by that?"

"Before, there were five of them, now there's only one," she mumbled, avoiding eye contact.

"This is undeniable progress," I said, unable to hide my joy. "But what we're interested in is whether the most aggressive one is still there. Do you understand?"

"Absolutely. And I can confidently say that the most rational and logical one is the one that remains."

"How does that manifest?" I squinted.

"He doesn't like being cooped up, and we've agreed to have our conversations late at night. During the day, he doesn't show up at all." Eleanora's voice trembled, revealing her agitation.

"What do you talk about late at night, if you don't mind me asking?" I inquired without changing my tone. Eleanora's eyes were no longer darting around. Even though she couldn't withstand my gaze for more than a few seconds, she seemed focused on the even stitches, a reproduction of a Bosch painting on the wall to the right, and the pattern on the carpet.

"We talk about life and death, good and evil, eternal human values," she replied.

"Really?" I couldn't hide my surprise. "Who talks more in your nocturnal dialogues?"

It was evident that Eleanora hesitated with her response. However, she soon stated quite reasonably, "I talk more. But when I ask him to tell me something, he speaks quite a lot, recounting remarkable stories."

"What are these stories about?" I asked, closing the medical history folder, already almost certain about her discharge. We can't keep all schizophrenic patients; there are too many of them. Therefore, patients with a sluggish form of the illness can leave the hospital at the request of their relatives. We usually think that the mentally ill are primarily dangerous to society, but that's not true. More often they harm themselves and very rarely others.

"These are stories of humanity." Eleanora fixed her tea-colored eyes on my white clothes longer than usual.

"I'm sorry?"

"Stories from the history of nations. About wars, betrayal, death, violence ... About the horrors of the past."

I opened the pale lilac folder again. Both parents were historians, both associate professors in the history department.

"And how do you feel listening to these stories? Do they sadden you? Anger you, perhaps? Offend you?"

"They don't evoke any of those feelings in me. I'm a historian, just like my parents, and knowing the truth is important to me. So I simply write them down."

It seemed like the truth.

"May I take a look at your notes?"

My patient had been seeing another doctor before she was transferred to me just a couple of months ago. Eleanora pulled out a stack of notebooks from her cloth bag. The handwriting in the first one looked quite round, which was encouraging. The letters leaned correctly to the right, with hardly any sharp angles. The overall lettering didn't strain the eyes, except for the absence of sentence divisions. I couldn't find any full stops in the text and consequently not a single capital letter except for names. The most common punctuation mark was the dash, coming to the rescue in any attempt to complete a thought and structure it.

It was clear that Eleanora had done well in school and had written a lot in her life. The other peculiarities were quite natural for someone suffering from schizophrenia, as the literal translation of the illness is *splitting of consciousness*. This is why the patient futilely attempts to unite everything, avoiding the use of separating punctuation marks. In the struggle not to lose the integrity of perception, the patient's brain might even combine several words into one incredibly long one. My eyes caught a few isolated prepositions combined into words, but even this was more than normal for Ms. Maze. Overall, it was the text of someone afflicted with schizophrenia, showing no tendency toward aggression or violence, which was what I was trying to determine.

Suddenly, at the very bottom, in the middle of a word, a Cyrillic 'Ш' appeared more and more frequently as I flipped through the pages. It multiplied, and words that included this foreign letter were written in more sweeping and impulsive handwriting.

"Do you have notebooks from when all five of them were talking to you?" I inquired.

It was important for me to see the difference in her internal state between "back then" and "today."

When fragile Eleanora was first brought to us, she would switch between voices and threaten the staff with violence. She used to endlessly argue and contradict herself. Covering her ears, she would scream for all four of them to speak one by one and not enrage the fifth. An hour earlier, she had attacked her father with a knife, accusing him of spreading lies. But now, for the past four months, the patient hadn't shown any signs of aggression; she had behaved rationally and only spoken in her own voice.

"This one—maroon. It's a bit messy; I'll have to rewrite it. They were all yelling, interrupting each other," Eleanora shyly admitted, placing a cherry-colored notebook with crumpled corners in front of me.

My right hand trembled. The Latin script, which had become so familiar to my eye, now featured letters from various linguistic groups. There were o's crowned with umlauts, s's with cedillas and a's adorned with accents. Hieroglyphs and cuneiform script appeared less frequently.

"Are you sure you'll be able to decipher this text without assistance?" I inquired, feeling somewhat embarrassed.

"Of course. I'm a historian!" Eleanora repeated with a forced smile.

Well, in my opinion, progress was evident. In six months of treatment, it seemed that our mentally ill patient had managed to reconcile with herself. Moreover, her parents had been writing letters to the consul for two months, pleading for assistance in getting Eleanora back home. Nobody wanted to oppose it. It seemed that if she left these walls, it would only make things easier for everyone. I marked the date and signed the discharge form.

Pressing one of the buttons under the desk, I called for an orderly to escort her. Soon the door opened and a tall young man walked into the room. In the corridor, a white head appeared—the next patient was waiting there. As she passed him, Eleanora briefly looked into his eyes and immediately lowered her gaze, clutching the bag full of unique knowledge tightly to her chest.

"She, she … Haven't you seen?" exclaimed the man. He was in a straitjacket, which he began to struggle against as soon as they lined up at the door. The patient spat after Eleanora and, the next moment, began to chant a monotonous prayer, spraying saliva around his mouth. His gray, disheveled hair made him look much older than the thirty-six years indicated by his medical history.

"Untie me!" he almost ordered.

"Please, have a seat," I said calmly, ignoring his request, and gestured to offer him a chair.

"Then at least wipe my beard," he asked in a calmer tone, looking at the orderly. The sturdy guy removed a towel from his neck and wiped the patient's face. "Don't tell me you've discharged her!" Victor stared at me.

"What surprises you about that? She, by the way, has been behaving much better than you for a long time." I pointed my finger at him as if talking to a child.

"Really? You didn't see anything?"

"What exactly do I need to see?"

"How her face distorted!" He furrowed his brow genuinely.

"No, I didn't see anything. Next time you see something, you can tell me?"

"Simpletons!" The man exhaled with exasperation. "How can you be so blind?"

"If you could continue without insulting me, I would greatly appreciate it."

"But there's a demon inside her! What's wrong with you people? She needs to be tied to the bed and have a priest summoned, not discharged."

Victor's hair had turned gray for a reason. He constantly encountered people possessed by demons, and when he was free, he had even tried to exorcise them. When he was brought to the clinic, he had had bottles of holy water with him, a massive silver cross, and images of various saints. He had believed he could find peace within our walls, far from the noisy streets and sinful souls. However, it turned out that, in his opinion, practically all the mentally ill were possessed by unclean spirits, and his presence among them was the most unfortunate turn of events possible.

***

In the middle of the night, the phone rang.

"Good evening, Dr. Richter. Is Eleanora Maze your patient?"

"Yes. What happened?"

"Her parents …" The police didn't mince words. "Mr. and Mrs. Maze were murdered in their sleep. Their daughter, Eleanora, armed herself with a knife in the middle of the night and inflicted forty-eight stab wounds on their bodies."

My hands went cold.

The court session was scheduled for four o'clock. It wouldn't determine Eleanora's fate. From now on, there was no hope of her leaving the hospital again. But it would determine my fate as a practicing psychiatrist. I wasn't afraid of losing my job, but I was trying my best to understand how this could have happened. How on earth could well-controlled schizophrenia turn into paranoia in just a week? How could Eleanora have crossed all acceptable boundaries of reason and brutally murdered her own parents in the middle of the night while they peacefully slept? Then she'd called the police and tearfully confessed, sobbing into the phone.

"Judy, are you ready? Representatives from the ministry will be here in one hour. The investigator is already on his way," my assistant informed me.

"I want Victor, my patient, to be present at the meeting," I said, rubbing my forehead with tension.

"But if he behaves like last time—"

"If he does, we'll take him away," I interrupted. She nodded and left my door slightly open.

Last night's events were vivid in my mind. After a long day spent with the police, I'd arrived at the hospital. I'd walked down the dimly lit corridor, half painted in an unpleasant shade of green. I couldn't shake the feeling that someone was constantly watching me from the high hospital windows. Even the sturdy bars couldn't stop that invisible, piercing gaze. It could penetrate anywhere, into any room, any corner of the Earth, and any soul. It made me uneasy; I doubled my pace.

Was I a believer or an atheist? Working here, I had to be both. In medicine, there was much more that couldn't be explained than the uninitiated could imagine. It ranged from miraculous healings through the power of persuasion to the momentary relief when twenty-one grams left the body as the brain died. And in psychiatry there were far more mysteries than in all other medical fields combined.

THE GULL CRY HOTEL

The heavy locks clicked open, and I entered the narrow room. Judging by the muscles in his face, Victor was pretending to be asleep. I walked to the end of his room and took a seat in the solitary chair. I gave an audible sigh to signal my readiness to begin the conversation.

"Aren't you afraid to be alone in the isolation room?" Victor didn't rush to open his eyes.

"If I saw demons, the last thing I would want is to share a room with them. If you didn't behave wildly towards other patients, you'd be in the common area right now. And if you didn't try to exorcise the people of this city, you'd be out of these walls," I responded.

"Who if not me? You're so blind that you see nothing," he retorted.

"You're right, I don't see their faces, but I see their works, and I have to live with that." I looked at the tall window, trying to hold back the tears welling up inside me.

"Did your patient kill someone?" Victor asked, lifting himself up on the bed.

"Did you figure that out from my words or from what you saw in her?"

"Let's call it intuition," he replied with a surprisingly genuine smile.

For some reason I felt compelled to listen to the details of his visions, and I instinctively leaned forward. He smirked, and the tension between us noticeably eased. The stout man in gray pajamas sat up on the bed and leaned against the wall. Now I could only see him in profile, without the ability to catch all his facial expressions if he intended to lie. But I didn't feel like probing. I had been working with him for almost two weeks and had never caught him in a lie. He genuinely believed in everything he saw. Perhaps that was why, in the prime of his life, he sat in solitary confinement in a psychiatric hospital, gray as an old man.

"If a person is possessed by a demon, you can focus on the spot between their brows and see the intruder's face. It appears like a semi-transparent overlay on the human face. If an unfortunate soul has several demons, they change their appearances like slides."

"And I can see them?"

"Yes, you can! Especially since you already believe in their existence."

"But you didn't have time to focus on Eleanora. Just a few seconds in the doorway ... Could that have been enough?"

"You're right. I see them differently. To my eyes, demons distort the human gaze, telling me things they don't tell others. They sense me, know that I can see them, so they don't hide at all. This fragile girl, she ...

Oh, let me remember her demon …" He paused for a few seconds as if recalling the moment they met.

I smiled ruefully and lowered my head. Suddenly my reason triumphed, and I stopped believing in this theatrical attempt to remember Eleanora. He must remember her. Where else could this eccentric see so many possessed people while sitting alone within these four walls?

"What puzzled you?" The patient instantly reacted, turning his head sharply and fixing me with a stern gaze. "I'm sure you remember Eleanora, and you could easily reproduce your vision, unless, of course, it's a product of your imagination. She's the last patient you saw."

Victor burst into laughter and said, "As long as you consider faith to be something that limits your understanding of the world rather than expanding it, that's how it will be."

I was taken aback for the second time. Victor was attacking from unexpected angles, and it made my mind roll slowly, reluctantly, but still moving to his point.

"Eleanora is far from the last of the possessed who spoke to me this week."

I bit my lip, regretting having come here. But the next moment, he said something that made me sink back into the chair.

"Not all the committed are locked up here." He nodded towards the door. "A couple of people around here are susceptible to demonic influence."

"Did visitors come to see you?"

"No. I have almost no friends. My family has turned away from me. But Greg's devil lately spoke to me."

The orderly working in this wing had been transferred to us from a prestigious clinic. He was fired for brutally beating a difficult patient, but he managed to find connections and return to work. At the time of his arrest, he said that the devil himself had entered him that night and made him do things he didn't want to do. Later he recanted his testimony and miraculously avoided punishment. In addition, he didn't choose a different field of work; he came back to work with the mentally ill. Yes, this muscle man wasn't particularly responsive or kind, but for working in these conditions, endurance, physical strength, and experience were much more important than kindness. How could Victor know such details? Who knows; maybe Greg himself had told him. Nevertheless, my interest in the conversation received a certain boost—enough to ignite it once again.

"Why did Eleanora show you her true face? Wouldn't it have been wiser to keep her demon secret, at least on the day of her discharge?"

"She was assured you wouldn't believe me. I'm just a madman in a straitjacket to you, nothing more."

"Victor …" I blushed and lowered my gaze; after all, he was speaking the truth.

"So she just walked by, and as she did, her demon revealed itself in all its glory."

"What did it look like?" I leaned forward to keep an eye on him during his story.

Victor cast his gaze to the right corner of the room. At that moment, his left brain hemisphere was at work—the one responsible for rationality, not imagination. So he must have been absolutely certain that everything he saw was true. His hands lay calmly on his stomach, and his legs hung relaxed from the bed. None of his movements betrayed nervousness or tension, which meant that his brain was recalling rather than emotionally inventing.

"Her eyes widened for a moment—larger than usual," he began. "They seemed unnaturally stretched sideways, and the black pupils expanded, overshadowing the eyeballs. Her nose retracted almost entirely and practically disappeared. Her skin took on a grayish hue, and her mouth suddenly gaped open, revealing a set of sharp fangs. They grew upon each other like wild vines, while a forked demonic tongue slithered through them. It coiled toward my lips, and a moment later, the mouth stretched into a malicious grin."

I stood up and approached quite closely, invading his personal space. "Did the demon understand that it was seen?"

"I doubt it." He shook his head. Usually, liars desperately avoid such gestures. "Only if …"

"What?"

I leaned down low and looked him straight in the eyes.

In response, he looked into mine. His pupils were of normal size, and the eye muscles didn't twitch as liars' often did.

"Only if he heard me screaming in your office like a madman."

I laughed.

Victor truly believed in his testimony. Even though the mentally healthy people around me lied about things approximately three times a day, this man was telling the truth. Whatever had happened between him and Eleanora, Victor's eyes had genuinely seen a demon.

"Why check with me? Wouldn't it be better to check Eleanora herself?" He merely shrugged at my inquisitive gaze.

I clasped my hands together and, taking large strides around the room, said, "Do you know what cacodemonomania is?"

"Is that my diagnosis?" Only now did I notice his sense of humor and his restrained, attractive smile.

"No." I smiled again involuntarily. "But it could be Eleanora's diagnosis. Patients with cacodemonomania sincerely believe that they are possessed by the devil. They react to holy items and Christian objects, threaten on behalf of demons and Lucifer himself, change their voices and expressions. They have seizures when hearing prayers; they simulate convulsions and spasms. They often attack clergy, inflicting serious injuries on themselves and others."

"But what if Eleanora doesn't know that the water in her glass is holy and there's a silver cross attached to the bottom of her chair?"

I paused, running my fingers through my hair. That evening, Victor not only made me smile but also made me think differently and therefore act pretty differently.

During my years practicing psychiatry, I've witnessed numerous phenomena that defied purely scientific explanations, and each time, I've tried to fit them into those explanations, just as every psychiatrist does. I'm no exception. In our demanding profession, leaving questions unanswered is not allowed. We often force ourselves to believe that everything unexplainable is nothing more than an unknown post-syndrome of an illness we're already familiar with.

***

The spacious and bright room felt unfriendly due to the ominous dimming of the lights. One of the transparent white curtains in the corner swayed in the strong gusts of wind signaling the approach of a storm. Round chandeliers hung from sturdy chains and undulated slowly as people entered, allowing the draft to take hold. I greeted the investigator, a stocky, balding man, and headed towards a separate table away from the committee and the patient. Just as I sat down, I saw Eleanora for the first time since her discharge. She entered the room calmly. Her dark, fine hair was pulled neatly back, and a deep emotional distress was reflected on her pallid face.

What am I doing? I thought. *She's a sick person ...*

At my suggestion, this girl had been served an overly salty breakfast that morning, and her water had been accidentally spilled by a nurse. She hurriedly approached the table, her trembling hand reaching for a glass filled with clear liquid, but she couldn't quite touch it. Her thin hand, marked with bulging veins, froze about two inches from the glass. Her eyebrows furrowed noticeably, and faint shadows spread beneath them, exuding a dull darkness. She leaned on the table with both hands, absently tracing her temple with her fingers—a gesture of nervous tension, a distraction from the situation at hand. Perhaps at this very moment she heard the voice. An order. A command.

I hurriedly took my seat at the table, feigning preoccupation.

Eleanora needed to answer a few simple questions: how she felt about me as her doctor, whether she experienced anger and rage after our meetings, and what we talked about when the voice recorder was turned off. The committee and the guardians entered the room. Everyone took their seats except for the patient.

"Please, Ms. Maze, have a seat," the chief physician's stern voice commanded as he gestured with a firm hand toward the standing Eleanora.

"I can't," she cut in.

"Why?" he asked, his gaze finally lifting from the papers.

"My body hurts unbearably."

"Is something troubling you? Do you want to undergo an examination?"

I still avoided looking at her, afraid of giving myself away. Just fifteen minutes ago, I had walked into this room and discreetly taped a silver cross to the underside of her chair. This symbol of Christianity had been confiscated from Victor when he was admitted to the clinic. In the same spot I had found holy water, which I had used to fill the glass.

She remained silent, and the pause extended. Then I lifted my gaze as if struggling to tear myself away from the horrifying details of the consequences of her severe illness. She stared at me intently. Her brown eyes completely dissolved into growing darkness. The rest of her facial features blurred and vanished altogether. Only her dark, creepy mouth stretched into a menacing grin. Time seemed to slow down—the heavy lamps swung in a leisurely fashion and the transparent white curtain billowed dramatically, allowing something ominous to enter the room with the wind. This vision completely paralyzed me. I was an excellent psychiatrist but a terrible exorcist.

The next moment, the black voids of Eleanora's eyes contracted into dark, gleaming points, and her forehead stretched unbelievably, revealing two elongated bumps. Her nose turned into a pointed protrusion, and her lips stuck together viscously, as if acid had been splashed onto her skin. I felt a rush of heat. I hid my gaze, full of horror. But what I heard next made my body tremble.

"Juuudyyy …" a voice called as if from the depths, carried by the wind. It sent shivers down my spine, but even this voice couldn't compare to what I heard from my patient.

"They're tormenting me within the walls of the hospital," Eleanora gasped. "Night after night I endure humiliation."

I lifted my gaze sharply. "That's not true," I croaked.

The judge cleared his throat. "Please continue. What exactly is happening here at night?"

"The orderlies are raping me and my doctor is observing it, taking videos," she replied with terrifying confidence.

The court was abruptly interrupted as Eleanora was taken for a medical examination. I left the room feeling sick, with an unbearable turmoil throughout my body.

"Why wasn't Victor brought here?" I inquired of the assistant standing by the wall.

"Judy, he passed away last night."

"What?" My head spun, and for a moment I felt like I might collapse.

"Heart attack."

"When? When did this happen?" I shook my head, struggling to believe her.

"Time of death was three-thirty," she replied, glancing at her thin folder.

"God …" I could barely believe my own ears.

I found myself standing in front of his room without realizing how I got there. The door was open. Inside, there was a rustling sound, and as I entered, I practically bumped into an orderly. He was holding a striped mattress stained with yellow spots and appeared slightly disoriented. We exchanged terse greetings, and I walked over to the chair where I had sat just the previous evening, conversing with the patient. Was he truly ill? Or had I been too blind to see the real causes of his affliction?

"Just yesterday, Victor was alive. He was not only my patient but also a deeply devout Christian," I remarked to the departing orderly.

"Yes—it's very unfortunate. He wasn't just unwell mentally," Greg replied as he turned to leave the room. The corners of his mouth twitched slightly—he was pleased with himself, making every effort not to reveal a smile. A few seconds were enough for me to concentrate and try to see his demon. His human face seemed to blur, giving way to a smoky outline. As confidently as I had started, I suddenly shifted my gaze to the empty metal mesh of the bed. Seeing more than two demons in one hour threatened to land me in one of these rooms, wearing gray pajamas instead of a medical coat. I covered my eyes with my hand and exhaled.

"Greg, forgive me. Too many deaths in the past week. You can go; I'll stay for a moment."

He left in silence. In my thoughts, the image of Victor came alive—his silvery hair and the beard that seemed too mature for his age. Right now, he sat before me like a saint. Yesterday, as a woman, I had felt comfortable in his presence, and it was oddly peaceful.

If only under different circumstances ... echoed in my mind.

THE GULL CRY HOTEL

***

I was suspended from medical practice for several months. Eleanora's allegations weren't substantiated, but I naturally chose to discontinue my practice for a while.

Supposedly, she had about five demons within her, according to the history of her illness. After reading unbelievable accounts of their exorcism, I couldn't bring myself to suggest such an alternative treatment to her relatives. I preferred to forget about her, Greg, and even Victor. But if someone ever asks me whether I have seen a real demon face to face, my expression will betray a lie if I decide to reply "No."

Chapter 5

Anna couldn't recall how she left Dr. Richter's office. The rain had long ceased, and night had fallen over London. She summoned an Uber and took in the evening's freshness. Ozone filled her lungs, helping to clear her thoughts. Everything she had heard in that stuffy office, saturated with the scent of medication and cigarette smoke, seemed unreal, like a scene from a movie, a chapter from a book, but certainly not a doctor's confession about her medical practice.

She rode in the car, her gaze lingering on the quiet streets enveloped in lush greenery, rows of two-story houses with pointed roofs, and the warm electric lights reflecting in puddles. Could Anna Walker discern what was real and what wasn't? In her life, there had as yet been no confirmation of Judy's words, yet neither medicine nor science could provide any direct refutation of them. As a writer, she knew one thing for sure: the story had touched her, stirred emotions within her, frightened her and inspired her. It had taken root in Anna like a seed, which meant it would soon sprout and show its first leaves.

Six months later, Anna found herself in the office of the chief editor of a major London publishing house.

THE GULL CRY HOTEL

"Books based on real events, they're very special books," Alison, the head of literary fiction, said. "Readers will love it!" She tenderly embraced the manuscript.

By this time, Anna was fed up with this novel. She felt sick of it. She had put this story through her own soul. She had changed the names, added a past for Eleanora and a future for Judy, spared Victor's life, and given them a chance of happiness just before he died from a heart attack. Like any writer, she had reworked the material beyond recognition, creating motivation for the killer and driving her to escape, giving the detectives more work. She had changed many things, leaving only that sense of fear that couldn't be faked. It transferred to the reader, turning the story into a bestseller. However, there were fewer intriguing novels to follow, until one day Anna found herself on the brink of burnout.

***

"What's this?" Alison twirled a thin flash drive between her fingers.

"All I managed to do … There are only a few chapters left. I promise I'll finish them in two weeks." Anna took a seat in the chair opposite the massive desk.

"I'm not just talking about deadlines"—Alison sighed wearily—"although that's a concern too. Anna, what is this?"

The novelist frowned, hesitating.

"Here is cliché after cliché—dull scenes and dialogues as if they were written under duress. And the characters, Anna!"

"What about them?"

"They're all lifted from your previous novels!" Alison Watcher pushed the portable drive away with a look of disgust. "It's like it wasn't really you who wrote it. So I'm asking, what is this, Anna?"

Four years of working together—forty-eight months of intense creativity, not to mention Anna's writing during vacations and regular calls from Alison, no matter where in the world Anna was. She had seriously believed there was no one closer to her than her editor. But now Mrs. Watcher looked at her with a cold, unfamiliar gaze. The same way she had looked at the young writer she had first met in the hallway. Back then, this person had been everything to Anna, while for Alison, Anna was absolutely nobody—a blip on the wall of the most popular publishing house in London.

And if you ever think your employer is your friend, know this: it's just an illusion. There are no friends in big business. Here, either you're at the forefront and mean everything to your publisher or you've fallen by the wayside and become a shadow.

"Alison, I ... I really don't know what happened. Maybe I need a break?"

THE GULL CRY HOTEL

"A break?" The stern lines of Alison's face became even more pronounced. "You have six months for the novel and a month for re-reading the manuscript to correct all shortcomings as written in your contract."

"But I—"

"No 'buts' and no 'I.' Deadlines are set, the advertising campaign has been running for a month, and readers are eagerly awaiting another bestseller. So, I have a question worth several hundred thousand."

"What is it?" Anna swallowed softly.

"Who will write the book, damn it? Who the hell will write this bestseller?"

"I … I will …" Anna said, taking the flash drive from the table and slowly getting up.

"Two weeks," a nearly robotic voice said. A voice devoid of compassion.

Anna Walker found herself in the long hallway.

"It's her, it's her." Young authors bringing their manuscripts to the editorial office nudged each other. How she wished she could get inside one of their heads and absorb that awkward freshness, incredible sensuality, and genuine revelation—all the things she had once had in abundance but somehow lost on the road to fame.

"Absorb their ideas?" you might ask. No, not their ideas. Ideas are always plentiful. What matters to a writer is their transmission. That observant eye is affluent at the beginning of a career when you haven't yet seen the world. When, like a child, you soak up the characters' personalities, live their lives, cry their tears. Breathe in the stale air of a room and sense the cold sea breeze of a chilly night. That night when a murder takes place; the night you can't escape until dawn.

A young woman jumped up with an open flyleaf and a ballpoint pen. "Anna, may I have your autograph? I admire you!"

"Thank you." Anna smiled. "What name?"

"For Kriss—Kriss Wallins."

"An excellent name for a writer."

"Thank you." Kriss looked at Anna with envy, and Anna looked at Kriss with the same feeling.

Anna tried to let go of her heavy thoughts as she gazed out of the car window at the old yet undeniably progressive city.

When she had first started writing, she had lived in a massive apartment complex. Her rather cozy flat could easily have been described as a spacious room. It was clean and bright. The entrance door to the grand lobby opened automatically, recognizing Anna's face. Then she, a modern city dweller, would dive into the east wing, passing along a narrow corridor with motion sensor LED lamps that lit up above her. She would stop in front of number 23. She knew the eight-digit code for the electronic lock, and after entering the digits, she would place the index finger of her right hand on the miniature scanner. The door would open without a key. Immense panoramic windows made of silicate glass provided complete protection from intrusion, overlooked the car park, and never opened. On rainy days she couldn't hear the raindrops, and when it was windy she was shielded from the rustling of the trees. She yearned to let the freshness of a summer evening into her abode, which she called home, but she only allowed filtered air by pressing the button labeled "boost."

Once Anna had managed to sell herself to a publishing house, she had taken out a loan and rented an old-style flat. There were large French windows here too, but now they opened wide. And when the publishing house signed a contract with her "on special terms," she moved to an excellent residential complex. The new glass buildings with spacious balconies and luxurious winter gardens captivated the heart of this inveterate pedant. They were clean, bright, and, most importantly, fresh.

For a whole year estate agents kept calling her, offering country houses at throwaway prices. But memories of English cottages, even the most prestigious and well-appointed ones, brought with them a persistent smell of mold—the fungus that permeated the brick houses in the humidity of the local air.

Anna loved her flat, a blend of high tech and Scandinavian minimalism filled with living plants. Here, it always smelled like coffee and rain.

She sank into the velvet cushions of her sofa and opened her laptop. She had written three sentences when her phone rang.

Roderick, it displayed, accentuating the old-fashioned name with a pompous melody.

"Hello." Anna smiled.

"Hey there! Don't forget about Ruby's cocktail party this Sunday," he said, smiling.

"Roderick, I won't be able to make it," Anna replied.

"What do you mean, you won't be able to make it?" he protested. The smile in his voice momentarily disappeared.

"The new novel is just not working."

"Don't be dramatic." Roderick's laughter through the phone sounded rehearsed. "Show Alison the manuscript and she'll surely love it."

"I already showed her."

"And …?" Roderick's unflappable tone took on a hint of concern.

"The publishing house is one step away from terminating my contract," Anna admitted reluctantly.

THE GULL CRY HOTEL

"Oh my … What are you going to do?"

"I don't know … Maybe it's time for a change of scenery. To go away for a while."

"Great idea! I'm sure everything will work out this time too …"

They fell silent, as if searching for a response in each other but not finding one.

"Will you come over?" she asked quietly.

"I can't today; it's the Liverpool vs. Manchester United match. How about tomorrow?"

"Tomorrow I might be flying …"

"Then have a safe trip! See you when you get back. And …"

"Yes?"

"Freshen up. Love you…"

"Love you…" Anna hung up the phone.

Freshen up … As if I'm about to apply a moisturizing mask, not rewrite a novel! Why is everything like this? Why can't he come up with a beautiful, incredibly touching phrase and say it? Is everything really that bad for us?

In reality, their relationship wasn't bad. It wasn't good either. It was hard to define their relationship at all.

Chapter 6

"If the book didn't have that disclaimer saying all characters and events are fictional and any resemblance is purely coincidental, I'd believe it was reality!" Eddie confessed. "Not the part about demons, of course." He chuckled. "But otherwise the feelings and emotions of the characters felt so genuine ..."

Anna swallowed softly.

"Of course." Anna herself didn't believe in Judy's demons. This story was sad and gloomy. But a writer isn't someone who knows a bunch of incredible stories. A writer is someone who can turn an ordinary story into something incredible.

Anna delved into the storyline, describing it vividly, but still she thought that Dr. Richter had gone off the deep end. She also knew perfectly well that if the author didn't believe in her own story, the reader wouldn't either. So Anna had literally lived her first novel, almost driving herself crazy in the process.

"How can you describe emotions like that? It's as if you've experienced everything yourself for multiple characters simultaneously," Eddie intuited. "How do you achieve such mastery?"

"I— I don't even know." Anna hesitated, blushing deeply.

"Do you classify them into psychological types? One of my friends, who is struggling to become a serious writer, told me that everyone is categorized in tables. A victim can never be a perpetrator, and it is quite unnatural for a sadist to be a masochist as well."

"Actually, it's much more complicated than that. Personally, I prefer simple observation to tables."

"And who do you observe?"

"Everyone." Anna shrugged.

"Your partner must be going through fits of jealousy."

"Um, yes … It's not easy for him," Anna lied. "And you? What brings you to Northern Ireland?"

"I'm meeting a friend there, and in a few days we're flying to Iceland," Eddie replied.

"Is he Irish?" Anna inquired.

"She is." Eddie chuckled awkwardly. "She is Irish."

"Right." Anna pursed her lips.

They loved the same coffee, enjoyed the same movies, shared similar outlooks on life, and talked incessantly until the very moment of disembarkation, like they hadn't talked to anyone in a long time.

Among other things, they were eerily similar in what they never managed to tell each other or any living soul.

Despite the extraordinarily warm relationship, Belfast greeted them with a biting wind. Eddie and Anna bid each other farewell. He was taking a taxi to the hotel, and she was rushing to catch the train to the coast.

"So, two weeks on a deserted island, is it?" Eddie shoved his hands into the pockets of his joggers.

"Deserted?" Anna shivered in the wind.

"Who could doubt that? I've been to Rathlin Island, you know."

"Maybe that's exactly what I need right now," Anna said hesitantly.

"You rented a house there? Planning to go fishing?" Eddie chuckled, masking his concern with curiosity.

"I booked a room at a hotel."

"A hotel?" Eddie clearly didn't know every nook and cranny of this vast planet.

"The Gull Cry Hotel."

"Brr—what a spooky name for a holiday place! How on earth did you find it?"

"Just got lucky."

***

THE GULL CRY HOTEL

Anna vividly remembered how she had found the hotel. It had happened just the previous night—eighteen hours ago, to be precise.

She placed her phone on the floor after her conversation with Roderick and allowed her heavy head to sink into the velvety cushions. Paradoxical as it may sound, in her relationship with his man, Anna felt more alone than when she was single. So what was the use of this largely physical friendship and soulless companionship?

When Anna had entered the elite circles of bestselling writers, her life had become filled with new acquaintances. Among them was a handsome man with a soft light beard, an impeccable haircut, and the sensuous gaze of blue eyes. He was stylish and simultaneously rugged—so, according to many, a suitable match for her.

She perused his social media page and gave herself away with a couple of *likes*. One Saturday, she personally met Roderick at one of Ruby's parties. A touching British song was playing, and Anna, wrapped in a blanket, sat on the swings. Billy graciously brought her a glass of wine, bowed dramatically, and led everyone inside. Everyone except Roderick.

She waited. He approached. He stood behind her and leaned in. He touched her cheek with his soft stubble and whispered softly, "I'm worthy of you, Anna."

She said nothing and couldn't help but cringe, blaming it on the wine. It was clichéd, even for the cheapest of romance novels, yet in response she took his hand. *Real love is something you can wait for your whole life and never find*, she decided, and she invited him to stay the night. And Roderick stayed.

Sometimes Anna seriously pondered whether their meeting was a work of fate. She didn't know if destiny had brought her and Roderick together, but she knew for sure that Ruby and all her friends were hardly Cupids.

Among other things, there was something more important on the agenda than the absence of emotions. Her failed manuscript troubled Anna the most—Alison's gaze of disappointment, to be precise, which still haunted her and sent shivers down her spine.

The transparent curtain lifted, letting in the night's coolness, but Anna didn't rush to close the balcony door. She pulled up her plush blanket and looked at her laptop screen again. This time, instead of attempting to write, she found the ten most inspiring places in the United Kingdom.

In addition to the Yorkshire Dales, Stonehenge, and the White Cliffs of Dover, the article suggested visiting the coast of Northern Ireland. Here, on the ad's banner picture, covered in velvety greenery, the picturesque rocky landscape rose above the mighty ocean. The low fog invoked fear and awe, centuries-old lighthouses guarded their secrets, and there was not a single living soul for miles.

THE GULL CRY HOTEL

A pleasant excitement spread in Anna's stomach.

This is what I need, she concluded and opened a list of quaint hotels along the coast. *Something cozy and secluded would be perfect. To step out into the mist after breakfast and wander through the boundless hills of this mysterious land of the Celts.*

In contrast to the city hotels, a three-story antique mansion stood out, built of gray stone. *Spectacular ocean view*, the description read. *The nearest settlement is nine miles away. Rustic cuisine and friendly staff. If you're seeking tranquility and seclusion, we invite you to visit the coastal Gull Cry Hotel.*

Anna went to the hotel's website and booked a room. The process took a couple of minutes, and it took another ten minutes to purchase a ticket to Belfast. From there, a train to Ballycastle and an evening ferry to Rathlin Island.

A taxi will be waiting for you in the port car park, they considerately added in the confirmation email.

Well, tomorrow I'm flying to Northern Ireland! Anna exclaimed, taking a deep breath and reopening her manuscript.

On the third chapter, after hours of thoughtful revisions and well past midnight, Anna closed her eyes.

Somewhere deep in her consciousness, the feeling persisted that she was still asleep when a gentle tapping came on the glass of the balcony door. She cast her gaze into the darkness, where a figure stood on the other side of the panoramic window. Thank goodness, in this dreamlike state, the balcony door remained closed. An unfamiliar antique key was visible in the lock, while a stranger's face flickered through the curtains.

For a moment it seemed like a child stood there. Yet within the stocky figure and disproportionately large face, Anna recognized a dwarf. His eyes gleamed with an unhealthy zeal, and his wide mouth occasionally exposed a row of sharpened teeth.

This character seemed to have escaped from a sinister circus. And he had escaped to Anna, to the metropolis, to the balcony of her flat. If she had momentarily forgotten that she lived on the ninth floor of a well-secured residential complex, she could have easily believed this.

Finally he spotted her through the curtains. A small yet strong hand grabbed the door handle and began to shake it hysterically. The guest was determined to get inside, but the key was preventing him. His hand clenched into a fist. Now Anna could hear much stronger knocking, and that was when she woke up.

She jumped up from the couch and rubbed her eyes. The feeling that someone had really knocked on the glass remained with her, but the balcony was empty. The partially open door had allowed weak gusts of wind inside. Beyond the translucent curtains, the leaves of decorative Ficus plants swayed occasionally and the sharp tips of dwarf thuja shook.

Anna rose and hastily turned on the lights. She caught her breath, checking every dim corner of the living room. Fear proved to be stronger than from just a nightmare, but that was precisely what she needed—real emotions, something that couldn't be simulated or forced. She brewed some Earl Grey tea and wrapped herself in the plush blanket once again. A pleasant excitement spread over her body, the same feeling she had experienced when writing her first book. Anna sensed deep within her the birth of something fresh, new, and genuine. She knew this state well—fear had given her the impulse, and now she had to obey her writer's instincts. Staring into the dark window, she recalled the horrific vision, which brought another vivid image with a chain of events trailing behind. Unaware of time passing, Anna wrote, hastily typing her thoughts, afraid to scare away the elusive trail left by the nightmare.

***

"May I have your phone number?" Eddie, it seemed, had to invest quite a bit to emit this straightforward sentence. "Perhaps a wind of chance will send me one day to Rathlin," he added, slightly embarrassed.

A wind of chance? You're flying to Iceland with your girlfriend! someone in Anna's mind whispered with a touch of skepticism. Nevertheless, she quickly retrieved her phone and recited her number to Eddie.

"Recently changed your number?" He grinned, his lips curling at the corners.

"No, I've had it for five years. I just don't keep numbers in my head."

"Really?"

"Saves space." She shrugged.

Eddie laughed. He didn't want to part ways with Anna, but he couldn't come up with a reason to stay with her either.

They shook hands once again; their farewell had taken longer than they'd expected. The taxi line had emptied, and the arrivals had stopped coming out of the airport building.

"Well, see you around?" he finally said.

"See you." She nodded.

THE GULL CRY HOTEL

Chapter 7

Belfast Lanyon Place was covered in dew. Anna pulled her windbreaker out of her bag. Now it was evening, it had gotten significantly colder—the platform wasn't warming anyone up in this weather.

Anna slid her hands into her pockets, but the wind passed right through the thin fleece. Her fingers tingled in the wind, and her face reddened.

The train appeared just as the first large raindrop fell on Anna's cheek. By the time the line of carriages came to a halt, all the travelers on the platform were already soaked. Anna extended the handle of her suitcase and quickly stepped onto gray floor. The train was warm and nearly empty. Anna made her way to the middle and took a seat by the window. The train began to move, and very soon slanting raindrops started to streak down the windowpane.

Till the end of the line, she thought. *I may even doze off.* Eddie's image appeared when she closed her eyes, and her soul became filled with a magical sensation. His mischievous gaze, his enticing smile, and his incredible inner magnetism ... This carriage would be hundreds of times cozier if Eddie were here.

THE GULL CRY HOTEL

The door behind her shut, and Anna jumped. She was certain she had heard the sharp sound distinctly, but the carriage remained empty.

Hmm, was it my imagination? She frowned.

Anna loved solitude, but for some reason being alone right now made her uneasy. She slung her bag over her shoulder, extended the suitcase handle once more, and walked toward the front into the adjacent carriage. One tight door, then another, and she found herself in a space identical to the one she'd left.

"No one," Anna whispered.

A growing sense of unease filled her chest, and an unnatural weakness crept into her hands.

Now she was almost running—running to get to the next carriage, to find fellow passengers as soon as possible and finally calm down. Another unsteady vestibule, tight doors, and she was in another carriage where a young couple of travelers dozed, pressed against the windows. She let out a loud sigh. The grip that had constricted her chest almost to the point of nausea had loosened.

Where is this panic coming from? Such an unfamiliar or utterly forgotten primal fear!

Anna sank into a seat. Outside, the darkness was relentless. The clouds grew heavier, casting out lightning, while the rain sent torrents down the windows. The rhythmic sound of the wheels, the gentle swaying, and the blurred landscape wrapped her in a sleepy haze. She closed her eyes. The train had nearly lulled her to sleep when the brakes suddenly screeched. She heard the grinding of iron and the rain tapping on the thick glass. This must be one of the few stops on the Irish Express—Anna didn't even want to open her eyes to gaze upon Antrim. But then, out of nowhere, she felt a piercing gaze. It happens sometimes, when someone looks at your back and for some reason you turn around. And then, inexplicably, in the crowd you find those exact eyes—the eyes of the one who's watching.

Anna almost reflexively opened her eyes, and she recognized through the glass a familiar face—familiar to the point of sheer horror. The train was departing from the platform when the stunned Anna saw the dwarf—the very same one who had appeared in her dream the night before. She couldn't forget those obsessed eyes in the disproportionately large face and the grotesque smile. She wished she could. But even through the blurred window, she recognized him—the character from her nightmare.

Time seemed to slow down, and the train seemed to stall. Anna leaned against the rain-splattered window.

"This can't be true ... I must be hallucinating," she whispered. Fear spread through her body, almost reaching the point of panic.

What's happening? Am I being followed? But by whom? The dwarf from the dream? What nonsense!

THE GULL CRY HOTEL

After a few more sobering thoughts, Anna began to worry about her mental health. The past years had been full of work, and the last few days had brought intense stress. What could she expect from her psyche now? It appeared that her previously sturdy nervous system had given way.

The laptop rested on her lap. Anna was in no mood for sleep now.

Black waves washed over her lifeless body, while the shifting sand rapidly swallowed her delicate wrists, gently concealing the traces of a cruel struggle. But could her pre-death battle with Georges be called a struggle? Just as much as you can call the meeting of a wounded doe with a cheetah a struggle ...

A wounded doe with a cheetah ... Anna frowned. *Is there something more poetic?*

She quickly typed the search term *predators and their prey* into Google. It struggled; the internet connection was slow. Anna, waiting for a response, scanned the tops of the seats.

The lovers! Where did they go? She was alone once again. Unpleasant anxiety was building up. She stood up and looked around—no one. She took a few deep breaths and stared at the screen. Slowly but steadily, the search engine began to yield results. *Boa and rabbit, hawk and mouse, spider and fly ...*

Hmm ... a spider could fit very well. However, I wouldn't want to compare Bate to a fly. Moth—too big ... Gnat—too small ...

A child rushed down the corridor, and Anna straightened like a taut string. She didn't see but clearly heard it. Quick footsteps followed one another until the train door shut behind them. Anna froze, unable to tear her gaze away from the bright screen. With a trembling hand, she reached for her phone and, her fingers sliding across the screen, pressed Roderick's number.

The phone kept ringing. Long, endless rings. Relentless static, and Anna's heart nearly leaped out of her chest. Suddenly, through the interference, the ringing resumed, changing to a drowsy voice. "Hello?"

"Rick!" That was what Anna called her beloved Roderick Scott. "Rick!"

Static. The cursed static returned.

"Anna, are you ... okay?"

"Damn it, Rick! I'm on a train. Something strange is happening ..."

More static.

"What?"

"There are no people here, but I think I hear someone's footsteps ... Rick! Rick?"

THE GULL CRY HOTEL

No, the call wasn't going through, and the phone simply went dead. Anna stared at her computer screen, where, just like her mobile, there was no internet connection.

"Oh God, oh God," she whispered, sinking into her chair when she heard the sharp slap of the door.

"Good evening, madam. Your ticket?" A neatly dressed man in uniform and a dark blue cap appeared in front of her.

She held her breath and, with trembling hands, retrieved a folded rectangle of white cardboard from her jeans pocket. "H-here you go."

"Thank you." The conductor took Anna's ticket. "Is everything all right with you?"

"Yes, of course," Anna replied, glancing around nervously, trying to control the overwhelming tremor of her hands.

"Hmm, then have a pleasant journey."

"Listen." Anna stopped him. "Where are all the passengers?"

"Don't worry—after Ballymena, you'll remember how peacefully you sat here alone." He smirked.

"Can't wait," Anna whispered, rubbing her shoulders.

The conductor hadn't lied. Just ten minutes later the town appeared, and her phone buzzed on the seat.

"Anna? Are you okay?" Roderick spoke with his usual calmness.

"Yes." She exhaled. "I'm on my way to the coast. There was such a storm here ..." She buried her fingers in her chestnut hair, carefully considering each word.

Should I tell him or stay silent?

Anna chose to remain silent, remembering how Roderick had strongly advised her to visit his best friend, a psychiatrist, for any misunderstandings—about any cause for worry, disagreements, secret or overt grievances, anything that adults can discuss without the interference of third parties.

"The storm frightened you like that?"

"Frightened? No, I don't think so," she said, concealing her emotions from him as she had done so many times. She was coming to her senses, looking out at the bustling platform crowded with people. Here, students, backpackers, elderly couples, and younger couples with children crowded together—there was hardly any reason to be scared now. Well, except for the lack of space, of course.

"Good to hear. I'm glad. I hope Ballycastle will inspire you!" Roderick replied.

"Rick, the hotel I'm heading to is on Rathlin ..."

"Yes, right! I hope everything works out for you there."

THE GULL CRY HOTEL

Anna made a disgusted face. Just this morning, in the taxi, she had been absentmindedly writing romantic messages to this man, but now, in the evening, every word he said seemed irritating for some reason—insincere and indifferent. Or maybe it wasn't just a feeling; maybe it truly was that way. It had always been that way. How could Anna suddenly see through it all and discern the catch? What had happened to her? The answer was simple—Eddie had happened.

They exchanged the usual pleasantries, gave formal assurances, said the customary "love you," and hung up.

"Eddie … Where are you, Eddie?" Anna whispered, still staring at the black screen of her phone.

Of course he wouldn't save her from these intrusive hallucinations, but Eddie may be the one person she could tell this story to. Maybe just as a friend. As a fellow writer.

The train quickly filled up, and soon an elderly couple settled down beside Anna. A cloying mixture of vanilla and lavender filled the air, striking her unexpectedly. Anna leaned her forehead against the cold window and lowered her heavy eyelids. At some point, her struggle with the suffocating aroma came to an end. Thinking about the airplane and her new acquaintance, she drifted off to sleep.

***

"Ma'am, ma'am! End of the line!"

What? So fast? Anna opened her eyes. Above her stood a red-haired railroad worker in a bright green vest. The carriage was empty.

"Oh, I'm sorry." She jumped up from her seat. After getting off the train, she ran through the station and out to the road.

"Taxi!" Anna waved her hand, and a black cab leisurely approached her. "To the port."

"Heading to Rathlin, are you?" The cab driver smiled in the rear-view mirror.

"Exactly." Even he knew where Anna was going, unlike Roderick.

"The weather's been terrible for the past week. Storming constantly."

"After the storm comes the calm." Anna frowned.

"True, but not in Northern Ireland." The driver laughed.

Near the horizon, the sun sneakily flashed between the clouds. But soon enough, rain drummed against the window once more. All hope of witnessing the sunset disappeared behind a high wall of gray cloud.

"I hope the ferry is running." The driver peered at the heavy sky looming over the town.

"I hope so," Anna repeated softly, wrapping a woolen shawl around her neck.

Chapter 8

"Ma'am, are you heading to Rathlin Island?" A stocky sailor with a cigarette clamped between his teeth ushered the passengers along.

The ferry was departing, trying to run from the storm. Anna fixed her gaze on the horizon. For a moment it seemed as if something ominous had risen from the ocean and was creeping inexorably toward the coast. Here and now she had the chance to say no, drop her bags, and forget about the trip. But she nodded, handed her suitcase to the muscular sailor, and, taking two steps across the shaky gangplank, stepped onto the ferry.

"Please, come aboard," the man urged, fighting with the wind.

Anna hurried under the shelter and removed her soaked hood. The drizzle had given way to a full downpour.

"Follow me," the sailor shouted, and Anna, catching her breath, dashed toward the heavy door. The young man swiftly entered passengers place with her suitcase, leaned it against the nearest seat, and rushed back. He was in a hurry, probably with plenty of work in this weather. Anna rushed to the salon, picked up her suitcase, and took a seat by the window at the far end.

THE GULL CRY HOTEL

The vessel set off on its journey. Dark waves curled, gaining strength and crashing into the stern. They immediately shattered into pieces, but others replaced them, just as powerful and soullessly gray, much like the sky, the shore, and everything around. With an ear-piercing creak, the ship rolled from one foamy crest to another. The rain intensified, teasing the already furious sea.

Through the storm, a striped lighthouse came into view. The restless ocean swept over it, tirelessly testing its durability. Mighty and grim in any weather, it shone with a bright beam. It greeted giant cargo tankers coming from Scotland, and each time, it saw off the blue ferry to Rathlin.

As the lighthouse faded into the distance, a thick mist enveloped everything, with only occasional flashes of a white beam piercing through. Just as her eyes were adjusting to the darkness, the spotlight would blind them once more, causing Anna to close her inflamed eyelids in pain.

Finally the light dimmed and the shore disappeared into the fog. Ten minutes later, the vessel tilted. The suitcases of the few passengers made a resonant journey across the rough floor. Anna grabbed the railing and reached for her travel bag, but she quickly abandoned the attempt and clung to the armrest with both hands. An emergency signal was activated, urging passengers to put on their life jackets. The jacket was under her seat, but unfastening even one of her hands proved impossible.

The ferry swayed, then steadied, but Anna still couldn't release her fingers. The stubborn door creaked open and slammed shut, letting in the scent of the sea, the splashes of the waves, and a soaked sailor. Leaning on the slippery handrails, the young man straightened up, and, with a gaping mouth, caught his breath. Soon he reached the passengers and retrieved their life jackets from under the seats. He left one near Anna and distributed the others around the cabin.

"Are we sinking?" asked an old lady in confusion.

"No, not at all." The sailor shook his head, "We're almost at Rathlin—nowhere to sink."

A balding man jumped up and pressed his face to the window, peering at the gloomy seascape.

"Sir, please sit down! It's quite challenging to dock in weather like this. Always a rough ride." The sailor gestured theatrically, then promptly grabbed the back of a chair.

The ferry tilted again, this time to the left. Anna clung to the seat back and fastened her life jacket while the suitcases slowly slid to the other side. "Oh God," she moaned, hearing the cries of her fellow passengers.

The elderly lady, the balding man in the neat coat, and a couple of tourists, now all clad in identical orange life jackets, were gripping their seats. The sailor rushed back and disappeared behind the heavy door.

The bow surged forward and Anna felt a jolt. A second later, the deck became covered in thick foam. Somewhere car alarms were going off, and ahead, through the gray mist, the lights of the pier appeared.

"Thank God," Anna murmured.

Suddenly the ferry started spinning counterclockwise. There was an impact, then another impact, followed by a low creaking of the bulkheads and an ominous screech of metal.

"To the exit!" someone yelled through the open door.

Passengers leaped from their seats, grabbing their bags, and rushed toward the exit. The elderly lady picked up her handbag and froze.

"What's wrong? Can I help?" Anna leaned over.

"I don't feel well," she moaned.

"Hey, sailor! Hey, someone!" Anna yelled, but no one rushed to help. Anna bundled everything into one hand, supported the old lady with the other, and tried to take a step. The ferry rocked again, and Anna, abandoning her suitcase, clung to the railings. "Someone help!" she shouted again, her voice muffled by the storm.

"Don't call for help, Anna; no one will come," croaked the crone in a sinister voice.

Anna still held her, unable to believe her ears. But at some point she let go. The stranger huddled down and, without raising her head, approached the exit. Each slow step rang in Anna's head. *Anna Walker, the mad writer.*

To the hotel! Urgently to the hotel! Rest, sleep, and it will all pass. It's tension, that's all—damn tension!

Drenched with salty spray, Anna came ashore. The storm had completely obscured her view, and, like a moth, she flew toward the artificial light of the dock.

Entering the spacious arrivals hall, she stopped, placed her bags on the wooden floor, and removed the wet hood clinging to her hair. She untied the woolen scarf that hung around her neck like a snake, carrying an unbearable stench.

Shower, tea, a warm bed ... Shower, tea, a warm bed ... The words circled in her head like a mantra.

Ferry workers rushed past her, and soon she found herself completely alone. She looked around when someone nearby coughed loudly, deliberately. It was a man in a black coat and a flat cap. When Anna finally noticed him, he extended a sign with her name on it.

Utterly exhausted, she waved in a welcoming gesture. The man sprang into action, rushed over, and picked up her suitcase.

"Green." The greeter extended a red hand. "Green Barkley. Welcome to Rathlin!"

His small dark eyes darted with embarrassment, and his narrow mouth with its peculiar little mustache broke into a shy smile.

"Thank you! Tough conditions you've got here, though."

"In London you rarely see this, but around here"—he nodded casually toward the dock—"when the sky breaks loose, the ocean follows suit."

They walked to the car park, and in Green's hand, like a magician's wand from a mystical parlor, a long cane appeared. Courteously opening an umbrella, he escorted his guest to the car, unlocked the door, and tossed the suitcase into the boot.

"It's old but reliable," he said defensively, sneaking a glance at Anna in the rear-view mirror.

"I swear this is the very best place outside of Belfast," Anna said warmly, leaning her heavy head against the worn seat.

The car pulled onto the deserted road and glided smoothly over the hilly terrain. In the darkness and rain, Green drove by feel, but he drove very well, as he had had a lifetime to get to know the place. The storm ebbed and flowed. The car climbed a hill, buffeted by harsh winds, and, after a brief resistance, descended into a valley. Soon the gusts abated and the downpour settled into a steady drizzle. Fog crept across the fields. Anna raised her head, directing her tired gaze into the white mist. Suddenly, within the fog, an indistinct dark silhouette took on an eerie shape.

"What?" she whispered.

"Fog! Oh yes, Miss Walker, get used to it. Fog is an integral part of Rathlin."

"Over there ... a person," she said, pointing at the window.

"A person?" Green frowned, wiping the fogged-up glass. "Are you sure? I'm certain you must be mistaken."

"There was a person out there!" Anna exclaimed just as the car began to climb another hill.

"I assure you, there can't be anyone there," Green replied calmly. "In the lowlands, there's a marsh, Miss Walker. Few in their right mind would go there even on a sunny day."

In their right mind ... echoed in Anna's head. *Shower, tea, a warm bed! Shower, tea, a warm bed!* The novelist whispered her mantra.

They drove past a rocky headland, ascended another hill, and passed a trail near a treacherous cliff. The rain intensified once more as a familiar stone mansion appeared in the window—one she had seen in photographs.

"We're here." Green confirmed her suspicions.

THE GULL CRY HOTEL

He parked near a wall overgrown with ivy. In the bright glare of the headlights, the plant lit up in vivid reds, and for a moment Anna imagined the entire mansion was soaked with blood. A strange sense of trepidation began to stir within her. Everything about this day was filled with eerie coincidences—everything except for Eddie.

The sight of the windows glowing with warm electric light put Anna at ease for a moment. She took a deep breath and even thought she could smell fresh bed linen and hear the rustle of starched sheets.

The driver graciously opened the car door and unfurled his black umbrella once more.

The lobby was filled with the scent of roasted meat. It was quite cozy here—as cozy as homes designed to mimic the Victorian style could be. In the center of the large living room a fireplace crackled. Someone was sipping whiskey in a high-backed chair, and a young man in a doorman's uniform dozed on the sofa.

"Casper!" Green bellowed angrily, and the man lazily lifted his head from the cushion.

"Welcome to the Gull Cry Hotel!" A cheerful voice rang out from behind the low counter. Anna turned nervously, immediately locking eyes with a voluptuous red-haired Irishwoman. "I'm Rosemary." She waved, looking at the computer monitor. "You must be Mrs. Walker?"

"Miss," Anna corrected. "Miss Walker."

"If you've come to check out a groom, this is an awfully unfortunate place for it." Rosemary laughed, placing her hand on her chest.

"No, no, I'm not looking for ..." Anna reassured her, fumbling for her documents.

"We don't have many visitors at the moment," Rosemary explained, "but hopefully the weather will clear up and the Gull Cry Hotel will become popular again."

"Heh—popular," someone croaked from a high-backed chair. "Dream on, dear, dream on ..."

Ignoring the mockery, Rosemary scanned Anna's driving license and processed the payment. "Seven days, six nights—is that correct?"

"Yes, that's right."

"Breakfast starts at half-past eight." Rosemary returned the plastic cards and placed in front of Anna an antique key with a fob bearing the number 15. "You'll find everything you need for evening tea in your room."

"Thank you. Good night."

"And to you. A pleasant stay and good night, Mrs. Walker."

Anna could only muster a weary smile. She had neither the energy nor the inclination to argue or even engage in conversation. She ascended the creaky staircase to the first floor, twirling the ornate key in her hand, still puzzled about why the item felt so familiar. It was only when Casper placed her suitcase on the subdued carpet and closed the door behind him that a fragment from her horrifying dream appeared in Anna's mind. Sticking out of the balcony door, obstructing the dwarf's entry, had been an antique key—exactly the same as this one but without the fob.

Chapter 9

Anna surveyed the room. There was a tall bed and sturdy oak nightstands that held vintage table lamps. Floral motifs adorned everything. Her eyes lingered on a cozy nook near three tall windows, where a plush armchair with a footrest stood. This was where she intended to work, contemplating the mysterious view of the ocean. Next to the standard lamp was a table with a kettle, a couple of mugs, and an assortment of tea bags. On the other side of the bed was the door to the bathroom. Adjacent to this stood a worn writing desk with a carved chair tucked beneath it.

Anna flicked the kettle switch and perused the colorful array of teas. The tea bags looked like something purchased from a local witchcraft shop; it undeniably set the atmosphere but seemed a bit too much like potions to be brewed by a sorceress.

Chamomile, linden, and even peppermint and licorice… but how I long for a simple Earl Grey!

***

"But she's not even married! And at her age … So pretentious and arrogant. Of course, no one would marry someone like that!" Anna heard Rosemary's voice as soon as she found herself on the stairs again.

"Shh …" Someone interrupted her, hearing the creak of floorboards.

Anna reached the landing, where the storm raged outside the narrow window, and turned to face the hall. Here, the fire crackled, illuminating with warm light furniture that had been quite fashionable some twenty years ago. Rosemary, now suddenly blushing, fumbled behind the counter, and the chair by the fireplace was empty.

"Mrs. Walker!" The manager's voice conveyed feigned surprise.

"I wanted to have some tea before bed," Anna explained, surveying the room for any sign of other guests.

"Yes, of course. Everything is in your room." Rosemary for some reason avoided looking Anna in the eye.

"I drink black tea with bergamot."

"Oh yes." The manager seemed to remember something long forgotten. "Please visit the restaurant." She pointed to a door on the same wall as the fireplace. "You will find everything you need in there. I'm sorry, but you're a bit too late for dinner."

"Thank you, I'm not hungry —" Anna said, but Rosemary, not bothering to listen, had already hurried away. Anna blinked, frozen by the table near the door, but eventually moved from her spot, walking across the woolen carpet to the door indicated and entering a long dining room with a row of panoramic windows. She was ready to greet someone. According to her calculations, the person with whom Rosemary had been conversing should be in here. But here was no one.

Cozy! Anna thought, approaching a tall table at the end of the room, which was adorned with bundles of tea bags and plates of biscuits and pastries.

Round tables, each paired with plush chairs instead of standard hotel seats, stood near the sheer curtains. Anna brewed some tea, grabbed a couple of ginger cookies, and settled down by the window. Beyond the glass a real hurricane raged, illuminating with flashes of lightning a steep cliff and a stormy sea.

Despite the oddities that had colored the day, Anna felt noticeably calmer now. She liked this place. It was unlike anything she was accustomed to. There were catastrophically few people here—a welcome contrast to the overcrowded London she had left behind.

One flash followed another, the rolls of thunder trailing behind, and rain drummed on the slopes. Anna watched the horizon as, in the brief light of the storm, heavy clouds appeared in an ominous formation. They spilled over the ocean, swirling funnels of tiny tornadoes. The peals of thunder no longer frightened Anna. Sipping her tea, she observed the dynamics of the storm. Suddenly another flash illuminated the ocean, revealing numerous tendrils descending to the water like the tentacles of a colossal sea monster. Anna froze, piercing the darkness with her gaze, unwilling to even contemplate such thoughts.

The next flash illuminated the ocean, and Anna saw how the nimble vortex arched and rose above the raging sea. The monster marched, and it marched towards the shore. Anna, without taking her eyes off it, stared into the black darkness that had descended on the island again. A rumble echoed somewhere very close, and she started. Her hand dropped the cup, which rang out as it fell onto the saucer, and the hot drink spread across the pristine tablecloth. Rosamary rushed into the room a moment later.

"Are you all right?" she asked, nervously clearing away the utensils.

"Yes. I'm terribly sorry. Just …" Anna dismissed the horror from her face. "May I have a glass of wine?" She lifted her gaze, realizing that after everything she had seen that day, sleep wouldn't come easily.

"Wine?" Rosemary turned around.

"Yes, exactly." Anna nodded.

"We … we ran out of … wine," the manager stammered.

"Ran out of wine?" Anna blinked rapidly. This strange phrase just couldn't fit into her mind. Perhaps London had spoiled her. Perhaps such things as good wine were meant to run out on a rainy night. Or maybe she'd expected something more from this place, just like she had from Roderick—something that neither the Gull Cry Hotel nor her lover could ever give her.

They stared at each other for a few more seconds until Rosemary broke the silence. "I'll order Green to go to the dock tomorrow and buy some," she said.

Both froze with unnaturally pleasant expressions.

"New guests tomorrow?" Anna asked casually.

"Americans," Rosemary whispered conspiratorially, sensing fertile ground for gossip.

"Mmm!" Anna's eyebrows shot up towards her hairline. "Then tell Green to grab a dozen cases of beer."

"Oh no." The manager waved her hands. "I hope they won't start getting drunk here!"

"Sure they will." This time Anna smiled genuinely. "Goodnight, Rosemary!"

"Goodnight," she mumbled. "If you need anything …" She seemed to snap back to reality, immediately donning the mask of hypocrisy, which seemed the same to her as hospitality.

"I'll make sure to dial the number written on the phone," Anna said from the lobby.

She entered her room and locked the door.

THE GULL CRY HOTEL

"The key! No wine and now this damn key!"

She looked at it again, sitting by the window, while preparing for sleep, even as she lay in bed. Relaxation proved elusive. Because of the key, Anna kept returning again and again to the nightmare of the previous night. Her nerves couldn't handle it; she stood up and moved the nightstand closer to the door.

***

The last time she had experienced the fear of a nocturnal intrusion was back in her teenage years. Then again, in university, she had shared a room with Ashley Roggins, the wildest girl in Portsmouth. It was a town of fishermen and football players, so both kinds frequented Ashley. Anna didn't want to dwell on those times. However, against her wishes, her imagination painted a picture of a small room with a tiny window. Two beds, two small nightstands, a rickety wardrobe, and a lamp that gave out a muted light. Laughter and shuffling sounds echoed from behind the door, which was covered in posters. Ashley desperately tried to unlock it, jokingly fending off an insistent companion. Finally a key, along with a bunch of jingling keychains, fell to the floor—a signal for Anna to put on her headphones, turn up the music, and cover herself with a blanket. The lock clicked and the door swung open. They burst into the room, shedding their clothes. Anna couldn't hear them anymore; she was pulling the blanket higher when she caught a familiar scent. Oh yes, scents overwhelmed her even then, and she had a very good memory for smells.

Joe? Joe Irwin? It was only from him that she'd caught a whiff of that cologne when they'd passed each other in the narrow corridors. A guy from uni, a rugby player, captain of the Blue Whales, and the only person in all of Portsmouth whom she deeply liked.

Reaching for the lamp, Anna turned it on. It seemed they didn't notice her presence or the sudden illumination at all. However, a moment later Joe halted. His eyes locked with Anna's. His strong jaw tightened. He released Ashley and started pulling on his T-shirt. He was breathing heavily, no longer acknowledging Anna's existence.

"Hey, what's wrong with you?" Ashley protested.

Anna didn't answer. She silently watched Joe, who was dismissively grabbing his trousers from the floor.

A sense of hurt constricted Anna's chest as Joe flushed with shame. He had dreamed of asking her out one day—Anna Walker was always the only girl in all of Portsmouth he never mustered the courage to approach.

***

The first betrayal. The inaugural one but certainly not the last. Yet the first one tends to etch itself more vividly in one's memory than the subsequent betrayals.

THE GULL CRY HOTEL

"Ah, Rosemary, a glass of wine wouldn't hurt right now." Anna fluffed her pillow, cocooned herself in the downy blanket, and closed her eyes, tired from the Irish wind that had stirred up the ferocious storm.

More than anything, Anna just wanted to peacefully fall asleep and avoid having any dreams. But tranquility eluded her entirely. Now, in her dreams, she stood on the edge of the cliff. A cool breeze brushed against her face, playing with her hair. Below, the jade-green ocean roared.

She surveyed her surroundings—a grand old mansion of a hotel loomed behind her, and near it, indistinct silhouettes of people. Women and men were distinguishable only by height and outline, though even that wasn't certain. Their eyes and mouths seemed fused together, and wet strands of hair hung from high foreheads. Anna shuddered. One of them, grotesquely tall, extended a massive hand, and then, as if on command, they all turned their gaze toward the horizon. She scrutinized them, trying to recognize someone, but no one was familiar. A strange mist deliberately concealed their faces. Almost alive, it crept to each of them and stole their features. Anna struggled to look away and, like the others, turned her gaze to the sea.

The sea receded. The water revealed the sand, occasional black rocks, and sunken boats. At the bottom lay dozens, perhaps hundreds, of rusty fishing boats. Hundreds, perhaps even thousands, of distorted barges, as if the sea had swallowed them all at once.

Jesus Christ. Anna's gaze was full of horror, even though she knew it was just a dream.

Suddenly, instead of water, fog crept in from afar. It emerged from the ocean, advancing in a massive wall toward the shore—toward the solitary hotel and all these people, and most importantly, toward Anna.

She peered at it anxiously. The white mist resembled a living organism approaching the cliff and ruthlessly devouring all visible space. Anna stepped back. She had only paused for a moment, feeling someone's close breath, when he pushed her from behind.

Her legs slid on the wet grass and, unable to hold on, she tumbled downward. Everything inside her contracted as she sensed the rapid descent.

Ann jolted upright on the bed.

Oh my God ... She tried to banish the horrifying dream.

Outside, deep in the night, the storm had finally subsided. The key stuck silently out of the door, and it seemed that everyone in the hotel was asleep. Anna listened carefully—the sound of the waves subtly broke through the ringing silence.

THE GULL CRY HOTEL

She rose and cracked open the window. A cold breeze swept into the room, the sound intensified, and the room became filled with the scent of the sea.

"Iodine is good for the nervous system. Breathe, Anna, breathe!" she commanded herself.

Having caught her breath, she closed the window and lay back in bed, drifting off again, this time without the anxieties of the past, without unnecessary thoughts, but with a lingering curiosity and a barely perceptible fear.

Chapter 10

Outside, seagulls shrieked relentlessly. They circled above the cliff, occasionally swooping towards the hotel.

"Half past five." Anna squinted at her watch. "What the hell?"

She tossed aside the blanket. "Cold—it's so damn cold!"

Shifting from foot to foot, she hurried to the armchair and glanced out of the window. Everything was shrouded in mist. Only a portion of the courtyard was visible—damp asphalt and no more than ten feet of green grass. In the white haze, noisy birds circled above the road, desperately diving into the fog.

"What have you got there? A corpse or something?" Anna grimaced and covered her head with a pillow. The noises subsided, and she sank into the sweet, plum-syrup-like sleep of early morning.

At half past ten, Anna finally awoke. Slicing through billowy clouds, the sun peeked through the windows.

"What a beautiful morning," she whispered, gazing at the tranquil ocean.

She freshened up, dressed, and descended for breakfast. There was no one at the reception desk, and the lobby was deserted as well. She noted that the daylight completely transformed the provincial inn, and the aroma from the kitchen added a touch of homely comfort to the place. Anna stepped into the long dining area. Rosemary was bustling about with the utensils, and only one table was occupied. In the farthest corner sat a tall man in a tweed suit. He was perusing the morning newspaper while slowly sipping his tea.

"A classic scene from a classic detective novel," Anna remarked.

It seemed like no one else in the world read newspapers anymore, but clearly they did in Northern Ireland. What could be better than the smell of fresh newsprint? Only the aroma of morning coffee!

Anna strode towards the spot that had caught her eye the previous evening.

"Mrs. Walker," Rosemary called out. "It's self-service here."

"Miss—Miss Walker."

It's best not to make Anna angry in the morning.

"Of course." Rosemary smirked. "Hot beverages here, eggs there, sides, bread, and bacon."

"Thank you," Anna mumbled, armed with a floral-patterned plate.

She breakfasted in silence, accompanied only by the rustling of the newspaper and the ceaseless cry of birds. Then her phone lit up with an incoming call.

"Good morning, dear." Anna squeezed the receiver between shoulder and ear, tearing off a piece of warm bread.

"Morning. How are you there?" Roderick's indifferent tone seemed even colder today.

"Me? I'm fine. Everything's fine. How about you?"

"I ran into Alison at the Ritz yesterday."

"You were at the Ritz yesterday?"

"Gregor invited me. What's the big deal?"

"Gregor invited you to a restaurant?"

"He had friends from the Netherlands visiting; they needed to be fed somewhere."

"You went to the Ritz with Gregor to feed his friends?" Anna's appetite vanished as if by magic.

"Yes." Roderick, now a bit flustered, began to get nervous. "What's the big deal? But it's not about them …"

"Of course it's not about them," Anna said through gritted teeth.

"Alison informed me that you're on probation. The publishing house is on the verge of canceling your contract."

Roderick gossiping with Alison about my contract? That's something new. Anna's blood started to boil in her veins.

"And I'm on the verge of ending our relationship!" she retorted sharply and quickly pressed the "end call" button.

Her stomach quivered; her hands trembled. Her knees groaned under the tension, and blood rushed to her face.

"Then why not take that step?" A velvety voice resonated from the corner.

Anna looked up. The speaker was still concealed behind his newspaper.

"Taking just one step is often the hardest," she replied, suppressing her emotions, trying to calm herself. Tears moistened her eyes from the injustice, and her throat constricted with a spasm.

When she reasoned with a cold mind, she saw that Roderick hadn't done anything at this very moment to hurt her so profoundly. However, apparently his offenses had accumulated, gathering trivialities like a snowball rolling downhill.

"Then don't take just one step, take several. Walk past without looking back. Let him savor the sight one last time," her unsolicited advisor persisted.

"I'm Anna." She tried to make out her interlocutor. "Anna Walker."

"Benedict." Her advisor didn't even think of lowering his newspaper. "Benedict Russell."

"Apparently, Benedict, you're not familiar with this feeling." Anna turned again to the window and took a sip of bitter coffee.

"Loneliness?" The silver-haired Irishman finally lowered the rustling pages.

"Love." Anna raised an eyebrow, locking eyes with Benedict.

"Well, no … It's not love at all." Mr. Russell closed himself off again with the sheets of paper.

Laughter drifted in from the kitchen.

What the hell? Anna fumed. However, it's worth considering that if the whole world is against you, most likely you're the one heading in the wrong direction. Don't like what comes out of it? Turn around and walk with it … It's all about you! It's always all about you.

Yes, Anna, in London, no one could care less about you and your problems. They don't care who you talk to on the phone, who you sleep with, date, live with, and especially what you think about all of it. Your life belongs only to you, and no one has the right to comment on your decisions. And it's not even about freedom and rights anymore. Truly, nobody cares about you. To each and every one, from the bottom of their hearts, your existence is utterly inconsequential. But get away from the noisy cities to a small town where the only performers are pesky seagulls and everyone is itching to pry into your life, to evaluate it and offer the murkiest of all known advice. Anna grabbed the plate and porcelain cup and left the restaurant. She went up to her room and put her breakfast on the table by the open window.

"Much better," she concluded, sinking into a plush chair.

Gripping the slim body of her laptop, Anna pulled it off the bed and placed it in front of her.

"Jeffrey couldn't find peace. Somewhere around midnight, fear took residence in him (fear for Juliana) and settled there—in the depths of his trembling heart…" Now Anna knew everything about that trembling.

She worked until lunchtime. It wouldn't be accurate to say that she was brimming with fresh ideas, but the gripping atmosphere of the previous evening and the eerie dream had undoubtedly left their mark on her text. The internet connection was very weak, but she still managed to Google whether there was a specific mental health diagnosis for unexplained anxiety and horrifyingly realistic dreams. Google obligingly informed her that that was almost all of them.

With a heavy sigh, Anna surveyed the steep coastal slopes and the surprisingly calm ocean. The distant northern sun only occasionally hid behind thin clouds, and the low trees were tinged with a pleasant yellow. In Ireland, only a fool would miss out on such a day—an ideal one for a stroll along the coast. Intentionally leaving her mobile phone on the table, she stepped out of her room.

"Yes, there's some Rick, I'm telling you," Rosemary reported, talking to someone on the landline as Anna reached the stairs. Putting the staff in their place wouldn't hurt. However, it was Anna, not Rosemary, who was on unfamiliar territory.

"Hush, someone's coming," Rosemary whispered. "For a stroll?" she asked loudly, replacing the receiver.

"Yes, for a stroll." Without even glancing at the reception, Anna proceeded to the foyer.

As the door swung open, a sea breeze brushed her face. It was a golden autumn on the northern coast, and today might be the last clear day until spring. Anna borrowed a black cane umbrella from the hotel's floor stand and stepped across the threshold.

"What an air," she couldn't resist remarking aloud.

THE GULL CRY HOTEL

Her lungs filled with the scents of meadow grass, juniper bushes, and coastal brine—such a rich and complex aroma for a city dweller. She strolled toward the cliff, leaning lightly on the black umbrella.

"Mrs. Walker, don't break it!" called a voice from behind.

"Go to hell, Rosemary," Anna replied, her response fading away, barely audible.

His Majesty the cliff enchanted her with its beauty. The towering ridge stretched to the very cape and beyond, leaving a thin strip of beach entirely inaccessible. Anna walked along a narrow path surrounded by plump seagulls. After twenty minutes of leisurely walking, a wooden bench appeared beneath a bush perpetually bent by the wind. Anna froze in front of the steel plaque screwed onto one of the dark boards.

Dedicated to my wife, Shifra, claimed by the sea. When I'm here, I know you're with me.

Frowning, Anna hesitated to sit. It was obviously someone's memorial bench. She crossed the gray asphalt of the road and found herself near a low forest. After walking a hundred meters, she came across a noticeable trail leading into the thicket. Thorny clusters of hawthorn closed elegantly above the passage, forming an arch adorned with blood-red fruits. How could she resist going down there? It was like entering a little world of elves. The reader might chuckle, but the farther from Belfast one gets, the more frequently one encounters a peculiar pagan cult brought from neighboring Iceland to the remote corners of the country.

Anna bent down and, after only twenty-nine steps, emerged onto undulating terrain. *Redwood Swamps*, explained the sign, and for some reason her heart quickened. This was the very swamp where she had seen a person from the road. She tightened her grip on the umbrella, tapping it on the green moss. It bounced off the ground, and Anna took her first step. After another two hundred steps she froze on top of a hill. This place seemed peculiar, and she aimlessly spun around, trying to understand why.

Right! It's too quiet here.

Anna descended the hill and, out of habit, struck the cane on the moss. The umbrella, failing to find the ground, suddenly sank handle-deep. The viscous waters closed in, and Anna lacked the leverage to pull it out. She fell to her knees, trying to hold on to the umbrella and horrified at the thought of retracing her steps blindly. In response the green ooze gurgled and swallowed its prey. Letting go of the cane handle with the cheap hotel branding, Anna braced her hands against the hill and caught her breath.

Now only a stick was a reliable tool to prevent a foot from sinking into the treacherous waters. Anna cautiously plunged a resilient branch into the green moss, and it instantly gave way. She took a step back and pulled on the makeshift cane. The marsh squelched, and from beneath the green cover, a raspberry-like bubble inflated.

"What on earth is this?" Anna frowned.

Her first strike at the unusual red object yielded nothing. But with the second slap, a perfectly white human hand emerged from the surface. Remarkably preserved, as if alive, it seemed like it could twitch at any moment and grasp the stick with its fingers.

Anna straightened up and pressed the stick against the object. The lifeless hand swung, and Anna screamed, immediately covering her mouth with her palm. Another magenta bubble bulged from the bluish-green sludge. Behind it appeared a collar and a sloping nape. The pale skin swelled as if it were a sponge soaked with water. Sparse patches of hair clung to the crown.

"Oh my God!" Anna recoiled.

Her foot slid across the mat of reeds and sank into the marshy ground. Anna dropped the stick and grabbed hold of the grass.

"Damn it, damn it, Anna!" she exclaimed in frustration.

Her boots quickly filled with water, becoming unbearably heavy. *A foolish, foolish death. To come to Northern Ireland in search of inspiration only to drown in a swamp on the very first stroll. Bravo! It's hard to imagine a more idiotic outcome, for heaven's sake.*

Her fingers clawed at the soil; the earth collected beneath her nails; her feet were deprived of solid ground. Panic surged, and when the cold water reached her knees, Anna screamed.

"Help! Somebody help!"

God, who am I shouting to? There's not a soul for a hundred miles!

Anna struggled to pull herself up on her elbows. Using them as anchors on the damp ground, she surged forward with her last ounce of strength. It carried her through one desperate lunge. As if in retaliation for her attempt to escape, the swamp gurgled discontentedly, swallowing her almost up to her waist.

How? How could I let this happen? Desperation welled up within Anna. *After everything that has happened to me, I'll just vanish on this nearly uninhabited island. Eddie ... I'll never see you again, my dear friend.* Tears filled her eyes.

The cold water embraced her waist, and something embraced her ankle with it—icy fingers gripped Anna and gently pulled down. Her body, without seeking permission, convulsed. Of course, she was aware of the harsh law of the bog—the more you resist, the deeper it swallows you. She let out a piercing scream as the Redwood Marshes engulfed her up to her chest.

Hold on! Anna didn't immediately grasp whether it was the voice of reason or someone else's voice from the outside world.

"Hold on!" It echoed louder, and she noticed a dark figure in a tweed suit on the path.

Benedict— what's his second name? Anna frowned, but the next moment her expression brightened, and she reached out her hand.

"How did you end up here?"

"I have no idea … Be careful! The swamp is right behind you."

"I know, I know … Come on, let's get out of here. Now, lean on your knee. Excellent. Now lift the other leg. Well done—splendid!"

Breathing heavily, Anna lay on the ground. "Thank you," she gasped.

"Oh, stop it!" Benedict waved it off.

"But how did you—"

"I followed you after lunch." Benedict had anticipated the question. "Thought I'd keep you company. I arrived and then saw this …" He shrugged comically, clearly intending to conclude the story with a joke, but he suddenly fell silent.

The tranquil Redwood Gardens of Peace spat out another corpse from the peat. It surfaced, framed by foul-smelling bubbles of hydrogen sulfide. On the adorned muddy surface emerged a triangle of blue skirt. Behind the skirt appeared a checkered coat, and behind it—the head of the drowned woman. Hair, like a reddish halo, enveloped the swollen face, which expressed no more emotion.

Anna screamed and lowered her gaze.

"Holy mother of God ..." Benedict touched his shaved chin.

"Behind you—another one," Anna croaked, swallowing loudly.

Benedict turned around and froze.

"Benedict, call the police."

"I don't have a phone," he said, not taking his eyes off the poor wretch.

"Damn."

"Where's yours?"

"I left it in my room."

"Come on, let's go and get it." Benedict reached out to Anna.

"I think I saw the killer."

THE GULL CRY HOTEL

Benedict froze, his muscles tense. "What are you talking about?"

"Yesterday, when we drove past this place, there was a man standing right here," Anna confessed.

Benedict exhaled and shook his head. "No, no ... These corpses could be quite ancient. The acids released by the swamp preserve the bodies from decay for decades—even centuries."

"In any case, we need to report it to the police. These people might be on the missing persons list and have families—loved ones who might still be waiting for them."

"Let's go." Benedict took Anna firmly by the forearm. "You're soaked. A storm is rolling in from the ocean, and there's warmth and a phone in the hotel. Sitting here won't help anyone."

The sun soon became shrouded in leaden clouds, and fog rolled in from the lowlands along the coastline. Anna wanted to believe with all her might that it was just getting darker because evening was near, but a new storm was brewing over the ocean. A pair of yellow headlights appeared on the winding road. The travelers briskly approached the hotel just as a car sped by.

Green was bringing guests from the port. Young and too drunk from their time in Belfast, they arrived to disturb the tranquility of the occupants of the Gull Cry Hotel.

Chapter 11

The scent of lavender filled the bathroom, gently permeating her airways. Steam settled on the tiles and mirrors like a sultry cloud. Anna relaxed, placing a rolled-up terry towel under her neck. Her body still ached, and the thought of the marshes weighed heavily on her mind. Before her eyes were the marble face of the deceased and the bewildered gaze of Rosemary, her hands frantically searching for the landline phone. Just a few minutes ago, shivering from the cold, Anna had recounted the bodies she had discovered, urging Rosemary to call the police. Finally the manager had armed herself with the handset and dialed the three-digit number.

"Hello, police department?"

After that, Anna didn't hear much. She had gone up to her room, discarded her wet clothes on the floor, and filled the tub with hot water. Now she turned the water off, intending to immerse herself in silence.

Rain pounded on the ribbed glass. Its hypnotic tap was occasionally interrupted by the revelry of the newly arrived American guests and the monotonous drip right by her foot. Anna closed her weary eyes. How could she sleep now after the horrors of the day? Perhaps ordering a bottle of wine to her room would help.

In the relative silence, which proved to be deceptive, she suddenly heard a strange sound. It was as if the door to her room had been carefully closed by an uninvited guest.

She opened her eyes, lifted her head from the towel, and listened. Someone stepped softly onto the carpet. The footsteps sounded as if a child were sneaking around the room.

The dwarf! echoed in her mind. Her eyes widened; her hands gripped the edges of the bath. "Who's there?" she uttered fearfully.

The nickel silver handle of the bathroom descended. Anna stopped breathing. The door was gently pushed, but it didn't yield. Paralyzed by fear, Anna was once again saved by an age-old habit—the habit of locking the bathroom. Yes, yes, from the time when she had shared living space with Ashley Roggins and, incidentally, with all of Portsmouth.

Someone cautiously stepped away from the door, trying not to make a noise. Anna slowly emerged from the bath and put on the hotel robe. Without taking her eyes off the door, she found her mobile and, with a familiar motion, illuminated the screen. *No service*, the sign in the top right corner indicated.

Maybe it's because of the storm, but an emergency call should work, the terrified woman muttered, running her fingers anxiously through her hair.

Her hands were trembling. Entering the three digits felt like an eternity. No ringing ensued as she repeated the sacred combination over and over. The monotonous howling of the wind was replaced by a loud thud against the glass. Anna jumped and dropped her phone. It fell at an angle and, bouncing about a meter, crashed screen down onto the white tiles.

"Damn! Damn!" Anna muttered, picking up the shattered Android. "Damn! How could this happen?" Her gaze slid over the nearby objects, seeking something heavy or at least fear-inducing, but she found nothing at all. Spinning on the spot, she spotted a cosmetics bag. Snatching the velvety pouch from the windowsill, she immediately found a tiny pair of nail scissors inside.

Good enough, she decided, lifting the miniature weapon into the air as she approached the door. Now it was one of two things: either she would see the imaginary dwarf with her own eyes or she would confirm the auditory hallucinations.

The lock clicked and, trembling with fear, Anna turned the handle. Her gaze fell upon the unmade bed, its oak legs pressing into the carpet. Opening the door a little further, a wardrobe revealed itself, its door slightly ajar. Anna silently stepped onto the carpet and peered behind the door, where an armchair sat peacefully beside a small round table. The storm raged outside the window, and someone could be hiding behind the thick curtains.

Anna took another hesitant step and, flinching at the creak of the floorboards, darted out of the room. After covering thirty steps of red-and-white lily-patterned carpet, she found herself on the staircase.

"There's someone in my room!" she yelled, running barefoot down the stairs.

"What? What are you talking about?" Rosemary froze in the middle of the hall with a tray.

"Someone was in my room just now!" Anna shouted. "Someone came in while I was taking a bath. And maybe they're still there!"

"That can't be, madam. All the guests and hotel staff are here right now," the manager protested.

In the glow of a couple of standard lamps and the fireplace, familiar faces appeared. Benedict Russell smiled, raising a glass of amber whiskey in a welcoming gesture. Green had joined him for a drink, still clad in his black cloak, and was now seemingly ready to leave the bustling hall. Seated by the window in an armchair was a plump older lady. Casting a momentarily wide-eyed gaze towards the staircase, she reached for the teapot, filled her flowery cup, and clucked disapprovingly.

"Modern ladies have no manners … appearing in a robe in front of gentlemen. Where is good old England heading?" she mumbled.

On the other side of the fireplace, a group of scantily clad young people froze. Just moments ago they had been coaxing Casper into playing darts and encouraging the lad to have a few drinks.

"Please, have a seat!" Benedict exclaimed, jumping up. He rushed to Anna and took her arm, leading her to an empty chair near one of the lamps, where she sank down slowly.

"You were so impressed by our swamp"—Rosemary gave an insidious smile—"now anything can haunt your imagination."

Anna wanted to confidently assert that Rosemary was wrong. However, recalling her horrifying dream, the chase on the train, and the old woman's whisper on the ferry, she hesitated to reply.

Of course, if she had gone mad, she probably wouldn't realize it. Perhaps her consciousness had long crossed that elusive line—the one that, once crossed, doesn't lead back to sanity. She alternately examined the faces of the guests and the unpretentious floral pattern on the furniture.

"Stress. It's all stress." Benedict squatted down beside her.

THE GULL CRY HOTEL

"Benedict, please!"

"I believe you, I believe you," he assured her.

Why? Anna thought.

"Mr. Russell," Rosemary protested, carrying the tray into the dining room. It held a neat circle of empty beer bottles. Despite her recent quarrel over alcohol, the hotel manager now looked cheerful and extremely hospitable; she had obviously been treating the newly arrived tourists.

"I'll go up anyway," Benedict interrupted.

"Mr. Russell! Mrs. Walker is perfectly capable of looking after herself. There's no need to reenact scenes from her books here," Rosemary urged.

They know about the books too ... Excellent! Anna smirked.

Benedict didn't reply. His eyebrows shot up towards the edge of his gray hair, but he quickly tried to wipe the bewilderment from his face and went upstairs.

"So, who exactly are we looking for? What did you hear?" This voice came from the high-backed chair near the fire. Someone was sitting in it—the same person whose presence Anna hadn't immediately noticed the night before.

"I heard a dwa ..." Anna started fervently before trailing off into a hoarse whisper. "A door opened. It sounded like someone entered the room."

A red-bearded darts player with a tattooed neck paused his game and surveyed Anna with a curious gaze.

"Would you like a drink? The bar's been restocked," Rosemary asked, frozen in the kitchen doorway.

"From the south of France, warmed by the sun." The stranger in the chair raised a glass of rich red liquid.

"Thank you, but I only drink white." Anna hesitated, examining the diverse guests in this remote Irish inn with unhidden interest.

"Quite a shame." The man leaned forward, piercing Anna with his gaze through rectangular glasses. "I don't consider this dew washed off the grapes as wine at all. Only red wine can mingle with blood and convey the warmth of a summer evening to the body. Especially on such a wretched night."

Anna could have argued with such a statement, but for some reason she didn't feel like contradicting this man. His entire demeanor vividly conveyed the definitiveness of his judgments and his inflexibility. Wavy wrinkles formed dense rows on his forehead with the slightest movement of his face, and deep nasolabial folds seemed to hinder any attempt to smile.

"What's your name, dear?" The tea-enjoying woman spoke, suddenly changing anger to mercy. Her pale skin was complemented by a lilac wool sweater, and in her gray curly hair, a thin olive-colored headband gleamed. "I'm Jill." She extended a hand, fragrant with lotion, for a ladylike handshake. "Jill Amsterham."

"Anna Walker," the novelist replied, rising to the greeting.

Dressed in pastel hues reminiscent of Claude Monet's *Water Lilies*, Jill lacked a single bright spot—nothing to capture Anna's wandering gaze and enable it to finally settle on something. Madam Amsterham beamed with a friendly smile, but she soon turned back to the window's darkness and took another sip of her dark tea.

"Casper, go to the kitchen and open a bottle of Chardonnay," Rosemary ordered sternly. "More wine, Father Kaiden?" she asked, leaning toward the chair with a gracious smile.

Father? Anna frowned and turned toward the fireplace. The black attire of the lean man was adorned with a white rectangle of a collar, silently indicating an affiliation, apparently, with the Catholic persuasion.

"Very pleased to meet you, Father Kaiden." Anna turned from Jill to the priest. "Where do you come from?"

"I live in the presbytery next to local church by the lighthouse. Unfortunately, the roof of the Lord's abode has sprung a leak, and Rosemary kindly agreed to provide me with one of the rooms while repairs are under way." He took a sip of wine. "And what brings you here?"

Anna accepted the glass from Casper. "The main goal, I suppose, is to be alone. One on one with my thoughts."

"You couldn't find a better place," Green chimed in.

"Aaahhh!" This sudden scream came from the darts player as he hit a portrait on the wall in the forehead with a dart. The guests patiently endured the emotional scene in the corner.

"Father, since you're a local, you must have heard about the missing people, have you?" Anna asked, sipping the wine. Fr. Kaiden raised his eyebrows, adjusted his glasses, and stared at his collocutor.

"What are you talking about?" Jill exclaimed, slapping her cheek with an affected blush.

"Just a few hours ago, Mr. Russell and I discovered a couple of bodies in the swamp," Anna replied, swallowing her drink.

"Bodies? In the swamp?" a blond American woman said with interest. She sauntered over to the priest and casually leaned on the back of his chair.

"What did they look like?" chimed in a broad-shouldered guy with piercings adorning various parts of his rather handsome face.

"Oh, come on! Don't you know what bodies look like?" scoffed a petite brunette in tight leggings, pulling colorful darts from the target.

"Camila, sweetheart, pass me the bottle." The redhead slumped onto the couch.

"In winter clothes, with no signs of violence …" Anna said thoughtfully, gazing at the black log smoldering in the fireplace.

"Quite an interesting description." Green raised his chin.

"I write a lot. Often detective stories." Anna slowly shifted her gaze to the driver. "That evening, Green, when you drove me here, I saw a person in the swamp. Possibly a murderer."

"Oh, please, Anna!" Benedict waved this away as he descended the stairs. "Admit that you nearly perished there yourself."

"Found anyone?" Anna stood up.

"No one. The room is completely empty. Here—I brought your slippers. And here's your key." Benedict courteously placed the footwear in front of Anna and took a seat on the couch. "It's quite obvious that the couple decided to take a walk along the deserted path," he continued. "Let's assume the gentleman stumbled and the lady tried to pull him out. She couldn't manage it and ended up in the marsh too."

"Thank you, Mr. Russell, for the explanation," Rosemary cut in, trying to close the topic.

"Have you reported it to the police?" Anna followed her with her eyes as she disappeared into the kitchen once again.

"Of course!" came in response.

"I want to see those bodies!" suddenly exclaimed the young man with the piercings.

"Me too!" chimed in the blonde, a crazy smile flickering across her face.

A lightning flash outside was followed by thunder a moment later. Jill flinched and hastily placed her cup on the saucer.

"I have no intention to disappoint you"—with evident disdain for the young people, Fr. Kaiden spoke up—"but the storms of Rathlin are among the longest lasting on the entire northern coast."

"Aaaahhh," Camila shouted to the sky, "what a bore! Why the hell did we come here?"

The young people exchanged glances. "Because this place is in the legendary top twenty hotels"—the red-haired guy rubbed his tattooed neck, and under the pressure of everyone's attention, he continued—"where ghosts dwell."

"Ghosts?" Anna frowned.

"Nonsense," Mrs. Amsterham shot back, grabbing her cup again.

Benedict struggled to contain his laughter, and the priest, turning towards the fire, only murmured softly, "Oh, Lord!"

"Rosemary, tell me, do ghosts inhabit these walls?" The blonde hit the manager with the question as she entered the hall.

"More wine?" A rosy-cheeked Rosemary didn't rush to respond.

"Yes, please." An unpleasant shiver ran through Anna's body.

"I would gladly refute such statements"—Green decided to answer—"but this is a very old building, and sometimes strange things happen here."

"What exactly has happened here?" one of the youngsters from distant Chicago chimed in.

"Well"—the driver hesitated—"sometimes hotel guests hear footsteps in the corridors." He cast a sharp glance at Anna. "Clear knocks coming from nowhere and creepy whispers that come with a howling wind."

"I told you we were in the right place!" Mr. Piercing exclaimed with excitement.

"Rosemary, confess, you made all this up to keep the hotel from being empty," Benedict prodded.

"Getting into this ranking, Mr. Russell, is not that simple," she immediately retorted. "The hotel owners must have substantial grounds for such statements."

"And you definitely have them?"

"Don't we?" She looked into Anna's eyes intently.

"Prove it!" Benedict wasn't backing down.

"Why should I prove anything, Mr. Russell?" She flashed him a cunning look. "The night will tell everything for me."

"Then I suppose I heard a ghost?" Anna interrupted the resulting silence. She was ready to believe it. Getting rid of a ghost seemed like a much more achievable task than overcoming mental illness.

"Yesterday you saw a killer; today you heard a ghost. I bet you'll be confessing to writing in the fantasy genre before long." Fr. Kaiden grinned, revealing his yellow teeth.

Anna turned towards the window and fell silent. Flashes of lightning occasionally illuminated the horizon, and the rest of the time she could only see her own blurred reflection. As for the ecstatic young people, their motivation was clear: Too many came to these damp lands to try a popular drug. Liberty cap, a psilocybin mushroom, was what these kids had come here for, and only Jill Amsterham was likely to believe in a ghost story.

"It's strange that you don't believe in ghosts, Father. They may be eerie, but still, they are a spiritual element of our world," she countered, albeit with a slight delay.

"You'd be quite surprised to learn what I believe in," Fr. Kaiden replied without losing his composure. "However, there must be a balance in everything. And this worldwide spiritual movement doesn't make true religion any more popular."

"Sometimes, to believe in God, one must glimpse the Devil."

"And where is this from? Some sensational blockbuster? How are we to know what the deeds of God are and what are the machinations of the Devil?"

"For instance, whoever is responsible for the deaths in the marshes clearly wasn't acting according to some divine plan," insisted Anna.

"Yet we don't know who those wanderers in the marshes were. Perhaps they deserved their fate." Father wouldn't entertain the thought of giving up.

This conversation is leading nowhere. Anna took another sip of wine, suddenly feeling a strong dizziness. She stood up and, swaying, grabbed hold of the standard lamp.

"Leaving us already?" Fr. Kaiden gloated.

"Are you okay, dear?" Jill whispered, trying to lock eyes with Anna.

"I'm fine, thank you," Anna lied, noticing how everything around her had begun to blur.

"I'll escort you." Benedict briskly jumped up, catching Anna around the waist.

"Mister, today is definitely your day!" The American winked.

For some reason the blonde burst into laughter, and Rosemary's distorted face imprinted a malicious grimace in Anna's imagination as she started to lose consciousness. Her disobedient legs struggled to climb the stairs, but after overcoming twenty feet of darkened corridor, she approached her room.

"Benedict," she uttered with a stumbling tongue, "could you …?"

"Go into your room?"

Anna nodded weakly.

"Of course! I should have suggested it myself."

Crossing the threshold, Anna felt a wave of suffocation. Her gaze wandered chaotically around the room, anticipating an attack. In the light of the lamp, the bed swayed like a ship in a storm, and the soft chair and round table seemed poised to move to the opposite corner at any moment. Benedict led Anna to the bed and she finally lay down, staring at the slightly open closet doors. He could sense her anxiety and for some reason he wanted to help her.

"Do you want me to check everything again while I'm here?" He leaned over.

"Thank you, and I apologize for all of this," Anna forced out with difficulty.

The elderly gentleman checked the closet, looked under the bed, pulled back the curtains, and inspected the bathroom. "No one here," he concluded and headed toward the door. "Rest well, Miss Walker! A good night's sleep will do you good."

"Thank you." Anna smiled sincerely. *For everything ...*

She couldn't bring herself to watch Benedict leave. She hadn't felt this unwell in a long time. Yet even in her semi-dazed state, she couldn't forget the fear of an intrusion into her room. If it was an ethereal spirit wandering the corridors of the old mansion, a locked door wouldn't stop it. But if it was someone very much alive, it wouldn't hurt to prop the door shut with a sturdy nightstand.

After resting and briefly overcoming her weakness, Anna stood on trembling feet, dragged over the massive bedside table, and propped it against the door. The last of her strength drained away and she collapsed listlessly onto the floor. Enduring several minutes of intense dizziness, she eventually crawled back to the bed. Grasping the neatly tucked sheet, she soon found herself back under the blanket.

"Much better," she almost whispered.

The ceiling seemed to alternate between receding and inevitably drawing near, while the chandelier continually eluded her gaze. A subtle tremor attacked her body, inducing brief spasms. A cold sweat broke out on her forehead. She wanted to call for help, but reaching for the landline phone, she dropped the device on the floor.

She was trying to crawl to the edge of the bed when unbearable pain squeezed her head in a vise. The next moment it seemed that inside her skull, shattered glass was trapped, ready to embed itself in her brain with the slightest movement. Breathing heavily, she fell onto her back. At some point, her body completely refused to move, and Anna lethargically closed her eyes.

THE GULL CRY HOTEL

Chapter 12

In her dream, Anna was walking on wet grass. Each step was a struggle.

So cold and slippery, like hordes of worms ... she thought, feeling water seeping between her toes.

In her dream, she trudged through the swamp—the same one that had almost swallowed her during the day. She didn't want to be there. She wanted to wake up, but, contrary to her desires, the nightmare persisted. A faint moan echoed nearby. When the moan repeated itself very close, Anna stopped. She looked around, hearing a squelching sound behind her. The sound grew clearer, and she realized—someone was following her.

Her footsteps quickened, yet her pursuer kept pace. Whispers surrounded her, urging her to run.

"Run as fast as you can ... Run, Anna, run from this place ..." the voices pleaded in unison. "But you can't escape ..." They contradicted each other as if driven by madness.

The grass grew taller, and the ground became damper. Before long, Anna discovered that she was standing knee-deep in water. The old-fashioned nightgown, worn perhaps only in her long-forgotten thirteen, was soaked and clung to her legs. And from beneath, someone persistently tugged on the wide sleeve adorned with frills. Ripping the thin cotton from the dead grip, Anna felt the fingers of another hand. It clutched at the hem, pulling her backward. She struggled to break free, but another hand latched on to the wet garment once again.

The bluish hands of swamp corpses pulled at her clothes from different directions, and Anna sank deeper into the loose soil. She saw drowned bodies slithering toward her like predators drawn by the scent of a living soul. A mist crept behind their pallid feet. She made no attempt to break free; she submitted to submersion, sinking beneath the water until slimy reeds brushed against her mouth. She lifted her eyes—there upon the hill a man stood above her. His face was shrouded in darkness; occasional glimmers of insane eyes broke through. He drove a shovel into the ground and spat on his wide palms. In an instant, she understood—he had no intention of helping her. There was no need to scream now; no one was coming to save her. Clumps of earth flew directly into her face, instantly clogging her throat. She gasped for breath, her numb body still feeling unbearable pain—hundreds of corpses tearing their prey to pieces.

Anna opened her eyes in horror. She could distinctly hear the hiss of her own breathing, as if she were indeed lacking air. As if she could actually suffocate in her dream. She tried to get up but couldn't. Her body ached, her head was splitting, but all of this faded in comparison to the nightmare. Her throat was parched, and the muscle pain was compounded by a deadly thirst. She shifted her gaze to the corner of the table, where a kettle of water and a lonely mug rested. Exerting considerable effort, she was able to stand. Reaching the narrow tabletop, she grabbed the kettle with a trembling hand. The task now seemed insurmountable to her.

This doesn't feel at all like alcohol intoxication. After a glass of wine? Hardly! But it does resemble poisoning quite a bit. But who, and why would anyone want to poison me? she pondered, draining a mug of water.

Clutching the furniture, Anna made her way back to the bed. Her leaden head sank into the pillows and she closed her eyes, intending to sleep through the night in peace this time.

Suddenly, from above, right overhead, there came a creaking of floorboards. Staring at the ceiling, she heard a short scream. The scream was followed by a crash—something heavy hit the floor and rolled. A thud, then another. A drawn-out wheeze through a constricted throat and then silence. Silence broken by the rush of steps. Someone upstairs crossed the hotel room and darted into the bathroom. Pipes gurgled in the stillness, and a stream of water hit the cast iron.

Antique mansions: during the day you can hardly hear anything, but when night falls, these houses come alive.

Anna remained still. She simply listened. A moment of graveyard silence, and something heavy struck the glass, making her shudder. Meanwhile, upstairs, the floorboards creaked once again.

Perhaps someone has come to help? Anna barely breathed. She froze, studying the cheap glass chandelier. No more sounds or cries emanated from the room above. There was nothing that could shed even a bit of light on the situation—nothing to narrate the unfolding events.

There was a creak near the wardrobe and something weighty began to slide across the carpet, followed by a familiar sequence of steps. This was followed by a bustle on the other side of the bed, a dull thud, rustling, and again the creaking of the decaying floor.

Finally everything fell silent. Silent as if nothing had ever happened.

Anna clutched her forehead. Blood pulsed in her temples, and her eyes burned with fire. Nausea gripped her.

"To the bathroom," she whispered disjointedly and, overcoming the pain, headed toward the restroom. Leaning against the high bedpost, she took a few steps. The door, painted a glaring white, blurred in a black halo. She grabbed the frame and, pulling up her unruly body, turned on the light. She washed her face with cold water, sat on the toilet, and pressed a wet towel to her forehead. Maybe it wouldn't last long, but she felt significantly relieved.

Outside, lightning flashed, dragging thunderous rolls behind the glass. Anna flinched. The eerie scene was intensified by her deathly pale face reflected in the mirror. She held her breath.

What is it, Anna? You wanted to be frightened. To immerse yourself in genuine emotions and saturate your book with them. So what scares you now? Listen carefully, sniff around, create! That's exactly why you came here ...

She closed her eyes and took a deep breath.

Remember it all! From this unbearable state to the creaking of the floorboards, she thought when something upstairs grated again. This time it wasn't the floor or the pipes. It sounded like a file or a saw. But what could they be doing in the bathroom in the middle of the night with a saw?

Anna Walker, an icon of Literary Publishing, had penned numerous blood-soaked episodes. In her novels, she spared no expense on elaborate scenes of cruelty. Sipping her coffee, she meticulously crafted acts of villainous brutality down to the smallest detail, choosing instruments and methods of murder more twisted with each stroke. At that moment, not a single muscle of Anna's face twitched—what she wrote had never been real.

But what was happening above her head now resembled real madness. With each sound of the saw, her legs seemed to sink into the cold tiles. Her fingers, cramped in a spasm, clung to the edge of the bathtub.

This went on for what felt like an eternity until the sawing finally stopped. However, in its place came something even more horrifying—now the shuffling was accompanied by splashes. The bathroom upstairs seemed literally flooded. But with what? Flooded with blood? Anna was on the verge of losing consciousness. The very thought of a dismembered corpse deprived the cramped room of air.

Reaching the narrow window, Anna cracked it open. A chilly wind brushed against her face, and raindrops splattered on her flushed cheeks. She could hear nothing but the tumultuous sounds of nature. The storm now concealed the bloody continuation of the night and cooled Anna's fevered mind.

The darkness of the hotel courtyard was sliced by the bright beam of a torch. Anna recoiled from the window, stumbling as she hurried to the switch. In a matter of seconds, her room was plunged into darkness. Thoughts of approaching the window dissolved, and Anna, hesitating, sank onto the bed. She sat in a trance for a long time, catching the faintest creaks and knocks that no longer emanated from the floor above. Perhaps they were caused by ghosts? Well, she would have given quite a lot for the old mansion to be inhabited by the ghosts of the dead instead of live killers.

Her wild thoughts danced in a mad whirl until the early hours. Startled by every rustle, Anna no longer closed her eyes. Eventually the impenetrable darkness of the Irish night was diluted by a saving blue hue. It seemed that with the blackness, the paralyzing fear receded, giving way to rational thoughts and actions. Anna rose from the bed and slipped into the bathroom. She quietly closed the window and approached the sink. Lifting her head, she listened again and froze. Even in the twilight, she could clearly discern a contrasting spot that had appeared on the once-pristine white ceiling.

"Sweet Lord," she whispered, immediately covering her mouth with her hand. "What is this? Blood? What else? But how can I check? It's foolish to wait for dawn in this weather."

She staggered to the edge of the bathtub, leaned her weakened hands against the tiles, and approached the stain. It had spread in a dark circle, emanating an unpleasant smell. Even in the semi-darkness, Anna confidently recognized it as blood. Her foot slipped, her forearms shook with a slight tremor, and she narrowly avoided falling into the perilous embrace of tiles, glass, and steel taps. "Damn, damn!" Shaking all over, she carefully sank to the floor and caught her breath.

Shivers ran down her spine, and an uncontrollable tremor spread from her abdomen. The faintly discernible scent of blood that she had noticed earlier now gnawed at her lungs. Stumbling, she returned to the bedroom and, shedding her toweling robe, hastily pulled on velvet trousers and an oversized sweater. In this outfit she had written all her bestsellers; in it she became the legendary Anna Walker. In this outfit she strode purposefully across the room and stopped at the door. In this very hotel, for the first time in her life, she had heard with her own ears a real murder.

As an author, she sighed with relief. No matter how much you try to escape from the truth, it will tirelessly remind you of itself in clichéd phrases, typical characters, and worn-out plots. Of course, she was afraid like never before. But what if her imagination had painted an inaccurate picture? Our brain takes only 20 percent of the surrounding world as accurate information. "And what about the remaining 80?" you might ask. That's what our brain extrapolates based on personal experience.

What was Anna's experience like? She had written about numerous murders and was eager to write about at least one more.

You need a breakthrough, Anna! That's exactly why you came here. And if there's no breakthrough, there's no need to hurry back to London. Without a grand new manuscript, no one is waiting for you. You can stay on this godforsaken island for the rest of your days ... You need fresh blood. So go and get it!

Anna pushed aside the oak nightstand and stared at the consistently bright ceiling. Was she frightened by the thought of being alone with a killer? Certainly she was.

But the fear of death dulled when she imagined that she had died as a writer.

I'll go upstairs, assess the situation, and head down to the phone, she decided as she turned the key. The deserted corridor was illuminated by dim lights, casting circles on the worn-out carpet. On the walls hung misty landscapes of Rathlin, and there was a narrow window at the end.

Anna listened intently and stepped out of the room. Like a secret agent, she pressed herself against the wall and once again surveyed the completely empty corridor. Pausing for just a moment, she walked silently to the stairs and peeked stealthily around the corner, checking each landing one after the other.

Nobody! At least not from this angle, she concluded, and in twenty-two steps, she was upstairs.

Before her was the exact same corridor with its relentlessly monotonous views of Rathlin. The first room on the left was the one directly above hers. Sneaking up to the door, Anna listened. Only the beating of her own heart pierced the silence. Forgetting all decency, she dropped to her knees and peered into the keyhole. Exactly the same room—the same furniture and a similar disorder. The unmade bed—the part she could see—seemed entirely empty, and clothing lay scattered on the floor in patches.

THE GULL CRY HOTEL

Identical corridors, identical rooms, maybe even identical keys? A whimsical thought compelled Anna to insert the key and try turning it in the lock. It clicked open effortlessly, and she cautiously turned the handle. The door obediently swung open. *That's the trick ...* Anna slipped inside.

There was no sign of a bloody struggle, and Anna slowly circled the bed. She stopped right where she had heard the crash. She hesitated when delicate glass crackled beneath her shoes. *And what's this?* She reached for the table lamp, but on the click of the switch, the room didn't become any lighter.

Of course—the victim knocked the lamp to the floor and the killer picked it up! Gently touching the table lamp, Anna felt the unusual smoothness of the wood, as if it had been smeared with something. From around the corner came the sound of a lone drop—it detached itself and, instead of bouncing off the tiles, fell into water. Anna's attention now turned to the door leading to the bathroom. Obviously, everything possible and impossible was hidden there—everything capable of shedding light on the events of the night better than any lamp.

Anna had deliberately delayed this moment, but she'd better not linger. She withdrew her hand from the table lamp, tiptoed around the bed, and approached the bathroom. When she pushed the door open, she was dumbfounded. A crimson sea of thick blood covered the entire floor and at least a third of the bathroom. The remaining space was dotted with grotesque splatters, stains, and streaks. Here, hands had grasped the tiles, dragging someone's remains; there, bloody fingers had unscrewed a vent; and here remained a trace of a shoe.

A metallic scent enveloped her throat and settled in the air. Anna covered her nose with her fingers and retreated, disoriented, leaving eloquent red traces on the carpet. The sweetish nuance of blood mixed with a cloying floral scent that seemingly came out of nowhere. The combination instantly triggered a throbbing sensation in her temples and started a migraine attack. Anna stumbled over a chair in the middle of the room, which promptly collapsed under the weight of the clothing left on its back. The sound echoed through the mansion, long immersed in the pre-dawn silence.

The police! I need to call the police! Anna burst out of the room and rushed down the stairs.

The lobby was dark and empty. Rain hammered on the wild ivy and iron ledges, cascading in waterfalls from the drainpipes. Anna darted behind the reception desk and grabbed the black receiver of the landline phone. She couldn't recall the last time she had used such a device, so it took her a moment to realize that the phone remained eerily silent, emitting not a single beep. She stood frozen over the rows of buttons but soon understood that the phone, like the entire mansion, had fallen mute. She found the cord and even the socket into which the plug was inserted. She checked all the connections, pressed numerous buttons, and after long minutes, finally realized that the line was dead.

Did it go dead because of the storm, or was it always like this? Then who the hell was Rosemary talking to when she was holding it, and most importantly, how? Is there no mobile phone here? Anna began to pull out drawers and shift folders of documents. *No—nowhere! I need to wake up the guests quickly!*

"Rosemary!" she shouted. "Green! Where are you all, damn it?" But nobody answered.

Anna ascended to the first floor and froze. She wanted to shout "murder," "get up," "help," or anything at all. But only a hoarse sound escaped her throat. At the end of the corridor stood a diminutive figure.

Loose-fitted trousers and angular boots adorned his frame, which was clad in a neatly tucked crimson shirt and topped with tousled hair. He took a step forward and the wall light illuminated his face. The last impression that was etched into Anna's consciousness before she lost it was the glassy gaze of the dwarf's nearly translucent eyes and his maniacal grin.

Chapter 13

A simultaneously familiar and utterly alien scent struck Anna's nostrils. With an effort, she opened her eyes. Above her, the ceiling gleamed white. Daylight rudely pierced through the gap in the partially drawn curtains. As soon as the weak electrical impulse reached the necessary neuron, Anna leaped from the bed and frantically shook her head.

"Easy, easy!" Fr. Kaiden was sitting at her feet. "Come on, lie back on the pillow. Maybe it's a concussion."

After a few seconds, once the initial shock had subsided, Anna felt a wave of pain rushing in like a black cloud. Her eyes filled with lead, and her head became significantly heavier.

"Okay, here we go." The holy father caught her by the shoulders and helped her lie down on the bed.

With a gesture, Fr. Kaiden asked Anna to watch the movement of his suspended finger. It was painful to watch, but she did so. Afterward, he leaned over to a leather bag and pulled out an old-fashioned blood pressure cuff.

"Are you a doctor?" Anna asked, the sound of the latex bulb punctuating her question.

"Yes," the priest curtly replied. "Hold off on the chit-chat."

He froze with the stethoscope in his ears, and when a solitary thump conveyed the numbers beneath the glass of the monitor, he nodded approvingly.

"Blood! Oh gosh ... Rivers of blood! So much ... It's everywhere!" Memories crashed over Anna. "Are the police already here?" She relived the horrors of the night once again.

"Blood?" He squinted suspiciously. "Did you have a nightmare last night?"

"A real nightmare! Someone was murdered in the room above."

The doctor held a long gaze on her and, swallowing hard, uttered, "I'll bring Rosemary to you or, even better, Benedict."

He exited the room, carefully closing the door behind him. Minutes stretched into eternity, during which Anna managed to distinguish the chirping of birds instead of the fierce wind. It seemed like the storm had truly dissolved all the horrors of the night, but she had a gut feeling that it wasn't the case.

Before her eyes flashed the bath, painted crimson. A gruesome crime scene—an example of inhuman cruelty. *What the hell was I thinking, going in there?* Anna pressed her palms to her temples. *What if the killer was still there? I must have lost my mind, putting my life in such danger.*

She tried to find justification for her insane act, but somewhere deep in her soul, she knew for certain—should the situation repeat itself, she would act in exactly the same way with the same fervor. Only personal experience and the torrent of intense emotions lived through can transform a set of words into a unique text—pages that can draw someone deep inside, immerse them in their dark waters. And for the reader to believe in the story, the writer must inevitably live it.

But the dwarf! Anna snapped upright and a sudden pain crushed the back of her head, forcing her to slump back onto the pillows. *The dwarf was alive ... and he was here, in this hotel!*

It seemed that Anna had lived through enough in the past twenty-four hours. And this morning, as she stared at the gap in the middle of the dark curtains, she suddenly caught a rapid flow of thoughts. Sentences circled in the air like dust particles in a solitary sunbeam, settling onto the laptop keyboard. For the first time in several years, she didn't need to search for words or attempt to artificially evoke emotions. Everything happened as if by magic. And perhaps writing is magic—a distinct form of sorcery woven seamlessly into everyday life.

Oh, Anna, don't push away the scent of those red droplets frozen on the tiles. You've witnessed such a bloody scene for the first time, and the first of everything is never forgotten. The first kiss, the first loss, the first corpse, whose face is imprinted in your memory more vividly than Michael's. Michael McKenzie—her companion with whom she had once ventured to the island of Bali.

***

It was an early Indonesian morning. Through the noise of the pool, the anxious voices of the staff could be heard. Anna listened, unable to make out anything, and turned onto her other side. The conversation grew louder; the hustle and bustle intensified. She opened her eyes and stared at the white tulle curtains gently swaying in the wind. In the courtyard of the hotel bungalow, azure waters murmured and equatorial greenery raged. Beyond the statues of Hindu gods lay a high hedge, separating their paradise garden from other gardens.

"What happened?" Anna asked the staff who brought breakfast.

"A girl named Lishan from the spa is missing. She left the hotel yesterday but never returned home," the hotel worker explained.

The tourists exchanged wary glances but soon forgot about the incident. After the tide had turned, they were set to go scuba diving on the coral reef. The boat departed promptly at three from the low dock at the end of the long beach. Anna ran, and Michael hurried her.

"Come on! If we're late, they won't refund us for the dive and training."

Anna seared his back with her gaze. She tried not to notice this triviality, this perpetual order even on vacation. On the whole, everything was fine, but Anna invariably felt … a romantic couple's vacation should look different.

An Asian man in wide trousers waved his hands. Michael rushed to the boat and handed him a backpack. The group of six set off. The latecomers took their places on the low bench, and Anna finally caught her breath. It was about twenty minutes to the reef, and from here, the shore was no longer visible. The feeling was that they would have to dive in the middle of the ocean—the Indian Ocean, one of the shallowest oceans after the Arctic, but the awareness of this fact did little to diminish her fear of the deep blue. Only when the water began to brighten, revealing the peaks of the coral reef, did the fear dull a bit.

The Europeans donned their wetsuits and strapped oxygen tanks to their backs. They took a couple of minutes to let the dizziness subside, and then they could dive. Anna wasn't exactly thrilled about doing it. However, Michael had assured her that everyone on Earth should, at least once in their life, descend to the ocean floor and, afterward, jump with a parachute. Now, standing on the rocking stern, Anna secretly hoped that she and Michael would part ways before reaching that second duty.

"Jump!" commanded the instructor, and Anna obediently stepped off the edge.

The azure waters closed over her head. *This is so fascinating!* Michael's enthusiastic exclamation echoed in her mind. Perhaps if you added sounds and smells to the mix ... Maybe it was an incredible experience when your view extended just a bit beyond the two ellipses of a snug diving mask. Perhaps ... But in those unbearable thirty minutes, which inexplicably stretched out for Anna, she felt no exhilaration. Everything she witnessed could also be seen in the enormous aquarium in the hotel lobby, perhaps even better.

While Anna explored the intricate coral formations teeming with colorful fish, she kept an eye on the oxygen gauge. When the indicator reached the red zone, she could release the final burst of carbon dioxide and begin the ascent. Suddenly something large flashed by her side. She tried to turn, but the swimmer constantly eluded her gaze. The pale blue hue hinted at a playful dolphin that had decided to befriend her.

Finally something interesting! Anna was invigorated. She pushed herself away from the reef and tried to maneuver her cumbersome fins to the side when suddenly, right before her eyes, a human face appeared.

The bluish skin reminded Anna of the god Vishnu, whose depictions she had seen the day before in one of the ancient temples. Narrow lids covered eyes veiled in mystery. The nose swelled, becoming a refuge for small fish, while the mouth was grotesquely sealed with a strip of black tape.

She wanted to scream. Desperately wanted to. As if a scream could carry the lifeless body miles away. She tried to swim away, but her fin got stuck among the coral, and now, thrashing from side to side, she was simply jerking in place. The waters pushed the corpse towards Anna, and it, as if pleading for help, reached out its black hair to the bewildered diver.

Someone touched her leg, and Anna waved her hands frantically. The rest was like being in a fog. The ascent to the surface, shouts in Indonesian, the sirens of a police boat. Anna turned her head only when they brought up Lishan. Her hands were tied behind her back, ankles tightly wrapped with black tape, clothes intact, and the visible parts of her body showed no apparent injuries. It seemed like she had just been immobilized and cold-bloodedly drowned.

In the lobby, soft music played. After glancing at the aquarium that evening, Anna wrote late into the night. Well, not quite like that! The manuscript seemed to write itself. She was just a conduit. Everything unfolded as if in a trance, as if without her participation. Anna once again immersed herself in the ocean—this time in the ocean of true creativity. That evening was also marked by Michael's deliberate attention, which had been so eagerly awaited but suddenly ceased to be desired. Now all Anna's thoughts and fantasies were consumed by the lifeless Lishan and the potential plot of her tragic death.

***

There was a knock on the door. Anna shuddered in horror but then bravely wiped the fear from her face. In her understanding, it was like this: the youth from far-off Chicago had indulged in hallucinogens and then, inspired by stories of ghosts, decided to finish each other off, like in that notorious horror movie about the rare mushroom, *Deadhead*. The only remaining question was about the dwarf, who had clearly emerged from her own subconscious.

Anna took a deep breath and called out, "Who's there?"

"It's Benedict."

"Come in!"

"Anna, dear, what's happened to you?" He appeared in the doorway.

"Happened to me?" she automatically replied. "What happened in the room above? Did the police catch him? Or wasn't he alone?"

"I'm not quite sure." He hesitated. "Our esteemed guests from America left early in the morning, as far as I know. Apparently more exciting places on this island await them. Green insisted that, in addition to backpacks, they had tents with them."

"Have they vanished? Just like that? Call the police, Benedict! We need to stop them before they leave the island!"

"And what charges, in your opinion, should the police bring against them?"

Anna's heartbeat intensified. Blood rushed to her cheeks, and, taking a deep breath, she furrowed her brow, hesitating to utter the word that echoed like a scream in her mind. *Murder! Unprecedented in its cruelty, murder!*

"But you haven't called me here to ask me about their departure, have you?" Benedict surveyed the room and fixed his gaze on Anna's pallid face.

"Benedict"—Anna swallowed—"last night I heard something up there." She pointed to the ceiling.

"You heard something?" He approached the window and touched the curtain. "It's a young business, you know."

"No." Anna looked down. "I heard something brutal. An altercation, some slaps …"

"Slaps?" Benedict turned around.

"And blows that ended in murder."

"Listen, dear Anna," Benedict said after a long silence. "I am just a guest in this hotel, like you. But, to my uninformed eye, an event such as the taking of one person's life by another cannot be ignored without proper attention."

"That's right. We need to call the police as soon as possible!" Anna quickly moved to the edge of the bed.

Benedict watched skeptically as she spoke enthusiastically. He looked again through the leaf-covered windows and, taking in a lungful of air, said, "You can call, but the officers will need some evidence that, in your opinion, something happened here last night."

"But isn't the blood-filled bathtub evidence enough?"

Benedict turned sharply. "What are you talking about?"

"I was there, Benedict. I went up and saw the bathtub filled with blood with my own eyes."

Benedict instantly started pacing from corner to corner, rubbing his nose. "Stay here," he concluded. "I'll get Rosemary and we'll check out the room."

"I'm coming with you." Anna planted her feet on the floor. Her head was spinning, and she stared blankly at the floor, leaning against the bed.

"Excluded! You'd better stay in bed."

Chapter 14

Now Anna couldn't work. She listened like a bloodhound, and Benedict's footsteps didn't take long to arrive. Soon the floorboards above creaked again. Her hands were suddenly covered in goosebumps. She rubbed her forearms, starting to worry about the old man she had befriended.

Someone followed Benedict. Anna fell silent. Almost holding her breath, she faintly discerned a couple of voices. They were clearly surveying the room, but no one screamed in hysteria, fainted, or hurried to call for help.

What the hell is going on in there? Do they have a bloodbath in the bathtub every Friday or something? Anna squinted.

At last everything quieted down, even upstairs. She waited, tormented by guesses, until there was a knock on the door again. "Come in!" she shouted.

Benedict appeared again. He looked at her apologetically and averted his eyes. Now he hesitated to speak. Moreover, he didn't even dare to make eye contact.

"Benedict?" Anna inquired persuasively. "Is something wrong? I mean, it is very wrong up there … but have you seen everything with your own eyes?"

Her words noticeably shook him, as if someone invisible had pushed him in the back of the head. Soon he turned and, without saying a word, began to examine the hotel room, only occasionally glancing at Anna.

"What? What, Benedict?" she demanded.

"I think even if I tell you, you won't believe me."

"Come on, spill it! Whatever the truth is! Who killed whom?"

"That's the thing, Anna. No one killed anyone."

The air in the room suddenly grew denser. Anna shook her head in confusion. "I don't understand … Then where did all that blood come from?

"There isn't a single drop of blood in the room or in the bathroom."

"But I saw it!" Anna almost shouted.

"Then it must have been your imagination," Benedict said, sitting beside her and gripping her hand.

"Imagination? You must be out of your mind!" she exclaimed but fell silent immediately.

For some reason, of all the things that happened to her, only the dwarf seemed unreal. But what if everything else wasn't real either? Could it really be like that? Suddenly Anna felt a wave of genuine horror. She gasped for breath and lowered her gaze.

"No, no, no," she protested with the last of her strength. "Such things cannot be imagined or dreamt ... I saw it! I saw with my own eyes! Where's Rosemary?" Anna jumped to her feet and headed for the door.

"Wait—you shouldn't get up yet." Benedict tried to stop her.

But it was all in vain. Anna could no longer stay another minute in her bed. Now she was not only concerned about the bloody altercation in the room above but also the possibility that the renowned writer, the legendary Anna Walker, had truly, seriously, and quite literally lost her sanity.

"Rosemary! Rosemary!" Anna strode resolutely toward the staircase.

"Miss Walker?" responded the manager from the lobby. "What's happened now?" She spoke much more quietly this time but still loudly enough for Anna to hear.

"I want to take a look at the room above mine."

Without waiting for Rosemary, Anna ascended the staircase and froze in the corridor on the second floor. Memories washed over her like an icy breeze—right there was where she had seen the dwarf and his horrifying grin.

"What's the matter?" Rosemary said wearily as she caught up with her.

"May I just ask you to open this room?" Anna said firmly, pointing at the door.

"You're lucky the guests have checked out," Rosemary mumbled as she unlocked the ill-fated room. "I wonder how I'd have explained your quirks to them."

"I'm afraid the dead don't need any explanations," Anna quipped and Rosemary turned sharply, her eyes wide.

Ignoring the bewildered manager, Anna stepped into the room. For a moment she hesitated, retracing the simple path she had taken the night before. The room was fresh and clean. An impeccably made bed stood on a perfectly vacuumed carpet. No bloody traces, not a single dent.

"Someone has cleaned up here?" Anna turned around.

"Someone?" Rosemary rolled her eyes. "Oh, please …"

"And you didn't notice anything suspicious?" Anna demanded, approaching the bedside table.

Without waiting for an answer, she touched the bedside lamp. It turned out to have been wiped clean, and the light bulb was screwed in tightly.

Okay. Anna breathed out.

"Suspicious? I haven't seen such a mess in a long time. But they paid for three nights and left after the first. It would be sinful to complain." Rosemary continued to prattle on as Anna circled the bed.

She bent down, examined the impeccable beige carpet, and approached the bathroom. Her stomach clenched as she turned the chrome handle. Yet, in an instant, before her eyes were pristine white tiles. In this small bright space with its narrow window, nothing hinted at the bloody atrocity. It was as clean as a bacteriological laboratory, devoid of any stains, rust streaks, or murky smudges. Nothing here could confirm the crimson tableau of dismemberment.

"But how is this possible?" Anna murmured, touching her fingertips to her sweaty forehead.

She felt unwell. Unwell as if this room was sapping the last of her strength. Just like a few hours earlier, she retreated, examining the carpet where she had left dark traces before.

Sitting down, she touched the pile. The wool fibers were damp. *Of course—natural carpets take a long time to dry.* It dawned on her. "Did you clean the carpet?" She gazed intensely at Rosemary.

"Yes. It was heavily soiled."

"With blood?" Anna jumped to her feet.

"With vomit," snapped Rosemary furiously. "Is the investigation over?"

"But ... but ..." Anna grasped at the back of a chair. "In my bathroom!" she finally realized. "In my bathroom, I saw a dark stain." She rushed into the corridor.

THE GULL CRY HOTEL

Stumbling, Anna descended the stairs and flew back into her room. She burst into the bathroom and raised her eyes to the ceiling. On the white plaster, a dark, uneven circle was visible. The same spot. The same stain. However, now it looked nothing like blood. More like ordinary water—a leak from the heavy rain.

In her head, tiny but insanely heavy hammers pounded one after another. She pressed her fingers to her temples, staggered back, and collapsed into the armchair.

How can this be? I don't understand ... I don't understand ...

"Are you all right?" Benedict hurried over to her.

Anna didn't respond. In fact, she didn't even hear him. He observed her torment for a moment, then withdrew, quietly closing the door behind him.

When Anna came to herself, the sun hung heavily in a misty halo above the horizon. She didn't know how long she had sat there, almost motionless, mentally replaying the insane events of the night and the no less insane events of the day.

The key! Memories surfaced, illuminating her eyes with an unhealthy gleam. *If anything of what I saw last night can be confirmed, then maybe I'm not that ill after all.*

She quietly opened the door, extracted the key from the lock, and peered into the corridor. *No one.*

Anna took a few steps forward and inserted the key into the lock. With a little effort, it turned, unlocking the room opposite. She raised an eyebrow and pushed the door open.

Empty, she remarked to herself, surveying a room eerily similar to her own.

But I did it! I opened someone else's room with my own key! Anna closed the door and stared manically at the hotel carpet. Its crimson hue was adept at concealing years of faithful service. However, where did those slight dents come from? She crouched down, changing her perspective. The hastily vacuumed pile revealed crushed traces leading to distant rooms.

Large size, tiny steps, Anna estimated. *How strange—I don't even know who is staying here and where.*

"What are you doing?"

Anna started and turned around. Behind her, holding a tray of food, stood Rosemary.

"Nothing," she stammered, quickly getting up. "And you?"

"Brought you dinner."

"For me?" Anna couldn't hide her surprise. "I could easily go down to the dining room. Besides, I would like to clarify a few things with you."

THE GULL CRY HOTEL

The manager frowned but quickly put on a friendly smile and gestured for her to follow. They crossed the completely empty lobby and entered the dimly lit dining hall.

"So, what did you want to clarify?" Rosemary set out two plates and utensils wrapped in a napkin from the tray.

"Dear Rosemary." Anna inspected the chicken leg in batter and looked up at the red-haired woman. "How is it that my key opens so many doors in this hotel?"

Rosemary froze but soon exhaled and shook her head. "You see ..." She spoke unusually softly. "Would you like some sherry?" Her eyes brightened, seeking understanding after a few sips of the intoxicating drink.

"No, thank you," Anna replied, recalling how unwell she had felt after the Chardonnay.

"I'll have some, if you don't mind ... You know how hard it is to run a hotel in such a remote place?" Rosemary disappeared into the kitchen but soon reappeared with a dark bottle in her hands.

"This mansion was in a terrible state of disrepair." Rosemary filled a glass and emptied it in one go. She exhaled into the back of her hand, and her eyes moistened. "No one knows what it took for me to start everything from scratch. To turn this desolate place into something decent. Something that would attract foreign guests, renowned writers." She sniffled and waved her hand, pointing to Anna. She refilled her glass and continued. "When I first walked in here," she said with a sigh, "the first thing I wanted to get rid of was the iron doors. So old and rusty, with dreadful dents." She downed a second shot and went on. "Doors that served as a vivid reminder of the horrors that took place here. With those, you know, creepy little windows for food and observation."

"Oh my God," Anna said. "What are you talking about?"

"A private psychiatric clinic." Rosemary finally lifted her gaze to her companion. "The mansion was sold at a bargain; no one wanted to take it. Oh, the things that happened here ... The owner, it seems, was a real madman. Experiments on people did no good for science but brought joy to a sadist who fancied himself a doctor and a scientist."

"Oh God ..."

"Darling, God left this place."

Anna had already forgotten about the keys as the manager continued. "So the first thing I did was change those awful doors. But after placing a big order, I faced the question of keys and locks. Initially, like you, it seemed to me that each one should be different. I contacted a big company in Belfast, and the next day, Jonathan arrived. Handsome Jonathan." Rosemary sighed wistfully and raised the sherry as if sending a mental greeting to the door company agent. "He was so

THE GULL CRY HOTEL

charming and talkative. I couldn't even get a word in—imagine that!"

It is hard to imagine indeed. Anna merely raised an eyebrow.

"So, he explained that their company has been working with hotels for many years, from small guesthouses like this one to renowned establishments with hundreds of rooms. Jonathan said that in the best case, even in the largest hotel, there would be only ten keys. Just imagine! Only ten combinations!"

As Rosemary spoke, it became increasingly difficult to believe her words.

"That's why electronic keys were introduced." She extended her hand, anticipating imminent questions. "Because if you think about traditional keys, no one in the entire world would manufacture five hundred different key designs. And hardly anyone among the guests would ever think that their key could open numerous other doors. It's obvious, explicit information that remains permanently concealed for most people."

"Interesting," Anna mused, touching her lips with her index finger.

"In the hotel business, there are other fascinating things, but perhaps I'll keep the rest to myself," Rosemary replied.

"A psychiatric clinic, you say?"

"You're a writer—isn't that intriguing? Besides, you can't even imagine how many prisons have been transformed into hotels. So a former sanatorium doesn't surprise anyone anymore. Listen, maybe you somehow felt the energy of this place and heard something dreadful. Only it didn't happen now, but a long time ago …"

Rosemary kept talking, but Anna no longer heard her. In her mind new, vivid pictures, events, and dialogues emerged. No matter how strange this place might be, it now seemed like the entire universe was on her side, inexorably guiding her manuscript to success.

Detailing the next chapter in her thoughts, she finished her dinner. The plot concoction, seasoned with the dark walls of the deranged house, was ready. All that remained was to reach her room and pour it all into docx files.

"Rosemary, when will the internet be back up?" Anna inquired as she got ready.

"The police officer mentioned that the base station is damaged. The landline is currently out of order. But we're hopeful they'll fix everything by tomorrow. How did you find out?"

"That doesn't matter now." Anna smiled mysteriously. "I'll go up to my room." She gathered her things, anticipating her favorite Earl Grey.

THE GULL CRY HOTEL

Rosemary graciously brought tea and was clearing the empty plates from the table when she glanced out of the window. Suddenly she froze. Her gaze pierced through the French windows to the darkening horizon.

As if hypnotized, she stared into the distance, where just after twilight with the onset of night, all outlines and colors would disappear. With the sunset, everything was plunged into darkness, creating the very real sensation that the mansion was adrift on a rocky fragment. It was lost, fallen into the abyss, and had found itself in another dimension—in a remote and dark place where there was no way to reach the rest of the world. Without the internet, these sensations were intensified, providing fertile ground for fantasies.

"What did you see there?" Anna stared into the darkening sea.

"Nothing," the manager replied without taking her eyes off the outside.

Studying it closely, Anna recognized the mist, a dense band rolling in from the ocean. Fog was not uncommon for Rathlin, but this seemed denser than usual. What scared Anna most was that this one seemed to have completely immobilized the energetic Rosemary.

"I think I'll go …" Anna said, afraid of losing the muse.

After scrutinizing Rosemary's unblinking gaze for a minute, she rose from the table. Tea in hand, she headed to the lobby, where she immediately encountered Green.

"Good evening, madam." He nodded hurriedly and moved aside, letting Anna pass.

She walked on and paused, casting a lingering gaze at the startled driver. He had always been stoic and taciturn, but even behind that curtain, she could sense genuine concern. Such emotions are hard to conceal from a seasoned writer.

She took another step, then paused again, listening intently.

"Do you see?" Green whispered, approaching Rosemary.

"Yes, I do," she replied, subdued.

Casper rushed into the hall from the street. Not seeming to notice Anna at all, he flew by. Entering the dining room, the young man began to mumble something but was immediately cut off by Green.

Anna lingered briefly at the bottom of the stairs, trying to make out the words and understand the general essence of the alarm. However, not catching a single word, she ascended to her room.

After placing her tea on the round table, she settled by the window and opened her laptop. Thoughts flowed in an uninterrupted stream, her fingers tapping rapidly on the keys. At some point she even sensed the stale odor she had written about. Her lifeless text came alive. It took in full lungfuls of air and began to breathe. Actually, it isn't the muse that resurrects slain manuscripts. Writers do it themselves. So often, after writing, complete emptiness sets in. A total absence of emotions, thoughts, and feelings—a sure sign that the writer has breathed life into their creation. They have given a part of their soul to something lifeless.

Finally, tearing her gaze away from the screen, Anna peered out of the window. She switched off the light and turned the bright screen to the wall. In the darkness on the border between sky and earth stood a white wall.

"Advective?" She squinted.

Like a massive wave, the mist loomed over the cliff. The wind had completely disappeared. It became suspiciously quiet. And, like everything around her, Anna froze, staring into the white veil. Suddenly a strange sound reached her ears. Dozens, maybe hundreds of voices merged into a whisper. The sound was so eerie that Anna momentarily stopped breathing. Struggling, she tried to discern the words of at least one of the speakers, but the speech seemed incoherent.

These hallucinations were endlessly terrifying. Where was that line that separates a mentally healthy person from someone with a disturbed mind? Where was that moment of realization that distinguishes what our brain perceives from the external world without distortion and what it generates itself?

Anna reached for the handle and opened the window. The cold air enveloped her face and shoulders. She listened. The whisper became more distinct. It seemed as if these blood-chilling sounds were brought by the mist from the eerie ocean.

THE GULL CRY HOTEL

Chapter 15

Anna closed the window. The last thing she wanted was to delve into the labyrinths of her consciousness. Not now. Not in this pivotal moment of her life. Perhaps it helps in the act of creation when reality is more frightening than any of one's fantasies can be. However, one must know how to balance on the edge. It's always easier to step aside and fall into the abyss than to continue walking the tightrope.

Anna wished she could talk to someone from London right now, even if it was the grumpy Rick or the infuriated Alison. But the internet was down, the phone was shattered, and the storm had torn apart the landlines.

"Breathe, Anna … Breathe." She rested her head against the back of the chair. *I'll finish the novel, submit it to the publisher, and fly off to the islands! I'll settle in a secluded bungalow in the midst of the jungle or right beside the ocean. Only those paradisiacal lands can restore sanity. And now back to work! You should make it! You should write another bestseller!*

She rubbed her hands and started to tap on the keyboard. She recalled the night down to the tiniest detail. Moreover, she added horror and emotions. The words flowed effortlessly and smoothly, weaving a talented narrative on the electronic page. There was no trace left of the previous work; Anna was creating something new, fresh, and, most importantly, based on real events. Of course, any of the hotel guests could argue about the reality of these events, but not Anna. For her, everything had happened. She saw all the chapters of her new book vividly, with her own eyes.

By the eighteenth chapter, she craved Earl Grey. She checked the tea packets near the kettle and, not finding that particular type, left the room.

From below, the murmur of conversation reached her ears. Trying not to make any noise, she approached the staircase in the hope of catching at least a snippet of the discussion. Despite the straightforwardness of all the characters, she sensed a certain mystery permeating this old building. She lingered, hoping to hear something that could shed light on the peculiarities unfolding in this place.

The acerbic tone of Fr. Kaiden was replaced by Jill's curt remarks. Her pitch ebbed and flowed, at times growing agitated. Soon the clinking of ice cubes in a glass resonated, followed by something uttered by Benedict. But what? Anna couldn't make out a single word. No, she distinctly heard every sound and every sigh. However, for some whimsical reason, the sounds failed to form words and words failed to construct sentences.

A new wave of horror engulfed her. What was happening? Were they speaking a different language among themselves? But what language? She had never heard anything like it. It didn't resemble Irish or any other local dialect.

"Good evening!" Anna finally decided to descend.

"Dervadar!" Benedict exclaimed, rising from the couch joyfully. "Kurdani suta alikfanchi?"

"I beg your pardon?" Anna stammered, hoping Benedict would repeat himself. To her great dismay, he didn't repeat it but continued, "Merdoki sigotivy …"

Frozen on the stairs, Anna was dumbfounded. *Are they speaking some damn Celtic language? Or— What the hell? Why can't I understand a thing?*

"Yes, sure." She forced a smile and cast her gaze downward.

Her breath grew heavier, her hands started to tremble, and her head filled with the same white haze that had enveloped the entire island. She no longer met the eyes of those seated. As if on cue, everyone turned their attention to poor Anna. She slipped into the dining room. In the kitchen, Rosemary was bustling around at the table. Casper was absentmindedly mashing potatoes with a fork.

THE GULL CRY HOTEL

Avoiding conversation, Anna hurried to the refreshment station and, tossing an Earl Grey tea bag into her mug, filled it with boiling water.

"Feeling better?" Rosemary inquired.

It seemed as if a stone hanging from Anna's chest had finally dislodged and fallen. She nodded hastily. She opened her mouth, preparing to ask about the strange language spoken in the hall, but changed her mind and turned away to the window.

The darkness of the night was veiled in a thick fog the likes of which she had never encountered in her life. She approached the window and peered into the mist through her faint reflection. Suddenly it seemed to Anna that her face had taken on different contours. Her cheeks were hollow, her eyes filled with darkness, and her mouth opened in a silent scream. She recoiled in fear, never taking her eyes off the horrifying visage. It wasn't her at all, it seemed. It was as if some sinister entity was staring at her from within the fog. Perhaps Eleanora herself had come to visit, accompanied by her demons …

What if, by believing in demons, you invite them into your soul? The thought was terrifying, especially considering she had penned an entire novel about them.

Anna blinked and the phantom disappeared.

"Did you see something?" Rosemary inquired curiously.

"See something?" Of course, Anna had no intention of confessing to any hallucinations. It was abundantly clear that even without the revived fog, she was behaving rather strangely.

"No, nothing ... Just ... it's so dense. I've lived in London for so long and never seen anything like this."

"Get used to it."

What's that supposed to mean? Anna frowned, but she preferred not to engage in prolonged dialogue.

She walked away. The hall fell into silence. Each person there was lost in their thoughts—perhaps cursing the fog or maybe the inexhaustible Anna Walker. She, more than ever before, couldn't care less. All that occupied her mind was returning from this place with an unparalleled manuscript. And, if possible, not losing her sanity completely.

"Anna?" came a voice from behind, and she flinched, spilling a few drops of tea onto the carpet. "Are you okay?" Benedict inquired.

"Thanks—I'm perfectly fine!" Anna replied, forcing a painfully fake smile.

THE GULL CRY HOTEL

Oh, Anna, who are you trying to fool? Your mind is far from fine; it sees differently, it hears differently. Its reality now diverges from the reality of these people. You're losing it! But none of the staff or guests must find out. They may suspect, but they don't know for sure. It has to stay that way. Hold on with all your might. Otherwise you won't make it to a decent clinic in London. Otherwise you'll be stuck in Ballymena, or at best, Belfast, for a very long time. Well, the difference isn't that significant, she thought to herself.

The taste of bergamot calmed her nerves, and she resumed her work. All she desired now was to finish writing and leave this place. However, after just the first sentence, she paused and glanced fearfully at the windows shrouded in mist. She froze, hesitating to make a move.

Could it be that, along with all the signs of madness, a touch of paranoia has crept in?

Now she felt as though someone outside was watching her. It was a strange sensation, as if she had been transported back to her distant childhood. She had had a nearly identical cardboard mansion—furniture and partitions made of thinner cardboard, wallpaper from wrapping paper, and carpets fashioned from old scraps of velvet. Once upon a time, she had spent entire days with her dollhouse. How unpleasant it was to suddenly find herself inside one of those cardboard houses. How eerie to feel someone's intense gaze upon her. A gaze that couldn't be escaped.

Trying not to dwell on the fog any longer, Anna drew the heavy curtains shut and climbed into bed. The desk lamp illuminated only a portion of the bed and cast a small halo on the carpet. The triple-layered curtains provided a secure barrier against any observer, yet for some reason the unsettling feeling persisted. Beneath this oppressive sensation, Anna managed to craft a scene of pursuit. And the chapters about the dreadful psychiatric hospital, shrouded in the fog that came from the ocean like a colossal living organism, turned out horrifyingly realistic.

It was well past midnight when Anna, with a sense of complete satisfaction, closed her laptop. Her eyes were heavy; her tired brain, worn out from intensive work, was literally shutting down. She slid onto the pillows and closed her eyes. She was sinking into the ringing silence when suddenly she heard a familiar sound. A dreadful whisper reached her ears.

"Anna ... Anna ... Come to us, Anna ..."

It seemed to emanate from nowhere, and then the words broke down into individual sounds that refused to coalesce into words anymore. Anna pressed herself into the bed, her body paralyzed.

"Go away," she answered. "Please leave me alone …"

A solitary tear trickled down her cheek, but the whisper didn't disappear. Desperate, Anna pressed pillows against her ears. The pillowcases were dampened by tears until she finally succumbed to sleep.

Three insistent knocks jolted Anna from her slumber. She sat up, staring at the door.

Maybe it's a dream, she thought as a child ran down the hallway.

Anna broke into a cold sweat. She had completely forgotten to prop the door shut with the heavy nightstand. It seemed that the fear of intruders had dimmed in comparison to the fear of madness. Well, if that was the case, the instigator of her insanity could rightly be called the grotesque dwarf. At the mere thought of him and the demonic gleam in his eyes, her heart fluttered with terror like a bird caught by a predator.

Listening intently, she once again caught the sound of rapid footsteps, the owner of which sprinted to the door, paused, and then dashed to the end of the hallway. When the prankster had distanced themselves to the maximum, Anna leaped from the bed and seized the oak nightstand. She pulled the hefty piece of furniture toward the door, hearing the midnight disturber approaching once again.

The sound of footsteps grew louder, then suddenly vanished.

And everything would have been fine, and she could even have pushed the nightstand back and jumped into bed again, except that stopping abruptly when you're running at full speed is simply impossible. The footsteps had disappeared as if the runner had been lifted off the ground. Anna felt a shiver run down her spine. Nonetheless, she braced the door and, with a trembling hand, quietly withdrew the key.

Where did he go? She hesitantly approached the keyhole.

Dim circles of light from the wall lamps fell onto the red carpet. There was absolutely no sound except her own heavy breathing. The corridor seemed entirely deserted when suddenly, from the other side, a glassy eye fixed its gaze on her, unblinking, inhuman, with the mad look of the dwarf from her nightmares.

Anna recoiled from the door, stumbled, and fell. She crawled to the bed, grabbed a pillow, and hurled it toward the door. It struck it and bounced off onto the nightstand. Now no one could enter the room, neither could they spy on Anna.

The throbbing in her temples persisted for an hour. She massaged her head until she realized that instead of touching it gently, she was forcefully scratching her skin. Soon the itch migrated to her shoulders, and she immediately dug her nails into them. The scratching provided relief, and the physical pain served as a distraction from the emotional turmoil.

Think, Anna, think! What would a psychiatrist ask you if you were in his office right now? Perhaps ...

"What triggered it all?" *Brilliant! So, what triggered it all?*

And more than anything else in the world, Anna would have liked to answer—the bloody murder she had heard. But she distinctly remembered that preceding that had been the guest in her room, the dreadful old woman on the ferry, the pursuit on the train, and the chillingly familiar gaze on the platform that sent shivers down her spine. But even before all that, before the cursed island and even before Belfast, she had seen the dwarf in London. On that fateful night when she had booked a room at the Gull Cry Hotel and then gone to sleep. It was then that she had seen her pursuer. Seen him in a dream.

"I've gone mad ... I've lost my mind," Anna repeated, rubbing her numb forearms. "I've gone mad ... gone mad ... I've lost my mind ..."

"You've gone mad, Anna," the walls echoed in a whisper. "You've lost your mind!"

At last, Anna understood them. Finally she deciphered their indistinct whispers. Finally she realized her own insanity.

THE GULL CRY HOTEL

Chapter 16

Outside, dawn was breaking. Anna was approaching the final scene. At some point, she reconciled with all the horrors unfolding around her and focused on her work. Thank goodness, as the sun rose higher, the corridor grew quieter, but not the room. No. Whispers continued to murmur and mutter there. That was when Anna threw on a woolen cardigan, grabbed her laptop, and left the room. At six in the morning, the lobby was empty, still smelling of whiskey from the evening's gathering, and unbearably cold. Settling into Jill Amsterham's spot, the writer stared at the screen. This armchair seemed to have absorbed all of Jill's creams—the ones that smelt so familiar to Anna this morning.

How quiet! she exclaimed with relief. *How wonderfully quiet ...*

An hour passed as if it were a minute. All the fears she had experienced found refuge in the mystical novel—a novel destined to revive Anna Walker's career and become another bestseller. She had heard many times that for a creative breakthrough, many writers turn to psychoactive substances. Some of them immerse themselves so deeply in their characters that after putting the final period in their manuscripts, they head to a rehabilitation clinic. Anna no longer cared about what would happen afterward. She was completely consumed by what was flowing from her pen right now.

"Good morning." Benedict appeared on the stairs.

In a neat tweed suit and a stiffly starched shirt, he looked as if he hadn't lain down since the evening before—the only gentleman among the rustic islanders. Anna never asked where he came from, but from the very beginning, she was convinced it was Dublin. Residents of the Irish capital always had three things: impeccable manners, innate kindness, and a retro style.

"Good morning, Benedict! I apologize—"

"Stop it, dear Anna!" he immediately interjected. "Believe me, each of us has reasons to be concerned. If you want to talk about it, I'm all ears. But if you prefer to keep it to yourself, I won't pester you with questions. Agreed?"

Anna nodded.

"Would you like some coffee?"

"Yes, Benedict, I really would." Anna perked up. "But let me brew it for us, and you can read this in the meantime." She turned the laptop toward her companion, and he hurried to take his reading glasses out of his breast pocket.

"Do you not fear showing the manuscript before publication?" He smirked.

"Stop it—you don't seem like a competitor. In reality, there are only seven plotlines. Ideas in books repeat all the time; what can't be replicated is the style. Immersion in the atmosphere, the utterly realistic depiction of unreal things and events. And that, Benedict, is impossible to steal and extremely difficult to replicate. Besides, every creator would like to hear a few kind compliments for motivation." She winked.

She was on the rise. She was genuinely enjoying what she was creating.

Anna turned on the coffee machine, stretched her back, and faced the French windows. The fog had lifted, but only slightly. Beyond the glass, a small patch of green lawn appeared like an island, and a strip of damp gravel was visible, followed by white mist. What was the point of having a room with an ocean view if the picturesque cliff was perpetually concealed by a dense haze?

Strangely, with the onset of day, the unsettling feeling that someone was watching her did not fade away. Anna stared, mesmerized, trying to understand the cause of such an eerie sensation. It wasn't the gaze of a human being. No, not anything resembling a creature like herself. The observer, it seemed, was immense. It loomed over the cliff. It appeared as if it had leaned over just to peer out of the corner of its eye into the long windows of the dining room and catch a glimpse of the tiny hotel guests.

Behind her, the machine screeched, and Anna flinched.

"Coffee, coffee, coffee …" She hurriedly grabbed the mugs and filled them with the aromatic beverage. "How do you take it?"

"Black, no sugar, thank you."

After adding just a bit of milk and a spoonful of sugar to her mug, Anna walked briskly out of the dining room. "Well, what do you think?" she asked, settling down opposite Benedict and anticipating compliments.

"You know," he said softly, looking, somewhat perplexed, into her eyes, "I'm not really an expert on contemporary literature."

Anna froze and frowned.

"Perhaps in London they'll give you more useful feedback," he concluded.

"But in general …" Anna gave a strained smile. "How do you find the atmosphere? Does it resemble the one here?" She tried to make a joke, but Benedict wasn't in the mood for laughter.

He took a sip of coffee and stared intently at Anna's questioning face. "I didn't get anything, Anna."

"What?" The word burst out of her constricted throat.

"I really tried to understand. But it's just a collection of words that don't make sentences."

Anna swallowed. "What are you talking about?"

"My dear, don't worry too much." Benedict set aside his mug and reached for her hand, but Anna immediately pulled it away.

"Benedict"—she was breathing heavily—"explain to me what you're talking about. What do you mean?"

Benedict seemed to understand the hopelessness of the situation and began to read. He was quiet and courteous, as always. He didn't want anyone else to hear all the nonsense that had seemed to Anna an unsurpassed creation. After the first paragraph, tears started to stream down her cheeks. After the second, a loud ringing appeared in her ears.

"Forgive me for all of this, but there was only one way to prove …"

She didn't hear him. She didn't feel the mug slip from her hands and crash to the floor. In slow motion, she saw Benedict rise. Automatically, she stood up and took her laptop in her hands. Ignoring the ambient sounds and commotion, she walked out into the courtyard.

The cold was no longer an unpleasant sensation. Oh no. On the contrary, Anna harbored unprecedented hopes for this chilly morning. Let it clear her mind, let it cleanse it of delusions. But something inside her hinted that the line she had crossed was far behind. No matter how much she searched for the way back, the fog obscured it—the path to her former sanity.

Now, Anna, you are no more sane than Eleanora, that unfortunate soul who heard demons and transcribed messages from them. You've turned into the heroine of your first novel.

Only once in her life had she teetered on the edge. Yes, once she had begged death to come and take her. That had happened a long time ago, yet the memories had not disappeared. That night, just like this morning, she had plummeted from ecstasy to terror in an instant. And that fall had nearly killed her. Nearly.

First job, first significant position, and first profound emotions. Everything blended into a cocktail of new experiences. Love at first sight that would only evolve after three years of professional interaction. It seemed like nothing could throw these two off the wheel of samsara: recurring encounters, workplace flirtation, and friendly embraces. But one day Richard was transferred to another office. For Anna, it was a blow. Even though she understood that her beloved now worked on the other side of London, every morning she hoped to enter the office and see his sweet smile—to have the opportunity to hug him, kiss his cheek, and hear the beating of his heart. Without this ritual, it seemed utterly impossible to work. Indeed, without Richard as a colleague, life became much harder to endure.

He would sometimes write emails, and they warmed Anna's soul like no scorching summer day ever could. At the end of July, she was sent on a business trip to Manchester. There wasn't much work to be done—just checking documentation at one of the company's branches and signing a couple of supply contracts. The trip fell on a Friday, and Anna decided to stay in the city of British football for the entire weekend. Her hotel in the city center was conducive to evening strolls and new acquaintances. Yet none of her promising new acquaintances could erase thoughts of Richard.

Anna approached the enormous window of her room and looked out at the night city. Earlier that day, she had sent an email to her colleague—an email in which she confessed her feelings. Many hours had passed, and she found herself in a foul mood, getting irritated over trivial matters and rapidly losing hope of saving their friendship, at least.

Behind her, an incoming text message chimed. Anna didn't hurry. It could be anyone, but more likely it was just a standard message from the network provider. However, this time her usually discerning guess was off. The message was from Richard. He was asking how things were in Manchester and what Anna was up to. She paced around the room, sat on the bed, and stood up again. She came up with a hundred different sentences but ended up writing only a few words about how everything was fine at the office and she wasn't really busy. Richard remained silent. So unusual. No warm "good night" or chilly "have a great evening."

"Sorry, bad signal!" he finally wrote. "I'm on my way to Manchester."

As Anna paced the room, she couldn't believe his words. Her cheeks burned, and the air was catastrophically inadequate.

"On business?" she asked.

And again, a long wait.

"To you," the phone revealed after a lengthy fifteen minutes.

He was coming to her. She read those two short words non-stop. She couldn't believe in the miracle that had finally happened after three years of delightfully unbearable friendship.

"Waiting," she replied. "Waiting eagerly," she added.

Richard was driving. He responded when possible and when there was a signal. Anna waited until dawn, but Richard never arrived. When she tried to call, his mobile phone was turned off and his home phone remained silent. On Saturday afternoon, she learned about the car accident that had taken Richard's life. The thought of suicide came suddenly, like a rainstorm on a sunny day.

Anna entered the bathroom and turned on the hot water. She slid onto the cold tiles, not feeling her body. Not understanding her feelings and emotions. Not sensing herself as alive and belonging to this world. What would have happened if she hadn't revealed her secret? Why email from Manchester when you can email from London? Why wait for damn three years, seeing him every godforsaken day? These heavy thoughts haunted Anna for many years. What if? Oh, if only she had known what was coming. If only she could have seen the sequence of events ahead. If only she could have foreseen that receiving an official email once a week was incomparably delightful than everything that had followed her heartfelt confession.

Stepping into it, you'll never come back. Judy Richter's words echoed in her head. *Going insane is truly terrifying. Moreover, you'll never realize that it has already happened to you. That's the cunning part of madness. The people around you will seem strange, their actions devoid of logic, their behavior unjustifiable. But in reality, it will be you who has gone insane, not them. That's why I agreed to this interview. Perhaps I can share this burden with someone else.*

Unaware of how she had ended up at the cliff's edge, Anna stared into the fog, so thick that you couldn't see into the distance or the depths below. Like a blanket you'd want to fall into and get lost forever. A stone, grating beneath her shoe, tumbled into the abyss. *No, Anna, you've never come this close to death before.*

Glancing around, Anna noticed a weathered bench beyond the path. Clearly whoever had affixed a message to it had lost their wife right there.

Well, I won't be original ... We'll meet soon, dear Shifra or whatever your name was, Anna muttered in her thoughts. She clutched the laptop to her chest and closed her eyes.

"Anna!" a familiar voice echoed. "Anna!"

She lifted her eyelids and turned her head. Emerging from the mist, Eddie walked towards her, burdened with a backpack.

Chapter 17

"Eddie? Is it really you?"

Anna seemed to snap out of her trance and stepped back from the edge.

"Can you believe it, not a single taxi! Luckily the ferry is still running." Eddie stopped and took off his backpack.

"What are you doing here?" Anna couldn't believe her eyes.

"I don't know." He sighed. "The last few days, all I've been thinking about is Rathlin. Better tell me, what are you doing here?"

"Going crazy." Anna smiled weakly. "Oh God, I'm so glad to see you!" She quickly placed her laptop on the bench and hugged Eddie.

"Me too—insanely." He hugged her back gently. "So where is he?" Eddie interrupted the prolonged pause.

"Who?"

"Apparently I'm talking about the hotel you were in such a hurry to get to in Belfast."

"No, no, let's sit here for a bit. I'm not ready to go back there." Anna slowly settled onto the bench.

"What happened?" Eddie raised his eyebrows. His carefree face instantly turned serious.

"I don't even know myself. It's a very strange place … I understand you've just come off the road and need to get to the hotel … Let's just sit here for a bit …" Anna spoke hesitantly.

"No problem at all—of course we can sit. Besides, I was in a hurry not to get to the hotel but to see you." Eddie lifted Anna's laptop and settled down next to her.

The cold morning compelled them to huddle together. Resting her head on Eddie's shoulder, Anna felt an unfamiliar sensation. It was tranquility. Suddenly, everything that had troubled her just ten minutes ago ceased to be a concern. All at once, she felt as good as when returning to her childhood home—the kind of home where you are completely protected, undeniably happy, and have no desire to run away. Anna squeezed Eddie's hand as if afraid he might be a mirage, capable of vanishing in an instant.

Along the coastline, the lapping of waves resonated, and somewhere in the distance, restless seagulls cried out. Anna's eyes inexorably closed—she had slept little that night. Through Eddie's steady breathing, the clicking of the keyboard became audible.

"What are you doing?" Anna blinked open her eyes. She straightened up and looked at the laptop screen. Eddie, on the other hand, didn't break away from his reading.

"You … This …" Anna hesitated. "Can you understand everything that's written there?"

"Well, I detected a hint of arrogance in you from the very beginning, but I assure you my IQ allows me to grasp bestselling texts—don't take offense—especially those from Literary Publishing."

"Oh God, no." Anna covered her face with her hands. "It's not about that. It's just that they told me …" She fell silent, hesitating.

"They told you …?" Eddie insisted.

"They said it's the writing of a deranged mind. It has words, punctuation marks—"

"Not all of it," Eddie interrupted.

"Not all of it." Anna chuckled nervously, scrutinizing his face. "But the main thing is that my text doesn't make sense. It's a senseless string of words."

"It's brilliant!" Eddie blurted out without a hint of a smile. "But where did you get all those reviews? Who convinced you of your own lack of talent?" He seemed quite puzzled.

"A friend …"

"A friend?"

"A venerable gentleman."

"The prison is crying over this venerable gentleman."

THE GULL CRY HOTEL

"What?"

"Here's an article: 'Incitement to suicide.'"

When Eddie had appeared on the cliff, Anna couldn't believe her eyes. But now she didn't believe her ears either. Obviously one of them was lying. And it was quite evident that Eddie wasn't the one.

"Do you think I don't see the state you're in?"

"You're talking as if you know my states," Anna said, pressing her temples.

"All right." Eddie closed her laptop. "Tell me everything step by step."

Once again resting her head on his shoulder, Anna dared to embark on a long narrative. She tried to lay out everything systematically and not miss any details. When she reached the part about the gruesome murder, Eddie visibly tensed and looked into her eyes. Anna stumbled and fell silent.

"Eddie?" She spoke after a prolonged silence.

"Hmm?"

"Thank you for coming. Our friendship means a lot to me, really."

"Don't talk nonsense," Eddie replied. "This is not a friendship at all. So, what happened next?"

As Anna tamed her rising emotions, she continued her narrative. But as soon as she had finished, Eddie started firing questions one after another.

"Did you hear the whisper somewhere else apart from your room?"

"I don't know," said Anna, puzzled.

"Focus—remember. This is important!"

"No, I don't think I heard it anywhere else …"

"Then somewhere beneath the wallpaper, there must be hidden speakers."

"What?" Anna recoiled.

Stop it, Anna. Don't even start with your "what" again, or Eddie will get up and go back into the mist. But he didn't notice her confusion and continued his questioning.

"And was the dwarf both in the carriage and on the platform?"

"Um …" Anna pondered. "Yeah, it seems so."

"So there were two of them. One might not have been the dwarf you usually see. After all, you didn't really get a good look at the one running through the carriage, did you?"

"No …"

"Just heard it?"

"Yes."

"Then we have one dwarf and his accomplice—either the same dwarf or a child given ten pounds. Or maybe it's just two guys and a couple of identical masks. You didn't see the dwarf from behind, did you?"

"No …"

"And the old woman on the ferry, she's definitely part of this gang. Haven't seen her around here, have you?"

"No …"

"She could have been standing on the other side of the window when you looked into the fog."

"But the face was hideous, almost inhuman!" Anna resisted.

"Believe me, if they darken her eyes a bit and ask her to open her mouth wider, under cover of night and fog, you'll see roughly what you saw. We used to scare kids with the same trick at the summer camp in Beaumont. Old trick."

Everything Eddie said was staggering. But he had no intention of stopping the flow of his thoughts.

"Wait—but if they want me dead, why would Benedict rescue me from the quicksand?"

"Meaning your swift demise wasn't part of their plan. Either he was ingratiating himself. But how they played you in the lobby with the non-existent language—that's the height of naivety. How could you fall for that?"

"Eddie …"

"Okay, sorry, I get it all."

"But what about the murder?"

"I can't say for sure, but I really hope that was staged too."

"I don't believe it—it's impossible!" Anna protested.

"What, exactly? To wash the bloodstains off the carpet? I agree, it's really challenging … but trust me, it's not on the impossible list!"

"Listen, there's one circumstance"—Anna began cautiously—"that I haven't mentioned."

"What is it? And stop hiding things from me," Eddie demanded.

"The first time, I saw that dwarf in a dream. Back in London."

"Hmm," Eddie pondered, and after a moment, he pulled his laptop from his backpack and opened it. He connected to the internet via his mobile phone and launched a web browser.

"Does your internet work?" Anna exclaimed in surprise.

THE GULL CRY HOTEL

"Of course it works."

"But Rosemary said—"

"They simply cut you off from civilization. So, the hotel, the screech of seagulls." Eddie typed rapidly. The screen displayed Anna's familiar hated mansion, and in the middle, there was an advertisement.

"Did you watch the video?"

"Yes," Anna blurted out, expecting new revelations from her miracle acquaintance.

"Then let's download it and play it back in slow motion."

"Why?" Anna grasped Eddie's arm and stared curiously at the screen.

"That's why," Eddie said, slowing down the video frame by frame. Between the images of local meadows, a sinister face with a glassy gaze suddenly appeared. Anna flinched, and her gut tightened with fear. Following the shots of the picturesque cliffs was a photo of an ancient key.

"And the key appeared in your dream?"

"Yeah." Anna swallowed. "But how does it work?"

"The twenty-fifth frame. A single slide isn't perceived by our consciousness, but the subconscious reads it. Of course, this method doesn't guarantee anything, but the information-sensitive brain—the brains of writers and creative people—is more likely to remember such messages. These psychopaths wouldn't lose anything if you didn't see the dwarf in a dream. But when you did, it definitely played into their hands."

"But why?"

"I don't know."

"So, are the Americans really alive?"

"I hope that's the one truth they told."

"But what if they aren't? What if they killed them?"

"If they went that far, I have to admit that killing people in the middle of the night isn't that simple. Especially since we're not just talking about murder but also dismemberment. Based on the timespan you're describing, most likely they were only working on one body in the bathroom. Perhaps someone else is still alive. And to do it so quickly with a manual saw ... Only an expert could manage that. A doctor, for example. Someone who knows where the tendons are attached. Without knowledge of anatomy, dismemberment takes up to twelve hours or more."

"Only a doctor ..." Anna rose from the bench. "But how do you know such details?" She frowned, taking a confident step away from the bench.

"Are you afraid of me?" Eddie chuckled. "I … No, no." He waved his hands. "Believe me, I'm just a well of useless information."

"Not that useless, apparently." Anna smiled. "So, it seems the killer is Father Kaiden? He's the only doctor in the picture as far as I know."

"He could have dismembered a body that was already dead, assuming there was a murder at all. The victim might have been killed near the bed, where you found the fallen lamp and stepped on broken glass."

"You know, its base was smeared with something. Something greasy and fragrant … like cream!" Anna exclaimed. "Could it be Jill Amsterham as well?"

"I hope I'm wrong, but it seems to me the whole hotel is in on it." Eddie shrugged. "Think about it—if someone else wasn't aware of what was going on, wouldn't they notice the strange behavior of this group? They're playing along with each other; they're all acting according to some plan."

"I'm a writer. I'm writing a book about their hotel. And it could play out as good publicity for them."

"No." Eddie shook his head. "Then your fine friend Benedict would have acknowledged the brilliance of the manuscript and actively encouraged you to finish and release the novel to reach as many people as possible.

Something doesn't fit here. They're pursuing some other motive."

"Yes, of course—you're right. What are we going to do?"

"For starters, let's call the police. We'll wait for them, and only in the company of an officer will we return to the hotel, gather your things, and leave."

"Where to?"

"Back to London! Or haven't you traveled enough around the Irish islands?"

"I've had enough, indeed." Anna sighed. "But what's their motive?"

"Their motive is known only to them. And what difference does it make to us? The main thing is to get out of here and let each one do what they do best. Writers write books, and the police investigate murders."

"Well, don't be modest. In less than an hour, you exposed them for what they really are."

Eddie flushed, but he tried not to show it. "I'm calling the police," he announced, dialing the three-digit number. He spoke at length with the Rathlin police department, who promised to send a car.

"Did you think about me?" Eddie murmured softly. It had clearly been bothering him since Belfast.

"Yes, a lot."

"Then why didn't you respond to my messages?"

"I broke my phone."

"Jesus, thank God I came!" He wiped the horror from his face, imagining all the irreversible things that could have happened that morning.

He hugged her too tightly for a mere friendly embrace. However, they didn't have to wait long. They could have sat there much longer, embracing each other, pondering what had happened, in a complete silence that didn't bother them at all. But upon hearing the car, as if on cue, they got up and approached the road.

"I'm Eddie Farrel, and this is Anna Walker."

"Witness?" The policeman squinted, extending his hand for a handshake.

"Yes." Anna nodded.

"Sergeant Henry Bathurst."

Anna examined Henry's face without embarrassment. The thought of how police officers had such typical faces for their profession never left her—as if they were chosen according to the same criteria, ensuring that Bathurst was a spitting image of Stevens, and Cooper resembled Gordon. But for what purpose? Apparently appearance, like uniform, must inevitably be standardized.

"So, what exactly did you see, ma'am?"

"I heard the murder. I saw signs of a struggle in the room and a bathtub full of human blood."

The sergeant glanced at Anna in wing mirror. "How do you know the blood was specifically human?"

Anna frowned.

"Did you see the body? Or its parts?"

"No." She shook her head nervously and looked at Eddie. "I didn't see it."

"Isn't the interrogation procedure supposed to be conducted by an investigator?" Eddie asked.

"I'm just trying to figure out, sir."

"Figure out what?"

"Whether it's worth calling the investigator."

This response clearly didn't sit well with Eddie. He grimaced, glanced briefly at Anna, and drilled the sergeant's nape with his gaze. The author of articles in a popular science magazine seemed to have caught the law enforcement officer out in something. However, engaging in conflict with the police wasn't in Eddie's plans, so he patiently remained silent. Anna touched his hand, interrupting his train of thought. He squeezed her hand and pulled her closer. Her breath quickened. She felt lightheaded and sweetly intoxicated, as if from a sip of sherry. It resembled a special form of addiction. In just one morning, she had become addicted to leaning on this guy's shoulder. It was calm and peaceful there. But if she withdrew just a meter, a sense of longing would immediately envelop her. Something enticed and drew her back to him as if the two of them had invisibly merged.

Eddie did not always do what he wanted to. But this time he was genuinely terrified. He was truly afraid that if he didn't do it now, he would never do it.

He looked into Anna's eyes, his gaze tracing her cheekbones, along her sharp nose, and stopping at her lips. She had been this close only to Roderick's lips in the past couple of years, but never had she desired to kiss anyone the way she wanted to kiss Eddie now. Strange Eddie. Amazing Eddie. The Eddie she barely knew yet who felt so familiar. As if she had known him all her life; as if she had been waiting for years for this moment.

Suddenly he leaned in and, bridging the gap of a couple of inches, kissed her. His gentle touch made Anna close her eyes. The vertigo didn't subside, and her body was engulfed in waves, as if she was leaping from a height every twenty seconds.

"We're almost there," Sergeant Bathurst intervened.

Reluctant to stop, Eddie did come to a halt. His dazed gaze vividly conveyed that Anna wasn't alone in her altered state. It seemed he had been hatching this plan since Belfast, since that very first encounter with her. That evening when he had arrived at his hotel, checked into his room, had dinner, and even attempted to work—whatever he did, his thoughts were far away, somewhere on the road to Rathlin.

Nuzzled against Eddie's neck, Anna closed her eyes and suddenly caught a subtle fragrance. It was the scent of freshly picked blueberries crushed between fingers.

"Your scent," she whispered.

"What about it?" Eddie tensed.

"You smell like blueberries."

A dimple appeared on his cheek. Suppressing his joy, he turned toward the window. Overwhelmed by emotions, he felt the urge to scream, but everyone might consider him insane too if he did that.

The car slowed down and veered off the road. Stepping onto the wet gravel, Anna saw an unfamiliar face in the hotel doorway.

"Miss Walker! What does all this mean?" The mustached brunet greeted Sergeant Bathurst and stared at Anna with a hint of reproach.

"What's wrong with you?" Eddie caught up with her.

"I don't know this man," she said quietly.

"Sorry, we didn't introduce ourselves." Eddie started the conversation, approaching the entrance. "Eddie Farrel."

However, the brunet with the eagle-eyed gaze ignored him. Instead of responding to his handshake, he didn't take his eyes off Anna.

"Where have you been? We were so worried and had to call the police." The stranger briskly crossed his arms over his chest.

"Who called the police?" She furrowed her brow in confusion. "We called the police!"

"Who's 'we,' Anna? Please don't start again."

The next moment Anna flinched, feeling a needle prick in her forearm. The image lost its sharpness, and soon the windows of the mansion floated before her eyes. The white sky initially blinded her, but within a second it was engulfed in a deep blackness.

"Relax, Anna, calm down …"

Strong hands gripped her wrists.

Chapter 18

"Don't try to break free. Don't make sudden movements ..."

Lifting her heavy eyelids, Anna saw her room and the brunet sitting next to her. She instinctively jerked, shuffling her feet and moving closer to the edge of the bed. "Who are you?" she said in fear. Her own voice seemed unfamiliar to her for a moment.

"You know me perfectly well, but if you wish, I'll introduce myself again. Just don't worry. There's no need for unnecessary concern right now. I'm Frank Barton, your attending physician."

"What?" Anna blinked. "What are you talking about?"

"You are in the private clinic named after Louis Martin on Rathlin Island."

"This is a hotel ... It's a hotel. Damn hotel," Anna whispered, examining her room with fear in her eyes.

You chose this truth for yourself from the very beginning. Since the day they brought you here.

"I wasn't brought; I came here on my own!" she blurted out, staring at Frank. His face showed no surprise; only his thick eyebrows twitched for a moment, then settled back over the weighty gaze of his brown eyes.

"Eddie! Where's Eddie?" she demanded.

"Well, we've come back to Eddie." The man sighed and, with a hint of disappointment, added, "You were brought here precisely because of him."

"What are you talking about? Where is he?"

"Anna, just so you know, I've said this many times before: There is no Eddie. This guy is a product of your imagination."

"No!" Anna laughed hysterically. "That's not true! I met him at Heathrow before my flight to Ireland."

"Dear Anna"—Frank squeezed her hand tighter—"I assure you, Eddie appeared in your life long before Heathrow. Roderick and Alison know about him; your parents and friends too. At first they, just like you, believed Eddie was real. But later they found out the truth. Mrs. Watcher sought our help. She cares about you and wants to see you well as soon as possible."

"I need to call her! Talk to her!" Anna babbled.

"Out of the question," Frank retorted without changing his tone.

"But why?"

"No calls to anyone in your close circle. Or do you want all of London to know about your ailment?"

"I need to talk to them—just hear confirmation from them of your words," pleaded Anna.

"Oh, Anna! We've been through this dozens of times. At first I allowed you to call London, but after seeing that we don't make any progress that way, I stopped it. Trust me and everything will be fine. I promise you'll return to normal life."

Staring at the wall, Anna froze. Her thoughts leaped from event to event as she desperately tried to piece together the lost fragments of her memories. But she couldn't.

"I don't believe you," she finally said. "I want to talk to Benedict, to Rosemary."

"Benedict had finished his stroll and is now taking a break in his room, as far as I know. And Rosemary is still in the kitchen, as always. You can always talk to them when you feel up to it," assured the doctor.

Anna's jaw grew heavier. She turned her unblinking gaze to Frank. "Are they patients too?" she inquired.

"Benedict is. Rosemary assists me with the chores around this clinic. She's truly indispensable. Looks like you've grown quite attached to her yourself." He smiled.

Anna once again gazed at the white wall. "And Father Kaiden?"

THE GULL CRY HOTEL

"Well, he's not really a priest, as you've probably figured out. I'll tell you his story some other time, if you don't mind. But there's no need to worry; the worst is already behind us. He's in capable hands and hasn't been a threat for three years now."

"The worst?" Anna raised her gaze inquisitively.

"Well, he managed to avoid prison, let's put it that way. Confinement with criminals wouldn't have been in his favor. His family, quite respectable and rather well known, took care of securing the best place for this unfortunate situation. I assure you he's completely harmless."

Anna sank back into her thoughts.

"I'll leave you … Get well soon." Frank rose from the bed.

"Wait!" she exclaimed. "When did he first appear?"

"Who?" Frank asked, as if playing a game.

"Eddie," Anna replied, subdued.

"A year ago. He showed up in your life exactly a year ago. Everyone's patiently waiting for him to leave. And you're the only one who can help him do that." Maintaining his intense gaze, the doctor approached the bed again. "We've heard a lot of stories about Eddie. In these two months—"

"Two months?" Anna interrupted.

Frank nodded solemnly. "During that time, almost the entire population of the clinic came to believe in his existence. Then there was silence. You talked about some murder, then you were occupied with the manuscript. Not a word about Eddie. We all brightened with hope. And now again ..." Frank sighed heavily. "I understand better than anyone how hard it is for you to fight him. But we'll help. You have to trust us."

Anna no longer lifted her gaze to her doctor, and soon he left her alone. She continued to stare at the wall, almost oblivious to the cries of annoying birds outside the window and the thick fog that seemed to have permanently shrouded the island. She traced her lips with her fingers, recalling the kiss. She still felt Eddie's presence, as if he were somewhere nearby, about to enter the room at any minute. Every time she closed her eyes, she sank into Eddie's blue eyes as if in a cold mountain lake.

Anna simply couldn't believe that such vivid emotions could awaken in her for an imaginary hero. Not just any hero from her novels but Eddie Farrel—an invisible character in her own life.

"No, no, no." Anna vehemently shook her head. "This can't be real."

She could have believed that she had ended up in a madhouse. That her only friend here, Benedict Russell, was as insane as she was. But Eddie! If Anna's imagination had given birth to Eddie Farrel, it would have obediently removed a couple of large tattoos from his forearms, trimmed his hair, and dutifully mended his worn-out socks.

No, Eddie didn't fit into Anna's perfect world. He was like a virus in the program, breaking all her stereotypes and convictions. She simply couldn't fall in love with someone like Eddie. Not even for an experiment or a hefty sum of money. Even in the most absurd of dreams, the image of Eddie would never captivate Anna's mind. Her connection with him was something else. Something uncontrollable and contradictory. Something that defied logic. A naked tangle of feelings and emotions. A state where rational thinking was impossible.

After the recent conversation, Anna wasn't sure about anything anymore except that no matter how unhealthy her mind might be, it simply couldn't create Eddie.

Her gaze roamed the room until it settled on the silvery laptop.

Edits! Well, of course—the revisions Eddie made to the text on the clifftop!

Anna slid off the bed and, with trembling hands, opened the laptop. The page loaded, displaying the timestamp of the changes made to the document: 7:14 a.m.—comma added, preposition removed, instead auxiliary part of speech typed.

He was fixing this—he was fixing it! Anna rallied.

A warmth spread through her body, but a moment later she was already flipping through page after page in search of similar rough patches. Well, all her "signature" mistakes were still in place. Only there, in that passage Benedict had characterized as senseless and Eddie hailed as genius, had the flaws been corrected.

But that wasn't enough for Anna. In a split personality, the ego doesn't remember the actions of the alter ego.

Think! Don't think like Anna Walker. Think like Eddie. What would he do? How would he act? If this is a conspiracy, they could have known about Alison and Roderick and about my life in London. But there's no way they could know what Eddie and I talked about when we met this morning.

"Don't give up! Don't play their games!" Anna clenched her fists, closed her eyes, and transported herself back to the evening when she had first heard the indistinct whisper.

To the right! It was coming from somewhere to the right!

Very soon she was moving cautiously next to the window, inspecting the curtain rod and the floral wallpaper step by step. She didn't know what she was looking for. She was just searching for anything that could shed light on the mystery of her obsession.

"I won't find anything like this." She sighed in frustration and rested her forehead against the glass.

THE GULL CRY HOTEL

The fog was thickening again. The gray silhouettes of seagulls had all but disappeared, just like the cliff and the road, along with Green's car. Only a strip of wet gravel and a section of brickwork overgrown with the blood-red leaves of wild ivy remained. If every day here was like this, going insane wouldn't be difficult at all.

Come on, pull yourself together! Don't succumb to despair!

Anna rushed to the door and listened.

Nobody ...

She quickly turned the key in the lock and rested the oak nightstand against the door. She darted back to the window, grabbed the round wooden table with both hands, and dragged it into the farthest corner. The chair followed suit, bracing the wobbly table with its high back. Stepping onto the chair, Anna climbed up onto the table. Gripping the heavy drapes, she delicately tapped the wall. Everything seemed ordinary—brick wall, probably plaster, primer, and old wallpaper.

Listening intently, Anna shifted slightly and the table beneath her feet swayed, making her lose her balance. Like an acrobat on a tightrope, she hung on to the drapes, restoring the furniture to its former equilibrium. At that very moment, a click reached her ear, followed by a familiar whisper that began to grow in volume. Her eyes rose to the ceiling and fixed on one of the faded burgundy peonies of the wallpaper. Anna descended to the floor, shifted the table closer to the wall, and moved the chair next to it. A minute's work and a new makeshift ladder was ready. She climbed it again, this time reaching the ceiling to confront her fears face to face.

He was right! They're deceiving me ... They've cut me off from everyone I know. They've taken Eddie away from me! A cold sweat washed over Anna, and, just about managing to reach the top of the wall, she began to scratch the paper furiously. Suddenly she stopped. *No one must find out that I've figured it out! I have to act cautiously. Until I find Eddie, I must play my part in this theater of the absurd.*

She hurriedly descended, dashed into the bathroom, and retrieved a pair of nail scissors from her cosmetics bag.

"High ..." She assessed the distance and moved the chair against the wall instead of the table. Leaning on the wall, she carefully climbed onto the velvety backrest. Now she stood directly in front of the faded peony. The blade of the scissors gently penetrated the paper and traced the burgundy outline. After cutting around half of the flower, Anna opened it like a little door. In the darkness of the neatly carved niche in the wall stood a miniature black speaker, its wires extending through holes into the adjacent room. Or ward, as Frank Barton would have said.

However, now, regardless of what Frank, Benedict, or anyone else in this godforsaken place might say, Anna couldn't care less. Now she knew the truth. Now she was capable of reaching the source of her hallucinations without anyone's help.

Someone carefully turned the door handle and, feeling resistance, attempted to insert a key into the lock. When that failed as well, a knock sounded.

"Miss Walker? Are you okay?" a female voice inquired.

"Yes! Who's there?" Anna hastily tried to restore the wallpaper to its undisturbed state, but it resisted, wrinkling and revealing gaps where it had been cut.

"Miss Walker, open the door! Your medication is waiting for you."

"Yes, yes, just a moment …"

Medication! thundered in her mind. *They've decided to put me on psychotropics! Damn maniacs …*

The delicate knock turned insistent, and Anna's heart raced. Tremors intensified in her hands, and the chair slowly moved away from the wall. She pulled the curtain towards herself and, miraculously avoiding a stumble, sharply descended onto the carpet.

"If you don't open up right away," the woman threatened from behind the door, "I'll have to call Dr. Barton and the orderlies!"

Having placed the table back in its original position, Anna awkwardly dragged the chair to the window and approached the door.

What if they inject me with a sedative again? What if they dress me in a straitjacket, strap me to the bed, and subject me to torture? But if I don't open up, I won't be able to find Eddie. Anna's gut trembled as she pushed the nightstand aside and turned the key. In the corridor stood a slender Irishwoman in her sixties, dressed in a neat dress and a starched apron. She had a peculiar smile and was holding a white tray with food and a small container that housed a couple of yellow pills.

"You look frightened," she declared from the doorway and stepped into the room. "And is this nightstand, dear, propping the door shut?"

"Yes," Anna blurted out, calming her nerves.

"And who are we barricading ourselves from?" The visitor smiled falsely, placing her tray on the round table.

Anna tried not to look at the corner, where the wallpaper was peeling with a soft crackle.

"The dwarf!" she unexpectedly exclaimed loudly. "He's haunting me. I saw him in London, then on the train. And after the train, right here, in this hotel."

"Oh dear, no need to get nervous. We'll definitely help you." The nurse feigned concern. "Let's take the pills, and I'll leave you alone with your steak."

Damn ... Anything but this.

"I promise to take them after the meal," Anna hurriedly reassured her.

"No, no, we've been through this already," the nurse interrupted.

When did we have time? Anna bit her lip in confusion.

"Come on, open your mouth." The nurse armed herself with pills and a glass of water. "And no more closing up, or we'll have to take the key from you. We wouldn't want that. Dr. Barton wants all patients to feel like free individuals; it's, in his opinion, one of the most important steps towards recovery."

Anna merely glanced at the nurse and took the pills from her. She placed two yellow capsules in her mouth and swallowed water, attempting to keep the medication in her cheeks. The Irishwoman smirked and with a skillful movement compelled Anna to lift her head higher and finish the glass. She felt the pills slide down her throat.

Damn!

"That should be better," the nurse commented, heading towards the door. "Eat and get some sleep—it will do you good."

As soon as the door closed behind her, Anna bolted from her seat and dashed into the bathroom. Leaning over the toilet, she stuck her fingers into her mouth and forcefully pressed down on the base of her tongue. The first attempt yielded no results; the second time, she felt the water rise from her stomach. On the third try, she tried to insert her fingers as deep as she could. A fountain erupted, slightly tinged with yellow. Two swollen pills, damaged by stomach acid, landed in the toilet.

Phew, thank goodness ... She slid to the floor and leaned against the tiles.

Why all this? What's their motive? she agonized in speculation. But perhaps the most frightening thought was that they might not have a motive at all. How many people came to this backwater? Obviously not many like her. However, as Eddie had said, it was none of their business. The main thing was to find him as quickly as possible and escape from this place.

The more she pieced together all the events, the more accomplices surfaced. The island police were also involved, which meant nothing had stood in the way of them killing the young people from Chicago. And that meant nothing hindered them from dealing with Eddie.

The mere thought of his demise brought unbearable suffering. It was that thought that lifted Anna to her feet and directed her towards the door. She listened; the corridor was quiet. She pulled the key from the lock and pressed the handle, but the door didn't budge.

It can't be ... She repeated the attempt, but evidently the nurse's threats had not been baseless. Somehow they had locked Anna into her room.

THE GULL CRY HOTEL

Chapter 19

Anna paced around the room.

How long are they planning to keep me here, and what have they done with Eddie?

Approaching the window, she quietly opened it and looked down. The height was intimidating, but for some reason this was the least of her fears. She took one last glance at the door, extracted the key from the keyhole, and tucked it into her trouser pocket. Leaning out of the window, she grabbed hold of the ivy and tested the plant for strength. Its twisting stem disappeared into the gravel, entwining with two others at the bottom. The idea of falling was frightening, but doing nothing at all was even more terrifying.

Clutching the stalks, Anna hoisted herself through the window. She tested the strength of the plant, which tightly embraced the entire façade of the building, and shifted her weight onto her right leg. Still gripping the window frame, she gauged the distance to the adjacent room and the ground below. Among the autumn-thinned red foliage, knots of vines and swellings were discernible. However, in the window of the neighboring room, something else caught her eye—a gap. It was open.

THE GULL CRY HOTEL

Anna didn't know who would be waiting for her there. But between the two options, reaching the window seemed to her a much more achievable task than descending to the ground from the first floor down a wall enveloped by ivy.

As she shifted her entire weight onto a couple of branches, she heard a loud crack. There was no time to hesitate; the ivy branches was tearing away and detaching itself from the bricks right before her eyes.

"Oh God, oh God," Anna wailed, shifting her body closer to the adjacent window. The vine beneath her foot gave way, allowing her to plummet almost a meter. She clung to the branches, reaching desperately for the windowsill.

There was a creak of wood and another branch snapped beneath her foot. Leaning against the wall on tiptoes, Anna pulled herself up and reached her hand through the partially open window. Clasping the windowsill, she heard the last vines by her window snap. In that very moment, she realized that descending to the ground via such plants was akin to a conventional fall.

Realizing her stroke of luck, Anna pulled herself through the narrow gap and surveyed the room. It was empty and rather unkempt. Someone's belongings were strewn on the bed, and shoes lay scattered on the carpet near the chair. Whoever occupied this room was currently absent, providing Anna with a chance to slip away unnoticed.

This room had the same carpet, the same bed, identical curtains and wallpaper to her own. However, unlike her room, here, wires descended from the wall, plugging into an old-fashioned cassette player. She sifted through the tapes neatly arranged on the bedside table.

"Indistinct whisper," "persistent chatter," "creepy scream," "footsteps and knocks," "Benedict."

Anna furrowed her brow, lingering longer than usual on the tape labeled "Benedict." She pressed the button on the cassette player and opened the deck. The cassette inside had a sticker with the inscription "Anna."

Damn psychopaths ...

She walked over to the bed, where someone's clothes lay. The blood-red color of the man's shirt and trousers caught her attention. They were cut shorter than usual and crudely hemmed.

The dwarf. Anna's hands trembled.

Leaving the clothes behind, she stepped toward the wardrobe. Almost mechanically, she opened its doors, and from the darkness, the mad gaze of glassy eyes stared back at her. She stepped back. Her heart raced and her palms grew sweaty. Only when she discerned the silicone halo surrounding the horrifying face did she realize that it was indeed a mask. Everything was just as Eddie had suspected—word for word as he had explained.

THE GULL CRY HOTEL

As soon as she was able to tear her gaze away from the malevolent grimace, she managed to discern strands of false gray hair, makeup, and a white nightshirt with bloody streaks. It seemed like this wardrobe held all the mansion's darkest secrets.

How could Eddie have been so sure about the speakers and the masks? Perhaps I've been here before and Eddie is indeed just a creation of my imagination. Either scenario could be true, but Anna had no choice but to leave the room via the door. There was no other way back.

Quietly stepping away from her discoveries, Anna retrieved the key and approached the door. She looked through the keyhole—the corridor was empty, devoid of any footsteps or movement. She inserted the key and turned it gently. As before, one key could unlock any door in this house.

Anna stepped into the corridor, surveyed her surroundings, and listened intently. Somewhere in the distance familiar voices could be discerned, but they weren't approaching; no one was hurrying to this wing. Running to the elongated window, Anna stopped in front of the last room. It was here that the indentations in the carpet led, the ones she had noticed earlier, meaning this could be the office of her treating physician, Frank Barton, a psychopath and charlatan in one.

She leaned in towards the door; it seemed that there wasn't a soul inside. Complete silence and tranquility.

She once again inserted the ornate key into the lock, and it turned effortlessly once more. If this was Frank's secret place, full of mysteries and files of non-existent illnesses, syringes with sedatives, and dangerous pills capable of robbing a healthy mind of its sanity, he would have taken care to install another lock, the key to which he would carry with him everywhere and always.

But logic didn't work in this place, and therefore behind the door could be anything.

Having exhausted all possible scenarios, Anna didn't expect what she did see. There was hardly any furniture in the room, and the curtains were tightly drawn. In the semi-darkness, rows of suitcases and piles of clothes could be discerned. Finding the switch, she illuminated the room. Various suitcases and bags, backpacks and trunks were meticulously arranged, leaving no free space and no hope that anyone had left this place alive. Nearby lay clothes with dried brown stains.

The air was saturated with the metallic tang of blood, the scent of human sweat, and perfume. Anna was paralyzed. The key slipped from her hand.

"Mom!" A child's scream jolted her out of her stupor. She turned her head to see a boy standing at the end of the corridor.

It took Anna a second to realize—it was the one who, by changing costumes, had frightened her to the point of unconsciousness.

THE GULL CRY HOTEL

Chapter 20

As soon as footsteps echoed on the staircase, Anna sprang into action. She caught up with the boy and pulled a pair of nail scissors from her pocket, the same ones she had stashed away after discovering the hidden speaker in the wall.

She grabbed the child and pressed the miniature blade against his neck. A few steps away on the staircase, Frank and Rosemary froze.

"Let him go!" demanded Frank.

"Get out of the way!" Anna countered.

"Calm down, Anna. You don't understand what's happening." The doctor reached out to her.

"That's right, Doctor, I don't understand. And you're not helping me to understand. Get out of the way!"

"Please." Benedict appeared on the staircase. "Let the child go, Anna. You're not a killer."

"No, I'm not a killer. But you—you're all killers." She examined each face.

"You don't understand," Benedict repeated.

"Release Eddie and let us go. That's my demand!"

THE GULL CRY HOTEL

"We can't do that." Frank Barton seared her with his gaze.

"Anna, believe me, whatever you saw or heard, it's all for your own good. Let go of my son; he's certainly not guilty of anything!" Rosemary pleaded.

Anna felt her grip weaken. Of course she couldn't do anything to the child, and everyone around was aware of it. She was trapped again; soon someone would immobilize and sedate her once more. It would all repeat, and God only knew how many times this had happened already.

"Let me go," she said, fighting against the rising anxiety.

"Frank, let her go." Benedict suddenly intervened.

"But she's not ready," Barton snapped.

"How would you know? Let him decide for himself."

Let who decide? Anna squinted skeptically.

"Fine." The doctor reluctantly agreed. He touched Rosemary's shoulder and descended the stairs to the hall.

Rosemary stepped aside and Benedict, on the contrary, approached the stairs. Anna released the boy and ran down the steps.

"Don't go," Benedict whispered. He gazed intently into her eyes. "Trust me like you did in the swamp."

Like I did in the swamp? A question echoed in her mind. *Run, Anna, run!*

Out of the corner of her eye she noticed a syringe flashing in Fr. Kaiden's hands. He was hiding under the stairs. Anna shoved Benedict aside and sprinted toward the exit.

She pulled open the tight door and, startled by the chime of the entrance bell, burst outside. Momentarily disoriented, she dashed along the gravel next to the wall. Behind her the door creaked shut, and the bell chimed like a distant siren. Anna ran at full tilt, and somewhere in the white cloud, the gravel was already crunching behind her.

They won't go any further, won't stray far from the building, Anna reassured herself hopefully. She had nothing to lose, and after covering fifty meters, she stepped into the damp grass. Her footsteps became quieter, and, calming her breathing, she continued her journey.

Unable to see anything, she counted her steps and, reaching fifty-six, came to a halt. She could hear her name being called, and she saw the beam of a torch flickering in the mist. She had no desire to go back—at least not now, with the mansion surrounded.

When she had counted a hundred steps, the pursuit ceased. No one was looking for her anymore, as she had

THE GULL CRY HOTEL

ventured into blatant suicide—on one side of the hotel a sheer cliff, and on the other, the swamp.

The fugitive sat down and closed her eyes. *What's my plan? What plan do I have?*

Anna well understood that by the time she reached the port and found a phone, Eddie might no longer be alive. Action was needed here and now, but what action? Of course, there was no plan. The only thing guiding her was the desire to stop playing someone else's game. The last thing she wanted was to be a puppet in the hands of a bunch of lunatics. Therefore her primary plan remained disrupting the plans of the hotel's inhabitants. But what should she do now she had succeeded in fleeing?

Indecisive about where to go, Anna turned around and sat on the ground. It was quiet here. Occasionally seagulls cried in the distance.

Suddenly footsteps were heard from behind. Someone was treading lightly on the damp grass, trying not to make a noise. Someone was creeping closer, as if miraculously able to spot Anna in the mist.

Soon the same sound reached her from the other side. And then another and another. Anna felt surrounded, as if she was once again in a trap. Only this time the people closing in on her didn't emerge from the mist. She could clearly hear their footsteps and excited breathing and desperately tried to make out their figures but couldn't see them. Her fear grew until it turned into panic.

There was an exhalation to the right, just above her head, and a soft step to the left, as if one person was sneaking up on her while the other distracted her.

"Run, Anna, run ..." A whisper echoed, freezing the blood in her veins.

Anna jumped to her feet, looking around and peering hopelessly into the mist. "Anna, Anna, Anna ..." The whisper completely enveloped her.

She spun in place, soon realizing she had lost the direction in which she needed to return. She froze and listened: a step to the right, another to the left, breathing down her neck. Almost losing her mind, Anna turned—no one!

A lone seagull's cry from the coast prompted her to break free and dash away. Now she ran full tilt toward the cliff, back to the mansion.

She only stopped when she recognized the outline of Green's old car. She approached and leaned against it, catching her breath. Checking the doors, she confirmed that the car was locked.

What was that? she wondered, and immediately answered: *Drugs! Of course—they injected me with drugs.*

"Damn psychos!" she exclaimed aloud this time.

THE GULL CRY HOTEL

Listening carefully, Anna discerned a painfully familiar voice. It came from the direction of the mansion. So crisp, friendly with an unmistakable touch of falseness. Familiar to her from the very first day. She carefully stepped onto the gravel and approached the front windows. Even at the risk of her freedom, she absolutely needed to uncover the conspiracy—to fully reassure herself of her mental health if she was lucky, to discover the motives of these people, and, of course, to find Eddie.

A few more steps and Anna saw movement behind the windows. Fr. Kaiden once again kindled the fire, tossed in a new log, and settled into a high-backed chair. Seated at the round table, as before, was the plump Jill. She sipped her tea nervously, staring intently out the window. On the couch were Green and his trusted friend, ex private psychiatric clinic patient Benedict Russell. Frank Barton was pacing around the room, his hands clasped behind his back, speaking while everyone listened. He suddenly fell silent when Rosemary burst into the hall with a tray. The Irishwoman, now flushed, disagreed and interrupted the doctor. He glared at her sternly but listened.

"He's here!" Jill exclaimed, and everyone turned their gaze to the window. This time they saw Anna, but they looked through her.

Backing away, Anna scrutinized the faces that had changed so drastically—faces that were both familiar and entirely alien to her; the faces of people she had often seen but did not know at all. No one hurried to bring her back into the house. No one tried to restrain her or administer another dose of sedative. They all, without exception, simply observed her, not uttering a single word, devoid of any expression or emotion and, it seemed, not even blinking.

What is wrong with you people? Anna desperately tried to understand.

Suddenly the seagulls fell silent and the roar of the waves vanished, never to come back. A strange silence enveloped the surroundings—as if someone had plugged her ears, or perhaps someone had actually pushed the ocean away from the cliff. Anna couldn't see, but she could feel—something was moving chaotically in the mist.

It felt as though it came from the right, then from the left; somewhere in the distance and even above her head. Her fears were confirmed when the onlookers turned curious gazes somewhere much higher than the usual human height. Anna's pupils dilated, and a chilling wave ran down her spine. She slowly turned and lifted her head. In the mist, dark limbs were vaguely discernible.

Their contours resembled nothing that Anna had ever encountered. In none of the worlds of fauna or flora had she witnessed anything similar. But what struck her most were the dimensions. Sharp black ribbons appeared either just above the ground or so high up that no one could believe they were parts of the same thing.

THE GULL CRY HOTEL

Anna didn't move. She simply couldn't. Fear paralyzed her entire body and her consciousness as well. The creature neither approached nor retreated; it didn't attack or try to study her. It only emitted a strange, quiet sound, akin to high-voltage wires.

Hallucinations. Her consciousness finally gave birth to the thought.

Long ago, in her youth, Anna was impressed by stories of friends who had run from electricity pylons come alive. They would catch mushroom pickers, taking giant strides across the fields, gripping with rebar and bending down to the ground. They snatched up with black ropes of wires terrified teenagers who had decided to try hallucinogenic mushrooms, making the mad run for hours from a danger invisible to the ordinary eye.

Hallucinations, Anna repeated to herself, but unfortunately it didn't help.

She closed her eyes. If she couldn't see, maybe it wouldn't be as terrifying. *But if these are my personal hallucinations, how did they find out about them?*

The rumble intensified. It made her head spin, and her insides trembled. Now she couldn't see the monster, but she sensed its immediate presence with her entire being. The sound became unbearable, and at some point breathing became difficult. The stifling, dense fog seemed to penetrate her skin. The incomprehensible roar pressed against her eardrums, triggering waves of nausea.

She remained frozen in place as slick tentacles slid along her neck, spreading a deathly cold from the depths of the ocean throughout her body.

Anna could no longer endure this torture. "Let me in! Let me in! Can't you hear me? Let me in!" she screamed, pounding on the door.

None of the onlookers budged. They continued to watch with macabre fascination as something indescribably horrifying approached the mansion.

When the black ribbons slid under her feet, Anna felt her descent. Her cheek brushed against sharp stones, and a brief pang of pain pierced her temple. She no longer resisted; she willingly plunged into the darkness.

THE GULL CRY HOTEL

Chapter 21

"Miss Walker." A masculine hand clapped her cheek insistently, and Anna opened her eyes. She fearfully pressed herself into the pillow, instinctively gripping the plush of the couch. Frank Barton loomed over her like an eagle, piercing her with a heavy gaze. He didn't rush to interrogate her. Instead, he took her wrist and counted her pulse.

"Why are you so frightened?" Suddenly the doctor's gaze softened, and his thin lips, trembling, formed a smile.

Anna once again felt like a puppet in a tangled game. Of course, no one would tell her what was truly happening here. She was just a victim—one of many. How many had this company of psychos dispatched, shielded by the police?

"Miss Walker," Frank persisted. "Did you dream something?"

Dream? Please! No one will believe your blatant lies now, you damn Dr. Caligari!

Yes, they were no longer hiding the red-haired boy and the nurse who had changed into an old woman on the ferry; they no longer drugged Anna with sedatives. Frank's eyes alternated between a mad gleam and a return to sanity. The doctor lowered his gaze and touched Anna's hand. He began to stroke her, and suddenly he squeezed his fingers like a vise, continuing to slowly apply pressure.

"What did *he* say?" His voice became guttural, more like a roar. "What does *he* want?"

The whites of his eyes reddened; his thin lips twitched and viscous saliva appeared at their corners. Anna's joints audibly cracked under the pressure, and she winced in pain.

"Please"—a soft voice sounded—"let me talk to her."

Behind Frank stood Benedict. He smiled kindly at Anna, seemingly oblivious to all the madness unfolding around them. While the doctor pondered, staring at Anna with a crazed look, Benedict pulled a watch from his breast pocket, as if waiting for a train, and compared it with the clock on the wall.

"Well, come on." He patted Frank on the shoulder. "We don't have much time."

The doctor flared his nostrils and exhaled like a wild beast. He reluctantly rose and stepped aside. Benedict took his place. Good old Mr. Russell continued to smile, but now his smile seemed treacherous.

"Dear Anna"—the old man, instead of the doctor, now held Anna's hand—"talk to me. It's crucial for us to know if you have a message for us."

Anna skeptically surveyed those present and nodded. No, of course, she didn't hear any messages, but only in this way could she keep herself and Eddie alive. To continue lying or to die?

If I speak, then what? Nothing came to her mind at all. She needed more information about what these madmen believed—a bit more about what they saw under the influence of the drugs they had injected her with this morning.

"Dear Anna! What did *he* say?" Benedict insisted.

Every one of them froze, staring at the paling novelist.

"Make everyone leave," she managed to say.

Benedict glanced at Frank. The doctor pondered for a moment, then gritted his teeth and silently shook his head. Everyone obediently headed towards the stairs, glancing back and whispering.

"What did *he* say?" Benedict repeated his question when the hall had emptied.

"Benedict, in memory of our friendship—"

"Why in memory?" he interrupted. "I'm still your friend, don't doubt that!"

"If you are truly still my friend, answer just two questions."

"Of course."

"Is Eddie alive?" Anna asked, squeezing Benedict's hand.

He glanced around nervously and nodded weakly. Anna was overwhelmed with joy. Despite all the nightmares, her soul now was filled with happiness.

"Your second question, dear Anna," Benedict said ingratiatingly.

"Why do you kill people?"

Just a moment ago, she had intended to ask something else. But for some reason, suddenly believing that her friend Benedict was sane, she uttered a question that would disturb the consciousness of any normal person.

"Didn't *he* say?" Benedict frowned, dismissing her words.

His trust was fading, just like his interest in the information Anna supposedly held. Her heartbeat quickened and sweat appeared at her hairline. She had to keep playing the game or she wouldn't be able to save herself and Eddie.

"That's precisely why I requested a face-to-face conversation. I haven't understood everything *he* told me."

Benedict's eyes filled with hope. "What? What did *he* say, Anna?"

"I'll tell you, but first I want to know what *he* is."

Benedict sighed deeply and rubbed his veiny hands. "*He* is everything, dear Anna. There's nothing that doesn't depend on *him*."

"Hmm, you speak as if he's the Lord God."

"Isn't *he*, though?" Benedict widened his eyes like a child. "Once people were made to believe that there's only one god, but they were mistaken. Our ancestors, who worshipped multiple gods, had a reason for doing so, believe me."

"Yes, I understand." Anna nodded, not understanding anything at all. "But Benedict," she whispered, drawing closer, "in the past, people believed that thunder and lightning were manifestations of the gods."

"My dear Anna, you didn't see exactly that lightning and you didn't hear exactly that thunder. So how could you know it was just a regular atmospheric phenomenon? Just like now, many who come here are only capable of seeing ordinary fog. Just regular fog."

Right! She exhaled. She couldn't find an immediate response, but from now on, she had to be careful about everything she said.

"But Benedict, think about it. Why do the majority of people not see gods in the fog?" Not giving up hope, Anna spoke again.

"Because they're not ready. Our brains substitute reality. And when our brain is accustomed to one truth, it simply doesn't see another. But change the usual course of thought, broaden the horizons of possibility, and our consciousness becomes sensitive. It's at that moment we can behold what was impossible to see before."

"So you injected hallucinogens into me?" Anna couldn't take it anymore.

"Injected? No, no. Psychoactive substances were in the pills, just to prevent fear from paralyzing your mind."

Before Anna's eyes appeared the image of the two pills at the bottom of the toilet. *How much did I absorb?* She agonized over these speculations.

These lunatics clearly believed in something, but Anna, even with her excellent imagination, still had only a vague understanding of the foundations of their cult. And now, so as not to lose Benedict's trust, she needed to quickly reason about topics of which she had not the slightest inkling. Maybe if she initiated the attack, Benedict would let slip some things that could shed a little more light on everything happening in this place.

"But why did you summon *him*?" Anna prodded.

"We didn't summon *him*." Benedict reacted instantly.

"Yes, I understand." Anna nodded, understanding absolutely nothing, as Benedict continued animatedly.

"They summoned …"

"Who?"

"All those who had been banned from this dreadful place for decades." He sighed. "Frightened, desperate, lifelong prisoners of a private clinic for the mentally disturbed. Broken by the endless tortures of a sadist, at first they prayed to God, then to the Devil, but instead, *he* heard. And *he* answered their call from the depths of the ocean. No one remembers how it happened, but one day the clinic emptied. Within a year, everyone disappeared, from patients to staff. When the investigation hit a dead end, the mansion was put up for sale at a rock bottom price. The Bartons didn't expect it to fall on their shoulders. Frank handled the paperwork and Rosemary transformed the interiors, turning the rooms into hotel suites. But the euphoria was short-lived. That month, the coast was shrouded in dense fog. The mist lingered and refused to dissipate, seemingly merging with the mansion, breathing with it, slowly but surely choosing its victim. The first one to see *him* was young Benjamin. 'Mom, Mom, a monster is coming for me,' the little one repeated tirelessly. Rosemary and Frank attributed their youngest son's excessive excitement to the move. Until …" Benedict swallowed. "Until one night they heard his piercing screams. The fog had entered through the window. It entered"—Benedict struggled to tell the story—"and took its victim. Blood was everywhere, remnants of his small body. Torn-out hair, shreds of pajamas …"

"Oh God," slipped from Anna's lips.

Benedict's words sent a shiver down her spine, but he had no intention of stopping. He ran his finger over his moistened eyes, blinked away the tears, and continued.

"The next morning, for the first time in many gloomy days, the fog dispersed. The blue sky welcomed the sun. Heartbroken Rosemary insisted on retribution. She no longer believed in what she had seen at night. She preferred an alternate reality: Their son had been abducted, and he was still alive. Frank, on the other hand, didn't know what to believe, where to turn, who to appeal to. He buried his son's remains in the swamp. He reconciled with his wife's madness and, it seemed, he lost a bit of his sanity too. At one point he genuinely believed that the family could overcome the tragedy. Yet three months later, the fog reappeared on the horizon. It advanced again, forming a wall along the cliff, enveloping the coastline, and reaching the mansion."

Anna scrutinized the storyteller, studying him as Judy Richter, the psychiatrist at the prestigious mental health clinic in London, would observe one of her patients. She desperately wanted to catch Benedict in a lie, but judging by his physiognomy, this man wasn't lying. He genuinely believed everything he was saying.

"When eight-year-old Matthew claimed that someone was hiding in the fog, Frank and Rosemary immediately understood: It had come out for its seasonal hunt. In those days they were fortunate enough to encounter a tourist who asked for shelter. This house became his last refuge. In an attempt to save their son, the Bartons made their first sacrifice—the first, but far from the last. Moreover, their shaken consciousness was able to perceive the one hiding in the mist. *He* spoke to them—spoke to each of us. Every season, *his* appetite grew, and the methods of sacrifices became more sophisticated. Each season *he* demanded a new contactee, a fresh mind capable of understanding *his* divine language—people on the verge of madness, seeing their god and hearing *him* for the first time."

"For God's sake, are you saving yourself by killing others?" Anna blurted out.

"No, no, my dear. Listen to me! Sacrifice became part of these people's lives, and eventually all of us, because if the mist couldn't satisfy itself on the coast, it went deeper into the island, through the swamps to the small towns of Rathlin. We all lost loved ones. Jill Amsterham lost her husband and Kaiden lost his wife. Shifra willingly jumped off the cliff to save her son, Casper. Frank, a doctor by education, wanted to turn the mansion into a clinic again. He thought it would be easier to conceal the disappearances. But Henry …"

"The police officer?" Anna whispered with numb lips.

"Yes, he has lost people too … Of course, the police are aware of the situation. Thank God, Henry understands how crucial our mission is. So he suggested opening a hotel. And for a long time it worked flawlessly. We killed and drove the victims to the swamp. Some of them was able to go insane, like myself, and then we could receive new messages. *He* approved of our approach; *he* accepted our offerings. And only you know what *he* wants this time, right?" Benedict stared into the frightened eyes of his interlocutor. "What does *he* want, Anna? Which sacrifice does *he* want this time?"

"*He* wants you to let us go with Eddie," Anna whispered.

Benedict swiftly recoiled. "I thought I could trust you," he said disappointedly. "*He* simply couldn't ask for that. Just couldn't!"

"You're right. I'm the one asking for it." Anna spoke persuasively. "Can we blame someone for a primal fear—for the strongest of all natural instincts, the fear of death? Aren't you afraid of death, all of you who are so terrified by *his* appearance? You who have lost your loved ones, why haven't you gone after them? After those you loved so much?"

"Because *he* won't stop!" Benedict shouted so loudly that Anna flinched. "Don't you understand? We don't kill for amusement. By killing a few, we save millions. We maintain balance in this world; we do what others cannot."

The old man's eyes sparkled. Red threads spread through the whites of his eyeballs. The wise and smiling Mr. Russell was now consumed by rage. Anna had never known him like this, if she knew him at all.

Oh, stop it! she wanted to scream, but she bit her tongue in time. *Better not argue with these cultists.*

"You're right," she conceded. "*He* wants my beloved—my Eddie."

Benedict squinted skeptically.

"*He* said that in my heart, there is love. And *he* wants to take away the person dearest to me so these walls once again will fill with unbearable pain."

Benedict's head nodded ever so slightly. It seemed that what Anna had spoken resonated as truth in his mind.

But the question that followed almost robbed Anna of consciousness.

"In what form will *he* take Eddie?"

"*He* wants him alive. *He* will do everything *himself*," Anna assured him.

"But how do we know that Eddie won't run away?"

"You surprise me, Benedict. You can't escape from *him*, can you? By the way, this is an island. And the police are on your side," she replied emotionlessly.

The cult members deliberated for a long time. Rosemary was becoming increasingly silent. Fr. Kaiden thirsted for blood. The venerable priest suggested cutting the tendons of Eddie's legs. Frank didn't like the idea of letting the man go alive.

"Wasn't your goal to learn the message? I've delivered it to you; what else do you doubt?" Anna struggled to maintain her composure, as everything inside her was tearing apart with incomprehension. But she simply couldn't see any other way. They had to leave the mansion, and beyond that, let it be what it is.

Benedict nodded approvingly as Jill Amsterham threw up her hands and wailed, "Poor child, to lose your beloved. To witness his death with your own eyes. To watch as the master tears apart his failed creation …"

Her shoulders trembled. Vulnerable and frightened, Madame Amsterham now seemed extremely excited about the impending scene of the bloody sacrifice.

Anna's face contorted for a moment. In her fury, she was ready to slap this unhinged woman into silence. But then they would surely break Eddie's legs and her plan would be ruined.

No matter how much composure Anna used to have in her previous life, now just one mention of Eddie stirred a storm of emotions within her. Whether they were good or bad didn't matter. Her body now had an instant reaction to anything related to this man.

At some point she stopped hearing voices around her. Thinking about Eddie's salvation and the possibility of her own, she stood up. One unsuccessful plan replaced another. She didn't notice when she approached the window and stared into the fog. Behind her, the nurse was loudly expressing herself, and Green was nodding in agreement. Anna didn't catch the words. Her gaze wandered over the window frames, which were devoid of handles or heavy objects that could be useful for self-defense. The fog was hypnotic. Eventually all sounds and thoughts merged into a single background.

Kill them ... A foreign voice echoed in her head. *Kill them all!* The nightmarish thought repeated itself like a broken record until Anna forced herself to snap back to reality. She closed her eyes, pressed her temples, and focused on Fr. Kaiden's voice.

"We'll make small incisions with the scalpel in the tendon area. He'll still be able to walk for a while, but he won't be able to run away."

When Anna finally grasped that the majority had endorsed the plan of the chief sadist, breathing became difficult for her, and her chest tightened with overwhelming emotion.

"Have you decided to defy *him*?" The infuriated Anna lowered her tone. She glared at them from under her eyebrows, hunching her head into her shoulders and spreading her arms defensively. "Do you really consider yourselves the masters? *He* wants to hunt on *his* own! *He* desires healthy, agile prey and you're offering *him* something with severed tendons? *He* is not a scavenger and never has been! Cut! Go on, cut Eddie's legs if you want to test the strength of *his* wrath!"

THE GULL CRY HOTEL

All of them, without exception, fell silent.

"Well, Father Kaiden"—Anna approached closely—"bring your plans to life. Show creativity … and Casper will disappear this very night."

The priest held on as best as he could, but soon he took off his steamed-up glasses and, with trembling fingers, pulled a handkerchief from his pocket.

"Who? Who else wants to suggest a brilliant plan? A plan different from the one-handed to me!"

Anna was clearly beside herself. With a heavy step, she paced around the room, scrutinizing the faces of the people she had feared just moments ago.

"Or is it you, Jill? Knock out Farrel with a rare lamp, smother him with your fragrant creams, and toss him into the fog unconscious. Only you also have someone to protect, don't you? Not here—not within these walls. But somewhere out there in the villages of Rathlin, or perhaps across the vast land. Isn't that right?"

The plump woman remained motionless, not glancing at Anna. Her cheeks flushed, and her powdered forehead glistened with beads of sweat.

"Of course, you wouldn't be sitting here like a sentinel in your damn chair near the window on this damn border of worlds … Although you're already too late. You can bring your sacrifice however you want."

Anna fell silent as everyone exchanged frightened glances.

Frank Barton frowned and scrutinized their faces, urging them to take action. Green leaped from his seat and strode into the dining room. The doctor quickly followed. Anna watched the men go, holding herself back from rushing after them. Soon the heavy hatch creaked, indicating they were entering the basement. A minute later, a piercing moan echoed. Anna shuddered and listened intently. Sounds signaled that the hostages were being brought upstairs.

Anna stared at Eddie without taking her eyes off him. He appeared subdued, his mouth sealed with a silver piece of duct tape, and a bruise marked his forehead. The guy next to him, the red-haired American, moaned and desperately tried to break free. His frightened eyes pleaded with Anna to take action, but she paid him little attention. Only occasionally she attempted to appear ruthless. Eddie scrutinized the onlookers, hoping to figure out what had happened in his absence. Of course, figuring it out was extremely difficult.

"What exactly we should do with him?" Frank approached Eddie, who widened his eyes in surprise and furrowed his brow.

"Untie his hands and out the door!" Anna ordered.

Green dragged the struggling American aside and Frank led the captive forward. Eddie was bewildered. He subtly

THE GULL CRY HOTEL

shook his head, signaling that he wasn't planning to leave the hotel without Anna. She lowered her gaze and turned to the window. She clenched her fists, suppressing despair. Her nails dug into her palms, and a solitary tear rolled down her cheek. Something flickered in the mist. Staring into the fog, Anna stopped breathing. Dark tendrils swept over the land and disappeared again into the dense cloud. Her hands grew cold.

Chapter 22

"No!" she shouted. "No, you can't go there!"

Turning swiftly, Anna rushed toward Eddie but was halted by Fr. Kaidan.

"Don't worry, we'll all meet in heaven," he muttered, immobilizing the rebel.

Baffled, Eddie walked under escort toward the door. It was clear that he didn't want to leave without the one he had come here for. However, he understood well—being free would give him a much better chance of helping her.

"No, please don't let him go!" Anna sobbed, but her hysteria only spurred Frank into action. Now the doctor was sure he was doing the right thing. He decisively opened the front door, loosened the knots at the hostages' wrists, and pushed Eddie out.

Oh my God, no! What have I done?

"You fulfilled *his* wish," Kaiden cut in.

"But I didn't know … I didn't realize …" Anna stopped resisting, and Kaiden loosened his grip. Weakened, she sank to the floor. Her head spun, nausea rising in her throat.

THE GULL CRY HOTEL

What have I done? Merciful God, what have I done? The key turned in the lock, momentarily breaking the silence that had settled in the hall. Through it, Eddie's footsteps occasionally reached them—he was moving along the gravel near the wall.

"Eddie, Eddie …" Anna raised her head. "Eddie, run! Run, Eddie!" She pressed against the window, her breath fogging the glass as she strained to see. "Run—can you hear me?" She rapped on the window. "He's somewhere there, right near you! Run! Can you hear me? Please run!"

"Enough," Jill scoffed. "Or we'll tape your mouth too."

A sudden impact startled the onlookers. Everyone, without exception, stepped back from the window, on the other side of which lay Eddie's body. His face was contorted in horror, a rope hung from his wrist, and his palms were dripping with blood. Anna screamed, waving her hands, and stood frozen in place as something invisible grabbed Eddie from behind and swiftly dragged him into the mist.

"No!" In desperation, Anna let out a primal scream. Unbelieving, she scrutinized the emotionless faces and stepped back towards the door.

"Stop her!" Rosemary shouted.

"Let her go." Frank waved it off.

Hearing this, the American bent low, then swiftly straightened his back. A dull thud was followed by the crunch of a broken nose. Grimacing in pain, Green recoiled, and a spray of crimson blood stained the carpet. Without wasting a second, Anna turned the key and swung open the door, through which the captive tourist was promptly ejected. Following him, Anna emerged. No one hurried to stop them. Everyone knew for certain: The master was on the hunt, and he would take as many as he deemed necessary.

"Eddie! Eddie! Where are you?"

"Mmm-mmm!" the American yelled, sticking close to Anna every step of the way. She peeled off the tape and the guy immediately started talking. "D-don't n-need to sc-sc-scream …"

She distinctly remembered—none of the guests from Chicago had had a stutter. But now this redhead couldn't utter a single word without stumbling.

What happened to him? Anna untied his hands and immediately continued pacing along the wall in search of Eddie.

"W-we n-need to r-run! It's n-not safe to go th-there …"

He grabbed Anna's hand and pulled her away from the hotel, which had become a real torture for him.

"No, no, I won't leave without him!" Anna resisted.

THE GULL CRY HOTEL

"H-he's alr-ready g-gone. Tr-trust m-me!"

Those words were unbearable for Anna. Within her mind she understood Eddie was dead, but her soul and heart refused to believe it.

Suddenly the gravel around them began to move. The sound resembled the wheels of a car, but instead of coming from a single direction, it echoed from all sides. The fugitives spun in place, trying to make out something in the dense fog.

The sound muffled and intensified, making it utterly impossible to predict where it would come from next. Anna stepped back, hearing its swift approach. She could have sworn that a speeding car would appear right in front of her at any moment. But nothing emerged from the fog. Only the quiet swishes cut through the air. Something enormous soared right above her, touched the stones behind, and slammed the red-haired guy to the ground. He screamed, rose into the air, and fell silent. Anna stood still. All her instincts strongly advised her to play dead or at least not move.

Someone touched her shoulder. She flinched. Arctic cold washed over her spine. Her legs wobbled. She turned around, ready to face death, but instead she saw Eddie.

"Shh." He pressed his index finger to his lips as Anna, ignoring all signals, rushed into his embrace.

He took a deep breath and then held her by the shoulders. He stared into her eyes, silently conveying the need to move. Staying in one place was too dangerous. Trying not to make any noise, they tiptoed towards the fields. The gravel betrayed their location with a treacherous crunch, but the one wandering in the fog seemed preoccupied with its captured prey.

Not far away, something thudded against the stones. Anna flinched and tightened her grip on Eddie's hand. The sounds continued. Horrific splats echoed all around. Anna couldn't see anything, but she sensed it—the red-haired guy was returning to the ground in pieces. Swallowing hard, she quickened her pace, but Eddie urged them to proceed without haste. Something powerful sliced through the air above them; Anna ducked and held her breath. Eddie put his arm around her shoulders as someone inexorably cut through the fog overhead. Large raindrops started to fall on the rocks. The rain intensified, but it wasn't water. Crimson splotches stained the gravel and the faces of the fugitives as they finally stepped onto the trampled grass.

"Now, run as fast as you can," Eddie whispered, squeezing Anna's hand, and they bolted away.

One hill replaced another, and at times shrubs, devoid of leaves, seemed to spring from the ground beneath their feet. They struck their ankles with prickly branches but were powerless to stop them. The mist was darkening. One might think that hell itself was engulfing this cursed island. Yet it was only the twilight descending upon the shores of Rathlin, filling the air with heavy dampness.

A sharp pain pierced her side and Anna collapsed on the ground.

"I ... I ..." she gasped pleadingly. "I can't ... go on ... any more."

Eddie straightened up and surveyed their surroundings. The mist still lingered across the fields, and there was no sign of pursuit from the mansion.

"We'll stop for the night later; we're still too close to the hotel," he said, sitting down beside her.

"Are you injured?" Anna grasped his hands anxiously.

"No, it's not blood ... Well, technically it is blood, but not mine."

"Not yours? I saw him attack you, dragging you away from the window. I thought you were gone!"

"Yeah, well ... I found blood near the house. The ground there is covered with dead seagulls. I picked one up"—Eddie hesitated—"snapped its neck, and smeared my hands with blood. Then I staged the whole thing."

"Staged?" She froze in astonishment.

"Well, sort of. Did you know you can throw yourself against a window as if someone has pushed you from behind? With the same success, you can push yourself away from the window as if someone has grabbed you and pulled you back. The fog provides plenty of opportunities for improvisation."

"You never cease to amaze me! I can't believe you pulled that off!"

"You're pretty amazing yourself. I almost believed you had decided to become an oracle for those cultists."

"Me? No way! But what they were talking about... Could it really be true?"

"I have no idea what they were talking about. Tell me on the way. Come on, get up—we need to keep moving."

And Anna told the story, making sure not to forget a single detail, repeating names as if saving them for a new novel—shocking, full of unbelievable yet real events.

"Everything was planned, just as you said. They deliberately drove me insane."

"But what for?"

"They said that if the mind is shaken, a person is capable of seeing and hearing things that a healthy mind cannot perceive."

"Well, you can't deny their logic."

Eddie listened but refrained from jumping to conclusions. When Anna fell silent, he seemed to replay her story in his mind before starting his own.

THE GULL CRY HOTEL

"When I was thinking of you alone here, I decided to check the hotel reviews," he began quietly, as if he hadn't thought he'd ever voice his thoughts.

"And what did you find?" Anna looked at Eddie with surprise.

"Almost nothing! There was hardly anything there."

"How? Why?"

"Apparently because not many people return from here." Eddie winked. "But there was a post on social media from someone named Dick Morris. In it, he described incredible things that are too hard to believe even after being here."

"About those psychopaths?"

"No." Eddie turned around anxiously. "He didn't talk much about the hotel itself. Mostly, he complained about being pursued by the fog. It was his first night in the hotel when he left this post online. He was writing emotionally, and that's always noticeable. 'Tonight, everything was covered in dense fog,' he said. 'I've never seen it so thick. Closer to midnight, it seemed to me that someone was watching me through the window, even though they had put me on the first floor of a tall local boarding house. Around two in the morning, something knocked on the glass. I almost believed it was a branch until I remembered that there were no trees outside my window. The knocking repeated, and to calm down my overactive imagination, I approached the window. I couldn't see his face. But I felt his ubiquitous gaze. He came for me, and it was hard to resist his will. We stared into each other's souls for a long time, and then he manifested from the fog as a blurry figure, woven from the muck that so adorns the coastal mud. He stood on legs, hunched to see me. I fell to the floor and crawled to the door. That night, he spared me. Didn't touch.'"

"And then?"

"That's where the post ends." Eddie straightened his arm, holding Anna back. His boot sank into the mire. This was where the swamp began.

THE GULL CRY HOTEL

Chapter 23

The evening descended. The mist thinned, revealing the dark green of the marshes. Arming themselves with sturdy sticks, the travelers ventured onto the quivering moss. Anna vividly recalled the moment she had almost perished there.

"Perhaps we should head towards the road?" she suggested.

"Problems with the swamp?" Eddie smirked.

"I almost got sucked in here on the second day after arriving," she confessed.

"It won't be boring traveling with you, that's for sure." Eddie laughed. "We'd be easily spotted on the road. Besides, walking through the swamp isn't that scary. Look, it's easy to distinguish water vegetation from soil. Aquatic plants look juicier and spread evenly. Soil-based ones are duller, bumpier, and mixed with remnants of last year's grass. Dealing with quicksand is a whole different story, even though identifying it isn't a problem if you're attentive."

"And how do you do that?"

"Insects."

THE GULL CRY HOTEL

"Insects?" Anna couldn't hide her surprise. It had seemed to her that she was the one harboring tons of useless knowledge. But this guy ... Well, the uselessness of his information could easily be debated in light of recent events.

"There are always insect tracks on the sand. If you're not on a dune and the area in front of you has the outline of a shallow depression, take a closer look. Insects easily identify voids in the soil and steer clear of them."

"Determining a marsh during the day might not be too difficult, but what do you suggest when night falls?"

Eddie had an answer for that too. "We'll camp here. No one will get to us in the middle of the swamp ... at least, not the living," he added for some reason.

"Are you sure about your plan?" Anna paused.

"Well, what's your plan?" Anna peered anxiously into the mire. The bad news was she didn't have a plan. But the good news was that she seemed to be able to distinguish soil-based plants from those covering the marsh.

They moved slowly, probing any spot of doubt with sticks. Low bushes and rotting stumps appeared on the terrain. A bit further away, in the sparse mist, tall trees emerged.

"We'll camp there," Eddie declared, scrutinizing a faintly discernible stone foundation.

Night was approaching from the coast, pushing heavy clouds. The sky darkened relentlessly, leaving only a hint of blue against which the tall crowns of black alders fluttered.

As they drew closer, the hidden ruins of a structure between the trees became clearer. With one final leap, they crossed a narrow strip of loose rock, bringing them close to the stones—gray masonry with a couple of elongated windows still intact. There were high steps and remnants of wooden beams from a pointed roof—everything in this building resembled a rural church.

"Apparently this is the abode of Father Kaiden, where the roof is leaking," Eddie observed.

Anna walked towards the ruined altar, but before reaching it, she stopped. "Look!" she exclaimed.

Before her a precisely scorched circle revealed itself, within which someone had burned symbols unknown to Anna.

"Anglo-Saxon." Eddie circled the spot, carefully examining each letter of the dead language.

"It seems they call them runes?" she questioned with skepticism in her voice.

Yes—it's Proto-Germanic or Anglo-Saxon or runic—many names for the same language. It consists of twenty-four letters and is considered magical in many cultures."

THE GULL CRY HOTEL

"And what does it say here?"

"No idea!"

Eddie squatted over the ritual site and touched the gray slabs. He rubbed something between his fingers and brought his hand to his nose.

"It's resin." Anna voiced his speculation.

"Where does such confidence come from?"

"The smell. I distinctly smell the scent of resin," she stated confidently without even sitting down.

"Well, this is no longer a case of osmophobia. It's a real superpower." Eddie laughed.

"If they finally kick me out of Literary, I can always join Scotland Yard." Anna smiled sheepishly.

"It seems like we're not being told the whole story. Who, you ask, summoned this …?" Eddie waved his hand as if flipping through a reel, searching for the right name for the force he had encountered.

"Patients of the mental health clinic."

"According to who?"

"Benedict."

"I wouldn't be surprised if it was the mental patients." Eddie sighed.

"And who did they summon?" For some reason, turning around, Anna was whispering.

"We don't need to know that. At dawn we'll leave this island forever, go to the city police, and try to forget all about it."

"Do you think the police can handle it? Not the people, but that ... what we saw."

"What about me? I saw nothing! Just mist and dead seagulls. So, what have you seen?"

"There was someone enormous. I saw tentacles ... and then he lifted the American into the air and tore him apart!"

"Hold on, hold on ... Did you see an actual tentacle? A specific physical part of the monster? Did you see it as clearly as you see me now?"

"Um ..." Anna bit her lip. "I guess just the outline. A blurry halo. But after! After, he lifted the redhead into the air and tore him apart!"

"Don't get upset, but did you see someone lifting the guy into the air? And tearing him apart?"

"He screamed, and then he vanished into the mist."

"But once he was lifted into the air, he fell silent. You didn't hear any more of his screams ... Is that right?"

"Well, yeah, basically … But even afterward … We both saw a rain of his blood …"

"We don't know whose blood exactly was raining. We don't know if parts of his body fell to the ground. We heard something cutting through the air, but essentially, my dear, we saw nothing. If we look at the bare facts, there aren't that many. Everything else is embellished by our imagination based on someone else's crazy stories."

"I don't understand."

"Hm." Eddie approached her. "Remember, you were sure that I had died. But here I am, right in front of you. And what you saw—an illusion. A flawlessly executed trick. Do you understand now?"

"And how many tricks do you have up your sleeve?" Anna blinked rapidly.

"Much more than Benedict Russell, for sure." He leaned in towards her lips.

With Eddie's touch, Anna's consciousness plunged into the mist, much like the cursed island. Her mind quickly forgot the horrors she had experienced. Even for her, the workings of it remained a mystery. Perhaps it was the healing power of love, or maybe it was the body's defensive response to severe stress. In either case, if it didn't erase, it certainly blurred the nightmares of Rathlin.

They found a sheltered nook, shielded from the wind, and embraced each other. Somewhere in the distance an owl hooted, and someone rustled in the bushes on the other side of the swamp. Anna's eyelids grew heavy, and at some point, completely losing control over them, she fell asleep.

***

"Grey! Grey! Ps-ps-ps-ps... Mr. Grey, where are you?"

The tall reeds sliced her tender palms, but eight-year-old Anna didn't notice the pain.

"Grey! Grey! Where are you?"

It so happened that upon arriving at Aunt Darla's, a place famous for its swampy expanses originating from the River Severn, Anna had lost her beloved pet. Grey had meowed restlessly all the way from London and, upon leaving his portable carrier, wandered around the unfamiliar house for a long time. As if waiting for an opportune moment, he darted between the legs of the postman delivering a package and disappeared into the marshes. His little owner, donning her boots, immediately set out in search of her pet. Her cousins helped, and by evening the adults had joined in, but it seemed that Grey had vanished without a trace.

Anna mourned him until late at night. Aunt Ruth was convinced that cats have no fewer than nine lives, if not more. She assured Anna that Grey would undoubtedly return when he had had his fill of adventures. Anna calmed down and tried to sleep. Suddenly, somewhere on the border between dreaming and wakefulness, she heard a familiar purring—the warm and cozy purring of Grey. He delicately padded his paws across her chest, searching for a sleeping spot. Although the fully grown cat weighed no less than four pounds, he still considered himself a kitten.

"Grey, you are heavy! Lie down next to me." Intending to nudge the creature away, the girl waved her hand through the air.

It was then that Anna first contemplated the existence of the soul—that it exists not only in humans, as they were taught in the Anglican church on Sundays, but in all living things. For many years, she recalled the strange incident that marked the beginning of her belief in the supernatural.

Like in her distant childhood, she found herself once again walking amid the tall reeds of the marsh. In her dream, she was no taller than three feet. Full of anxiety, she searched for her beloved Grey.

"Grey! Grey! Ps-ps-ps-ps!"

Not far away, someone splashed through the water, leading Anna deeper into the marshes. This time, at the strange whim of the lord of nightmares, her feet were bare. She cautiously took one step at a time, walking on the black water and shuddering as her feet touched the cold, viscous mud.

"Where are you, Grey? Come here; don't make me take another step," lamented Anna.

Splish, another splash—the cat showed no intention of stopping. The girl continued to advance further until her gaze settled on a figure as black as pitch. He stood there like a statue amidst the reeds, and Grey treacherously rubbed against his legs. The stranger lifted the animal and, stroking it, cradled it in his arms. His face showed no emotion; only his eyes sparkled like two red coals.

"Give him back to me." Anna reached out her hands, but the demon did not reply.

Then the young Anna approached and touched his black hand. A part of the forearm burst into dozens of living flies. Buzzing unpleasantly, they scattered, surrounding Anna, but soon regrouped and settled back into their previous positions. It wasn't a body at all—the creature consisted of so-called flesh or carrion flies.

***

"Meow!" echoed distinctly near her ear, and Anna started.

As she woke up, she heard it just as vividly as she had heard the owl's cry while falling asleep.

THE GULL CRY HOTEL

"Grey?" she instinctively called. But, of course, no one answered.

How cold it is! Anna exhaled a cloud of vapor. High in the sky, distant stars shimmered. Eddie, resting his head on the wall, was sleeping peacefully. Anna slipped out from under his relaxed arm and, huddling against the unusually cool night, listened.

From afar came the sound of rhythmic tapping. Anna stood up and approached one of the elongated windows. She shivered and was rubbing her forearms in an attempt to warm up when, in the darkness of the swamp, she noticed lights. There in the distance, driven by the wind, several torches flickered. In their light, black figures clad in long cloaks flitted about.

"Oh no, not this!" Anna rubbed her eyes. "Eddie, wake up! They're coming here!"

"Who?" He stretched, still half asleep.

"Obviously Frank and his patients."

"What? But how did they find us?" Eddie instantly sat up.

"Maybe because we chose their ritual site to sleep." Anna shook her head with a hint of reproach in her voice.

"Damn! Through the swamp at night! They're truly insane."

Chapter 24

Fear weakened her legs. Her thoughts became muddled. The fragile hope that the cultists wouldn't reach their ritual site was rapidly fading. The lights drew nearer, and one solitary voice became increasingly distinct. Jill Amsterham's voice, so familiar to Anna, now sounded different. With a groan, she filled her lungs with air, exhaling with a low bass, uttering something incomprehensible. A gust of cold wind once again stirred the treetops, and her words remained a mystery to the two frightened observers. Regardless of what the fearful Jill had rambled about yesterday, today she had transformed into something formidable. Leading a group of men, she guided them straight toward Anna and Eddie. Without uttering a word, they hurried to take cover behind the walls of the church. The crescent moon provided little assistance in discerning the narrow gap in the massive stones. However, upon reaching it, Anna could hardly make out any outlines in the pitch darkness.

Without electric light, we are blind at night, especially those among us who grew up accustomed to the lights of the big city—those who were raised in a place where it is never completely dark and absolutely silent. The rural darkness frightens and disorients such people.

THE GULL CRY HOTEL

Eddie tripped over a stone. Anna heard him land on the grass, stumble, and curse quietly. A moment later someone grasped her legs. She started.

"It's me," Eddie whispered, and Anna clutched his sturdy shoulders.

They huddled against the damp stones, trying not to make a sound. Soon, from the other side of the ruins, a fiery glow emerged. Anna no longer felt the cold. The chilly wind didn't pierce to her bones; instead it refreshed her flushed cheeks. From now on, her entire body burned like the torches held by these people. She recognized them all. Only Benedict, Rosemary and her son, Casper, and the nurse remained in the mansion. The others, however, had voluntarily ventured into the deep night of the swamp. Well, to be honest, not just ventured. They had navigated them successfully, wittingly or unwittingly getting as close to the fugitives as they could.

Without wasting a moment, the cultists closed in on the circle. Jill lowered her hood and stepped into its center. Four men took their positions at the cardinal points and, as if on cue, ignited a ring of resin. Jill's pale face took on a menacing crimson hue. She raised her hands to the sky and let out a cry. Her cloak cascaded in large folds, revealing grotesque gashes that covered her chubby forearms like swollen scars all the way to her wrists. Her eyes rolled back and her jaw hung loosely. She fell silent and froze. Suddenly her voice changed, becoming otherworldly. On the exhale, a painful rasp tore from her throat, sending shivers down Anna's spine. Clinging to Eddie, she continued to observe the terrifying transformation of the respectable Mrs. Amsterham. But it was Frank Barton who spoke first.

"Where are they? Tell us, where are they?"

Jill wasn't in a rush to respond. She stood frozen, her face turned toward the sky. Shadows flickered on her face in the dance of flames, pupils darting, her chest heaving in a chaotic rhythm. She breathed loudly, emitting a moan as frothy saliva was expelled from her mouth. One didn't need to be a doctor to understand—the woman was having a seizure. However, even when she fell onto the stones, legs drawn up, swinging like a pendulum from side to side, no one rushed to help. The quartet of statues remained motionless, observing the convulsions of their oracle.

"Speak, damn it!" Green demanded, unusually cruel. Green, the timid driver, was unknown to Anna in this light.

"Here …" Jill hissed like a serpent.

The men started to look around.

"Where? Where exactly?" Fr. Kaiden demanded.

"Here …" the woman, oozing with saliva, croaked. "He's here … The Lord is here …"

THE GULL CRY HOTEL

She ripped the cloak off her exposed body and sprawled in the center of the blazing circle. Her pale form was covered in grotesque scars. Some were straight crosshatches, as if she had been whipped. Others resembled bites from human teeth. Amidst the ugly marks, specific magical symbols proudly displayed themselves, carved by a blade or a delicate knife. But whatever was happening to this wretched soul, it was undoubtedly happening by her will alone. In the throes of ecstasy, Jill tossed her head back, unleashing maniacal laughter from her foamy mouth.

"He's here! He has come!" she screamed, shaking the Irish night with a horrifying cackle.

Eddie tugged Anna's hand, urging her to leave. His fearful eyes gleamed in the torchlight, and his lips silently repeated, "Let's go … Come on!"

Perhaps this was the moment when it truly was time to leave. To hell with curiosity—best to quell their unhealthy interest and abandon this cursed place. Eddie lived by a simple principle: don't believe everything, especially if seeing it with your own eyes has the potential to drive you mad, if it threatens the balance of your life, if it has the power to irreversibly alter your existence.

He had made an effort to erase the events that transpired on Everest on that stormy night from his memory. He had never again allowed his imagination to run wild. He had never crossed the line between real and unreal again.

Maybe, by leaving now, they could still return to a normal life, praying to one day forget it all.

"I want to know ..."

Eddie read her lips, but it took a moment for him to realize that Anna Walker was truly intent on seeing this monstrous spectacle through. Such was Eddie Farrel's path—a traveler and an explorer, seeking logic in everything. Anna's path was different. She always knew that the world was more than we could see or even feel. It was more complex and mysterious than a person could imagine. We observe countless signs, but over centuries of existence, we've failed to piece together a reliable picture of the Creation from these signs. Anna had long been disillusioned with religion; she had forgotten how to believe in God, let alone how to pray to Him. She always needed a little more answers, a little more evidence ... and today she could get them.

Eddie took a step back, but Anna didn't budge. She still held his hand tightly, still loved him as much as ever, but above all, she wanted to unravel the mystery—the secret of Rathlin Island.

From the very beginning of her career, from the day she had stepped into the mental health clinic for that meeting, she had grappled with a haunting question: Was there a shred of truth in Dr. Richter's story? Where was a line that separated the mentally ill from the sane? And had demons truly possessed Eleanora's soul?

THE GULL CRY HOTEL

Now Anna had the potential to become one of the few who held the answers to the universe's most enigmatic questions. Confronting the Devil, she hoped to catch a glimpse of God.

Eddie swiftly pulled her close and whispered into her ear, "Please, let's go! A minute more and it might already be too late."

Anna hesitated. Only he could persuade her to act differently, but not now. Not this time.

"Stay with me," Anna whispered in response. "We need to know. We can be among the few who know the truth!"

Eddie was never a hero. He wasn't a traitor or a coward, but a hero? No, not him. He believed everyone made their own choices, of course, unless they were wounded or a child. On Makalu, he had once left his best friend behind. His friend wanted to reach the summit when Eddie knew for sure they wouldn't make it. At the 5,000-meter mark, he felt a slight jolt. The mountaineer understood: one underground shake would inevitably be followed by others. Arguments and pleas were in vain, and then, finally, Eddie gave in. With a heavy heart, he descended to the mountain's base, only to learn that night that an avalanche had swept down the trail on the eastern slope. Rescue teams worked until evening but found no one. Eddie's friend had perished, along with hundreds of other reckless daredevils determined to conquer yet another eight-thousander.

In addition to keen observation skills, Eddie possessed a special instinct—an instinct for danger. He could sense trouble like a wild creature detects the slightest change in its surroundings. And if someone else had been in Anna's place right now, he would have left. He wouldn't have abandoned the scene entirely; he'd have stayed nearby, ready to lend a hand if things spiraled out of control. But Eddie would unequivocally refuse to be a mere bystander to what was unfolding. Right now, he wanted to know and see everything that Anna would know and see.

For the first time, selfish Eddie cared deeply about someone. For the first time, he fretted not only about someone's life but also their emotional well-being. After traversing half the globe, Eddie Farrel now knew with absolute certainty that he wouldn't find anywhere else in the world the spectrum of emotions he experienced when he was with Anna. It was naive to believe that love, by its nature, was selfless and unconditional.

Love is always about us and our needs. No, Eddie didn't want to love her madly, irrationally, with a flame that would burn forever.

He wanted her just as he had first met her at Heathrow Airport—slightly tired but unfailingly sweet, with that gaze that made him instantly uncomfortable. Other women would falter in front of Eddie, but not Anna. She didn't try to impress him; she didn't crave compliments. She didn't need company. She seemed perfectly content with herself and her solitude.

THE GULL CRY HOTEL

Studying him lounging on the chairs, her eyebrow raised—of course, she was sitting here. But now, instead of searching for a new place to hide, her brain greedily absorbed every detail of Eddie's vivid image. But why? Clearly to weave into one of her books. He agreed. He wanted to be there: in her books, in her life, in her mind. And what will you say now—love is selfless? Hell, no; everything in this world looks after its own interests. We stay with our loved ones only because we feel different with them—more alive, happier, fulfilled. And we want everything to be good for them simply because we need them to stay the way we fell in love with them.

Chapter 25

A whisper reached Eddie's ears. For a moment he thought it was Anna. However, he soon realized—a quiet yet ominously haunting choir surrounded them. Hidden in the mist, the whisperers converged on the church. Their murmurs were indistinct, but on closer inspection, one could see bodies blackened with dried blood, eaten by someone. They should have been dead long ago, but something had stirred them from eternal slumber. Someone had disturbed their rest, summoning them into a ritualistic circle.

Scratching at the massive stones, the dead emerged from the swamp. Like black serpents, they slithered toward Jill, thirsting for the taste of living flesh. They were swift, moving lizard-like, freezing in anticipation. Behind them the fog trailed, swallowing thin leashes to which the corpses were tethered. Thin threads converged into a powerful hand. Rising above the mist, the master strode through the mire. His colossal figure rippled, scattering with the gusts of wind and then coalescing once more.

A familiar sound grew in Anna's ears; not an engine but the hum of a billion flies.

"Merciful God ..." Eddie whispered through numb lips.

"What's there?" Anna tried to turn around, but she was held back. Eddie held her tightly, restricting her movements. "Eddie, what's there?" she asked.

"Nothing."

His breath became deep, his temples and forehead damp; his fingers dug into her body.

The mist could hide many things, but when Jill's next heart-wrenching scream pierced the air, imagination filled in the missing details with vivid colors.

"Run," Eddie commanded.

"But …"

This time, Anna had no choice. In the brief pause between the piercing screams, she distinctly heard the crunch of bones behind her. It was as if a human skull had cracked under unimaginable pressure. A short cry from Fr. Kaiden followed, abruptly silenced by a dull thud against the rocks. Death had caught up with one of them, and when the next cultist attempted to flee, the sound resembled a liquid-filled balloon bursting. Anna trembled; Eddie, opposite her, was frozen in place.

The moist Irish air filled with the scent of blood and smoke. Silence descended, but not for long. The next moment, the white expanse was illuminated by Frank's blazing cloak. Roaring like a beast, he traversed the entire distance from the ritual circle to the crumbling steps, and by the sound of it, he splashed into the swamp.

However, he remained smoldering, consumed by the mire and flames. The last thing Eddie saw was an immense dark figure exploding into a cloud of buzzing flies and settling into a sea of blood.

His ankle touched something slimy. Bony fingers clamped onto his leg, and teeth sank into his calf. He shoved Anna away and began ruthlessly pummeling the undead with his fists. Two more closed in behind the charred corpse. With each blow, he felt the teeth of a lifeless one shatter. Their grip weakened, but pain shot through his body in rapid waves. In an instant, he and Anna were running. The pursuing whispers and Jill's fading screams echoed in the air.

Neither darkness nor the swamp terrified them anymore. They had seen and heard enough to be plunged into utter horror by what had transpired. Thorny bushes, tearing their clothes, dug into their bodies. But the fugitives felt nothing more than primal fear. They raced, stumbling, falling, crawling a few meters and rising again. It seemed nothing could stop them. Nothing except the swamp. Anna's boot pressed into the ground and got stuck, rendering her immobile. In an instant, Eddie wrapped his arms around her waist and pulled her aside. Lying on the damp grass, gasping for breath, they dared to look back for the first time.

There in the distance, within the black church walls, the ritual fires were dying down. The mist still lingered over the swamp but no longer concealed the ominous creatures and their ferocious master.

"He killed them … killed them all," Anna breathed, her voice catching.

"And for some reason spared us." Eddie anxiously surveyed the part of the marsh illuminated by the bonfire.

It all seemed like a dream. A disturbing nightmare. Unpleasantly realistic hallucinations. They would have believed in one of those versions if not for the bite. Eddie's leg was bleeding profusely, saturating his trousers. In the darkness, the extent of his injuries was impossible to discern, but it was possible to wring out the blood-soaked fabric.

"How the hell did they do this?" Anna exclaimed, trying in vain to tear the hem off her cardigan.

"Who?" Eddie frowned.

"Actors," Anna wondered. She grabbed her shirt and, with all her might, tried to tear along the seam. Not a single stitch gave way.

"The lining is thinner," Eddie mumbled, sprawling on his back.

Pulling at one of the inner pockets of his jacket, Anna felt the creaky fabric finally give. A small but sturdy tourniquet emerged from the scrap.

"What's our plan?" she asked, tightening the makeshift bandage.

"Lie here until dawn," Eddie replied, breathing heavily. "If there's no one chasing us, there's no point venturing into the swamp."

He seemed weak, his speech faltering. His body grew hot with fever. Anna laid his head on her lap, gently stroking his damp hair and anxiously surveying their surroundings.

Well, it was not only Anna who received answers that night. Eddie, in turn, had wondered for many years whether the walking dead on Everest could have caused him real harm. Were they a threat to life or just a spooky designation from the afterlife for someone who defied centuries-old traditions?

Adrenaline pounded in Anna's temples and she kept watch until sunrise. Eddie breathed steadily, occasionally groaning and muttering something in delirium.

As the sky brightened, Anna leaned down to examine his leg. Gently lifting the crimson fabric, she was stunned. Eddie's skin had become almost translucent, revealing rivers of black veins flowing toward the wound. Her hands, instantly growing cold, lost their strength. Nausea rose from the depths of her stomach, and her head spun wildly. What to do now? How to get to the dock and from there to the mainland and, most importantly, to hospital?

THE GULL CRY HOTEL

"How did this happen?" the doctors would ask.

"Eddie was bitten by a corpse," Anna would have to answer.

Her eyes welled up. Tears of despair rolled down her cheeks in large drops.

She jumped to her feet and ran ahead, presumably toward the road. But after covering about a dozen meters, she stopped. She would succumb before reaching the deserted highway, and Eddie would perish before she could find help.

Why had she come here in the first place? To meet her love and lose him immediately? But if she hadn't embarked on this journey, she would never have found Eddie. Perhaps that would have been for the best. In that case, he would have remained alive and well. Of course, there was always another option—change plans and skip the train to Kells. So what had stopped her from taking his hand back in Belfast, offering him company, and abandoning her trip to Rathlin? Nothing but her own ego and English haughtiness—ephemeral things, non-living, immaterial. Things that might not have existed at all, which would undoubtedly have played in Anna's favor. Self-hatred weighed heavy on her chest.

She wanted evidence and she'd got it. One could argue about drugs, hallucinations, and staging. However, Eddie's body was saturated with cadaverous toxins, making it impossible to come up with any more convincing proof.

How often we wish we could rewind events like a videotape—go back to the starting point and choose a different path. Had the insights that Anna had gained altered Eddie's life? Only now did she fully grasp that the life of a loved one is not worth these revelations.

We never know if there's a Devil until we witness his deeds. We never know if there's a God until we encounter true love.

"He's not to blame for anything; I should be in his place! He shouldn't have come at all ... Do you hear me?" Anna shouted, releasing a cloud of breath into the cold air. "He's innocent in all of this! It's between you and me. And if you want to take him, take me too! Hey, whoever you are! Come on, show yourself! Did you chicken out? What are you afraid of? Or are you tired? A demon tired of tormenting the people who worshipped you. So where are you? Finally appear! Show yourself in all your glory! Show me who you really are!"

Her cry of desperation echoed through the countryside. But there was no response; no one came. Only the fog, seemingly alive, crept up to their feet and soon swallowed all the colors of the dawn. Fearing getting lost completely, Anna returned and lay down with her head on Eddie's chest. His heart beat rapidly, feverishly shaking his weakened body. His muscles contracted as he shivered. He hadn't regained consciousness; his lips had taken on a lavender hue.

Anna didn't take her eyes off him. She kissed him, holding back his convulsions. His body relaxed again; his heart slowed. Under the rhythm of it, Anna's eyelids grew heavy. Enveloped in mist, hopelessly frozen, she felt a profound fatigue. Unable to resist the pull of sleep, she closed her eyes and sank into darkness.

The best way to die is in your sleep.

***

Anna was awoken by the distant cry of birds. They chirped, celebrating the sun, which had risen quite high and managed to warm them up. She leaned on the wet grass with her palm. Eddie was nowhere to be seen. He had disappeared somewhere, dissolved, having thoughtfully placed his jacket under her head.

"Eddie …" Anna quickly got up and looked around.

He was standing nearby, facing the swamps. He stood on two legs, one of which bore the dark stain of dried blood. Anna's breath caught. She didn't know which feeling dominated her: happiness or fear.

"Eddie?" She timidly called her beloved.

Eddie swiftly turned and strode toward her. His face, free of any signs of illness, radiated joy. He wasn't limping. He was smiling broadly.

Chapter 26

"You ... I don't understand ..." Anna murmured, studying Eddie as if seeing him for the first time after a long separation.

"What's wrong? Is something wrong?" He approached, growing closer.

Anna wanted to respond but couldn't. What to say? How to explain it to him?

My love, you should already be dead!

Does sudden resurrection bring these words? Do people express gratitude for their fate in such a situation? However, Anna understood clearly that a deadly poison can incapacitate a person within a few hours. Revive? No! So who had breathed life into the half-dead Eddie? Who had presented her with such a gift? And what would she have to sacrifice in return?

"What happened?" Eddie crouched down.

She didn't hold back. She was too frightened to ask for permission. She hiked up his blood-stained trousers and froze in amazement—there was no trace of the bite.

Where was the wound? And if by some miracle it had healed, where the hell was the scar?

THE GULL CRY HOTEL

"Darling, what are you looking for? The trousers come off the other way." Eddie grinned shamelessly. Eddie—quite the joker. A miraculously surviving, visibly rejuvenated Eddie.

"Where did the blood on your trousers come from?" Anna fixed her anxious gaze on him.

"Um, if you recall, I had to get my hands dirty with seagull blood. It turned out there was too much blood in it."

He was lying. Eddie was brazenly lying. But perhaps he wasn't lying at all—maybe it was Anna's sanity that had gone off the rails.

Eddie, in turn, had seen much more than she had last night. But he was also adept at hiding much more than she could. He didn't explain anything; he simply embraced her.

"It's all over. Everything's behind us." He stroked her hair. "We don't need to think about it. It's better for us to forget all of it."

Anna shook her head. Eddie gently but persistently stopped her. He held her tighter, almost restricting her movements.

"It's gone, it's all gone. We're alive. What could be more important than that?"

And indeed, this was exactly what she'd prayed for. What she desired more than her own life—to rewind the tape, change the course of events, correct the fatal mistake.

We survived. We miraculously made it through. Why tempt fickle fortune? The wisest thing to do is to get out of this God-forsaken place ... Anna buried her face in her beloved's shoulder.

His sweater carried the scent of damp mohair. She was leaning into his neck when suddenly she caught a hint of— not just smoke—no, not smoke. Burning resin. The aroma infiltrated her nostrils and disappeared in an instant just as she managed to register it. She pulled away, looking at Eddie with concern. He still embraced her with love, contemplatively surveying the ruins of the church. It seemed like his thoughts were somewhere far away. Not just half a mile away but much farther.

These are just remnants of our nightmarish ordeal. She preferred to explain it that way.

Perhaps Anna hadn't witnessed Frank Barton burning alive, but she distinctly sensed the smell of charred flesh. Indeed, in just one night, both of them had been thoroughly saturated with the spirit of death.

"Well, get up. Let's go!" Eddie stood up and pulled Anna to her feet. "We're chilled to the bone here."

And he was right. Now the adrenaline in her blood had subsided, a sudden malaise overwhelmed Anna. She kept going until the very end. Leaning on a stick, she examined the swampy stretches, hoping to discern solid ground. She held on for three hours until her legs finally gave in.

Her weakness and dizziness intensified. Everything around her blurred, and her body temperature relentlessly rose. The day on the coast and night in the autumnal swamps of Northern Ireland had taken their toll. Eddie caught hold of his companion and led her on. Anna watched as they left the swamp and covered several miles of the road. She could smell the ocean and still managed to walk, leaning on Eddie's shoulder. The old waiting room at the port stirred memories of that fateful evening when she had first arrived on Rathlin. She sank onto a low-backed wooden chair and closed her eyes.

"This lady needs urgent medical attention. We got lost—lost our passports and phones in the swamp," Eddie explained to someone. "We need to get to Belfast. Here are my details. Can I make a call from your phone to my bank?"

He waited for a long time, spoke a lot on the phone. He brought Anna a couple of paracetamols and a travel blanket. She shivered from the cold, her disobedient hands clutching a hot-water bottle. All sounds merged into one meaningless hum. She lifted her leaden eyelids and looked ahead. About twenty steps from the registration window stood Eddie. He was explaining something to someone, reading printouts and signing documents. Minutes stretched, and Anna sank into darkness. Her head slowly descended to a critical point, after which her whole body jerked, bringing her back to consciousness. This repeated until the horn of the departing ferry sounded. At that moment, Eddie picked her up with the blanket and carried her towards the exit.

The shaky footbridge, the rain, and the narrow metal staircase—that was all she managed to remember in her semi-conscious state. Rocked by the waves, she sank onto the sturdy plastic seat, rested her heavy head on Eddie's chest, and tried to fall asleep. She lifted her eyelids; her gaze focused on the window splattered with droplets, beyond which nothing was visible except grayness.

The ferry continued to sway. Opening her eyes for the second time, Anna suddenly found herself lying in a bathtub. It was warm and comfortable. Her body no longer ached, her legs were no longer in pain, and her head did not throb. With considerable relief, she exhaled.

All behind me, like a nightmare ...

Anna leaned her head back on the folded towel. Condensation dripped down the tiles, enveloping the cramped room in a white haze. Suddenly, through the tiny clouds, her gaze fell on a bright spot. Crimson blood stained the plaster above her in an uneven oval. Anxious, she sat up and looked around. It was the same detested

THE GULL CRY HOTEL

bathroom from the Gull Cry Hotel. Only now, instead of water, the bath was filled to the brim with blood. In an instant, wild streaks, splatters, and imprints covered the entire tiles, reminiscent of what she had once seen in the room one floor above.

As Anna examined her bloodstained hands, she suddenly saw a black fly land on her index finger—one of those persistent ones that miraculously escape a swat and continue buzzing around. Another appeared next to it, and then a third, until a whole swarm hovered over the bathtub. The insects swarmed her hands and buzzed around her eyes. They relentlessly tickled her nostrils, seemingly diving deeper with each breath. In a panic, she struck her face and tore at her hair until strong hands gripped her wrists.

"Anna, Anna! Snap out of it! Come on, wake up!"

It was Eddie's voice. Anna struggled to lift her eyelids, and when her eyes were pierced by unbearable pain, she saw bright lights on the low ceiling of an ambulance. Rubber tubes hung like pale yellow intestines. There were blinking machines and a man in a bright green gown with a syringe in his hands.

Questioningly, Anna shifted her gaze to her beloved—he had immobilized her. He attentively studied her face as if he didn't know her at all. Her eyes shed two large drops and moistened again. Everything around her blurred once again when suddenly Eddie smiled. He did it as if he didn't know what emotion to express in such a situation.

In surprise, Anna opened her mouth. She was too weak to speak. Her only thought before falling into oblivion was the question "why?" Why did he smile so strangely? Her savior. Her greatest love. Her Eddie, and at the same time, not hers at all.

The first thing that reached Anna's consciousness was a rhythmic beep. There was no pain, only a heaviness in her chest, which, however, paled in comparison to the agonies she had endured. The hospital room was illuminated by a strip of dim light along the perimeter. There was almost no furniture except a low folding chair in the corner. However, the entire headboard seemed to be dotted with buttons, regulators, plugs, and stands for various equipment. Anna lifted her heavy head and examined her hands—a silicone tube protruded from the left, taped with a plaster. A clamp was attached to the index finger of her right hand, extending with wires to a small white panel where numbers changed and zigzags ran.

Behind the door, footsteps echoed. A dark silhouette froze in front of the corrugated glass. Anna kept her eyes on the visitor and a few small points suddenly detached from their dark halo. For a moment, the figure seemed to break into atoms, becoming more mobile, not as solid as a person should be. The monotonous beep accelerated; the heart rate number increased. Anna blinked when the vision disappeared as if it had never been there. Behind the glass, a person was still standing. They waved to someone at the end of the corridor, then quietly turned the door handle. For a moment it seemed to Anna that all the nightmares of Rathlin had come to visit her, but it was just Eddie.

"Awake?" he whispered, quietly closing the door behind him.

Anna blinked. It was the same Eddie with a playful gaze, a slightly ironic but consistently sweet grin. She exhaled, restoring the annoying beep of the equipment to its previous rhythm.

"What happened to me?"

"Bilateral pneumonia." Eddie sat on the edge of the hospital bed. "The worst is already behind us."

"We survived … It's some kind of miracle! Did you report it to the police?"

"No." Eddie straightened his back.

"No?" Anna stared in surprise.

"Darling, think about it. Who would they arrest? Only Rosemary, Benedict, the nurse, and the two children are still alive! But most likely, if we report all this, they'll accuse us of something. They'll find evidence among the things we left there. There will be witnesses, I'm sure—Sergeant Henry Bathurst will take care of that. It's better for us to keep silent."

"Are you suggesting we leave everything as it is?" Anna protested.

"I don't know." Eddie lowered his head. "I think we need to think everything through before telling anyone."

Of course, Eddie was right. If they spoke openly, both of them risked ending up in a psychiatric clinic. If they only told half the story, the police would have plenty of questions.

"Our story goes like this: you got lost in the marshes, and I was studying newts there. You got stuck in the mud, I came running when I heard your cries, and while I was pulling you out, I lost my backpack."

"But why didn't we go back to the hotel?"

"Because of the fog," Eddie fired back without hesitation.

"Then why didn't we take a cab from the pier to pick up my things?"

"There wasn't time for that; you needed urgent medical attention," Eddie explained immediately. He had thought of everything. He didn't leave Anna the option of choosing a different scenario.

"Any more questions, detective novelist?" His focus shifted from seriousness to flirtation.

He rose, pushed aside the IV drip, and approached. Then came a long kiss on her lips, her neck, and her clavicle. All of this made the equipment beep at an enviable frequency, and Eddie reached for the clip.

"Let's turn it off." He smiled and looked at her with the same gaze that weakened her knees.

His gaze dissipated all thoughts and brought a pleasant weightlessness to her stomach. What immense power he had over her. How much she could dismiss as mere imagination with just one touch from him. Her beloved, her cherished Eddie. The one who used to smell like blueberries, but lately there was a faint hint of smoke lingering on him. But let everything burn when he kisses her. When he goes lower; when they drown in this ocean of passion. By morning, the relentless waves had washed away everything: the horrors, the strange visions, and even the barely perceptible scent.

Chapter 27

"Alive! Oh God, she's alive!" wailed her mother, embracing Anna. "Where on earth were you?"

"Daughter, is this how you behave? We were nearly out of our minds!" her father grumbled, exhaling smoke through the slightly ajar window.

Well, not only you ...

He couldn't help but smoke. A couple of years ago he had almost quit drinking, but he hadn't kicked the smoking habit.

Too late to quit when it's time to die ... was his favorite phrase after he, gasping for breath, coughed and spat into his handkerchief.

"At first there was no signal, then I smashed my phone, and finally I got lost in the swamp," Anna repeated in a bewildered tone for Alison, her friends, and even her parents.

The same old story—emptiness in her eyes and rehearsed phrases. However, no one noticed the catch.

"And here comes our savior!" Mrs. Walker beamed at Eddie as he entered the room.

"Madam!" He kissed her hand and shook Mr. Walker's.

They were pleased to see him. Eddie instantly charmed them, just as he did everyone. They bombarded their daughter's new acquaintance with questions, completely forgetting about Roderick as if he had never existed. Eddie Farrel swiftly entered Anna Walker's life and claimed his place there. Moreover, he seemed to have always been there, just temporarily absent, and now he had been found, as if the missing puzzle piece had finally been discovered.

Anna's parents had already reported her missing; they hadn't slept for several nights. Upon hearing about their daughter's reappearance, they couldn't wait for Anna to be discharged from the hospital in Ballycastle. They insisted on her undergoing a complete examination in London, which meant another night in the hospital ward.

"Don't rush it," Alison had reassured Anna just a couple of hours ago. "Deadlines aren't an issue; we'll push everything back and reschedule. Diego is already crafting your unbelievable disappearance story; it will hit the shelves at the end of the week and stoke the reader's interest …"

Alison kept on talking and talking, but Anna no longer registered her words. A faint smile and a distant gaze were frozen on her face. How odd: Perhaps if she had truly just gotten lost in the swamp, she would have been less nauseated by all this babble. She silently nodded and averted her eyes when Alison squeezed her hands against her flat chest. How she despised her now. Everything irritated her about her editor—those sinewy hands adorned with bulky rings, the short dark hair styled in a French manner, that unhealthy equatorial tan, and the sharp scent of perfume that seemed to poison the entire space.

Anna yearned for the moment when Alison would talk herself out, navigate through the London traffic, and leave. She dreamed of never seeing her again, but thanks to Diego's skill, that seemed unlikely. They would handle everything perfectly. They would create such a sensation that Anna need not worry much about the manuscript anymore. With such a preface, anything would become a bestseller. The audience loves the buildup. People enjoy the anticipation of a good story much more than the story itself. That's the law of marketing, in which Alison could rightfully be called a deity.

Roderick showed up only after the infamous "Anna Walker disappearance story" had graced all the morning papers. He didn't hesitate to pick up some flowers on his way to the hospital. His arrival was laden with a surplus of cheap theatrics. That summed up Roderick entirely. He simply couldn't share his life with someone less renowned than a person gracing the headlines of the city newspapers.

Despite all of this, Anna couldn't recall Roderick dedicating himself to any particular profession or being fabulously wealthy or famous. He wasn't gifted or uniquely talented. Perhaps his sole talent lay in skillfully attaching himself to people who were noteworthy in the circles of city society.

She had to give him credit—Roderick had an exceptional talent, a knack, a skill. It required no investment, no hard work, no sleepless nights. All he needed was an unwavering belief in his perfection and indispensability. It was a sort of destiny—to be the soulmate of a well-known person. For a while, he too would be known, and tomorrow brings a new day and a new rising star toiling away half their life to become worthy of Sir Roderick. That's the paradox. That's unshakable self-esteem. And who would dare call this guy talentless after all this? Even Anna didn't dare, although she saw right through her former flame that day.

She didn't wish to prove anything to him, let alone explain. She had no desire to engage with this man in any of the senses she knew. Because he was like a tick—as soon as he sensed someone trying to extract him, he would burrow deeper. How hadn't she seen this before? Even Benedict Russell, hundreds of miles away from London and having never met Roderick, had figured it all out: It was always loneliness, always a thirst for love, but never actual love.

Benedict Russell! He could have been a great friend if he wasn't a psychopath. Although was he really that much of a psychopath in light of recent events?

"It's over between us," Anna declared firmly.

"Are you still holding a grudge against me for the Ritz? Stop it. Jealousy is not your level."

Anna was furious. Her breaths grew deeper; she pressed her lips together and crossed her arms over her chest. *What the hell, Roderick? Who gave you the right to dictate someone's emotions? And what does "your level" even mean? At what point did you start believing you could do anything and then come and tell your beloved what her "level" is?*

"No." Anna tried to calm herself—not to say too much. "I just don't love you."

He set the flowers down and blinked rapidly. "I don't believe you could stop loving me. You're just angry."

"Stop loving you? Anna raised her eyebrows ironically. "I never loved you."

"Hmm, so what does that mean? Have you been lying to me all this time?"

She wanted to reply with "not entirely" or "I thought I did." That was how the old Anna, suddenly feeling pity for her ex-lover, would have answered. But the current Anna was different. Roderick had worn her down too much—right now, just by showing up! He irritated her; she felt no sympathy. She only wanted one thing—for him to leave as soon as possible. From this room, from this building, from her life.

"Yes. I lied," she responded coldly.

"And what do you suggest we do with the wasted two years of our relationship, thrown away like garbage?"

"Good Lord, Roderick." Anna rolled her eyes. Two futile years during which she had never grasped how petty he was. "You can reminisce about them at your leisure." She glanced pointedly at the door.

"But how do you ... How can you be sure that you never loved me?" he started to stammer in indignation.

"Because I love now. And it's an entirely different feeling, so distinct from what I felt for you. Just like you feel towards me."

"I never said ..." The visitor boiled over.

Exactly, Roderick. You never said anything. And perhaps you should have ... Although no, of course, you did everything right."

"What, exactly?" He looked confused.

"You were yourself."

He gazed at her for a long time, clutching the bouquet. Finally he dropped the flowers and left the room. The past was done with. The future was already standing outside the door holding a pizza box.

"Someone important?" Eddie tensed, trying to maintain a cheerful mood.

"What is it?" Anna rubbed her hands together, inhaling the aroma of baked goods.

"Tuna," Eddie replied contentedly.

There was no need for further explanation. They understood each other so well that words sometimes seemed superfluous, having little significance.

As the last slice of pizza left the box, Eddie placed the laptop on Anna's knees. Without saying a word, she stared at the silver casing.

"I'm not sure I can work on the novel again."

"You have to," Eddie firmly declared.

"But Eddie, after everything that happened there …"

"I'm not asking you to read it. I'll proofread it myself. I'm just asking you to finish it."

"Finish it? But everything I wrote is back there in that eerie hotel room."

"There on the cliff, I sent the novel to my Gmail just in case someone dared to whisper to you again that it was worthless writing."

"You did that? I thought all was lost … and I thought, let it stay that way!"

"Hell, no. All this must see the light, even if only in a fiction novel."

THE GULL CRY HOTEL

Somehow Anna was back at work, pouring the sticky memories of that horrific night into her writing. They sucked her in like the redwood swamps—like a swift whirlpool woven from blood, screams, and deadly fog.

Once she had started, Anna Walker couldn't stop. She worked until the evening and her discharge. And even afterwards.

She was typing on her phone, waiting for the city bus. During rush hour, it was the fastest mode of transport in the metropolis. The scent of rain-soaked streets made her look away from the screen and embrace Eddie. November in London is gray, cold, and rainy. However, it's precisely November that adds an extra dose of warmth and coziness to the houses. Only the rain can drive away the crowds of city dwellers and tourists from the streets. How she loved London. Eddie loved Dublin—the place where he had grown up, where everything dear to him remained. Although after meeting Anna, his native Ireland was steadily losing its former allure.

They stepped onto the red double-decker bus and took two vacant seats. Outside, it quickly darkened, and the rain started again. Eddie contemplated the lights of the big city. Anna was writing the final chapter—the ending, perhaps the most crucial part. It must be concise and emotionally powerful. It has to carry answers to any questions that might arise in the reader's mind. It's destined not only to evoke strong emotions but also to persuade and at times even to re-persuade. The ideal ending is considered one that is destined to become a quote.

Anna's gaze wandered over the blue velvet of the seats, the orange handrails, often pausing on the monitor that broadcasted real-time footage from all corners of the cabin. You cannot hide or escape from the cameras in London. They are everywhere, relentlessly monitoring everyone and everything. You have to get used to it: At first it feels like you are in a reality show, but at some point you stop noticing them altogether.

Here's the upper deck with a couple of people on the back seat. The same top floor with footage of a sleeping man across from the observation window. The lower deck, and there's an old lady with a grocery bag, a couple of teenagers, and a man with a sturdy case in his hands. Here they are with Eddie, and it all repeats again.

A couple of people sit upstairs, their faces illuminated by phones. There's the sleeping man, the old lady with her colorful wheeled bag, and the pair of teenagers sharing earphones from a phone. The young man with the case and the motionless Anna in a dark green windbreaker, and instead of Eddie—a black swirl of smoke, arms crossed over the chest, and instead of his blue-as-the-sky eyes, two glowing coal-like embers. Three seconds and Anna's gaze once again returned to the upper deck.

Anna hesitated and turned her head. Eddie was dozing, leaning his temple against the fogged glass. Somehow the

THE GULL CRY HOTEL

cameras had managed to catch a glimpse of the one who now inhabited Eddie. Anna was shaken by a sudden chill; her limbs weakened. The phone slipped from her fingers and loudly hit the floor. Her companion jolted and opened his eyes.

Chapter 28

Eddie rubbed his eyes and picked up her phone. "Are you okay?" he asked, noticing Anna's visibly pale face.

She silently scrutinized him. Something otherworldly should have manifested—something that the monitor had revealed a moment ago. But it was the same Eddie, just with eyes reddened by the wind and flushed cheeks. Her intense gaze made him automatically adjust his hair. He worried for no reason—he was attractive to Anna regardless of how tired he seemed, what he wore, or what secrets he concealed. Perhaps that's where the true power of love lies.

Eddie's jaw tightened. He couldn't comprehend what was happening with Anna, and it troubled him. There couldn't be something that he was incapable of understanding between them. His breathing grew heavier, and his nostrils flared. He clenched his teeth and turned away to the window.

Anna gently touched his hand. Even if someone had taken up residence in him, Eddie was completely unaware of it.

"It seems like I'm having hallucinations," she finally uttered.

"Wake me up next time. We'll check it out together," he responded instantly.

"Agreed." Anna swallowed, realizing that her promise was unlikely to come true.

Six stops later, Anna once again strode through the stone jungle of her beloved apartment complex. She had missed this modern space and the secure feeling it brought—the scent of the spacious lobby filled with living trees, glass, and suspended LED constructions. But when she stepped over the threshold of her flat, true happiness took hold of her. Scientists claim that humans can identify their homes just like animals—solely by scent. We cannot dissect the complex mix that makes up the aroma of the place we live. Still, we can perceive this very special scent with sensors that instantly send a signal to our brains, letting us know that we are home.

Here is the scent of what we eat, what we launder, but above all, the aroma of our own pheromones. Moving into a new dwelling, we sense a foreign smell that we eventually stop noticing. It's not because we've become accustomed to it. It's simply because we've replaced the previous scent with our own.

"I like it here," Eddie observed. "It's undeniably your home. Cold outside and so cozy inside." He watched Anna bustling around. "And you seem to have missed it a lot."

"Oh yes! And you? Don't you miss home?" she asked enthusiastically.

"I try not to get too attached to either homes or people." He slouched onto the couch.

Anna was no longer surprised; that was all Eddie. She just glanced at him and smiled warmly.

"Good thing every rule has exceptions." He caught her hand and pulled her closer. More than ever, he wanted to stop time—stay in this passionate kiss forever and in this home, which for some reason didn't feel unfamiliar. They were carried away again on an ocean of tenderness and emotions.

Here and now, Anna was unquestionably happy with him. Only one thought cast a dark shadow over her—the dreadful fear of demonic possession. His or hers, which was inexorably becoming part of their reality.

Anna woke up suddenly, as if from a sharp sound that seemed to be there, yet seemed not to be. She remembered falling asleep in Eddie's embrace but now found herself alone in bed. Did she want to go and look for him? No! What scared her most was the final and irrevocable acknowledgment that the demon truly existed. And not just existed but resided directly in her Eddie.

"Darling?" she called softly, but there was no response.

THE GULL CRY HOTEL

Suddenly a weight constricted her chest—an irresistible desire to rewind life like a reel and return from the cold, lonely night to the fiery evening where passionate embraces and searing kisses wouldn't let her go. When she knew for sure that Eddie was just Eddie—that he belonged only to her and no one else.

But what? What if he needs help? A fleeting thought instantly propelled Anna to her feet. *What if the demon has decided to take Eddie after all?*

Stepping out of the bedroom, she glanced around. The living room and open kitchen were empty. Just like the balcony, the hallway, and the bathroom—no one! Anna walked up to the window. Even in the middle of the night, many London windows were lit. This city is never completely dark, empty, or quiet. Tonight its streets reflected the glow of electric lights. The chilly night was permeated by a drizzling rain. A rare mist crawled from the river. Not the best weather for a stroll, but Eddie, it seemed, thought otherwise.

Where could he have gone? And, more importantly, why? Anna returned to bed and wrapped herself in the blanket, noticing that her boyfriend's phone had been left on the nightstand. However, she didn't consider calling; if someone wants to go somewhere late at night, it's better not to interfere. Sleep refused to come, and after tossing and turning for about half an hour, Anna sat up in bed. So many thoughts swirled in her mind, yet not a single clear one.

"Can't sleep?"

Startled, Anna looked up—Eddie was standing in the doorway, barefoot and in a robe over naked skin. Anna's back reflexively straightened, her mouth slightly ajar.

"But ... Where were you?" she said softly, not trusting any of her five senses.

"On the balcony, getting some air," Eddie admitted casually.

Anna blinked. She might have believed it if she hadn't checked every inch of her flat.

"Getting some air?" She frowned.

"Suddenly felt suffocated. I woke up with a strange sensation in my throat. You know"—he thoughtfully scratched his neck—"as if a mosquito or a spider got in there."

"A spider?" Anna shook her head.

"Yes—probably a spider, and I ate it." Eddie grinned naively. "We all eat spiders at night," he continued as he noticed the widening eyes of his beloved. "Don't tell me you didn't know. Spiders occasionally crawl into the airways of sleeping people. It's their natural instinct: to find a deep, moist burrow for the birth of spiderlings. So they find it. Every person eats more than twenty spiders in their sleep throughout their lifetime. Each one of us!"

Anna could only stare at him in amazement. She had no idea what to think about all of this.

"So you woke up because you ate a spider?" she finally uttered.

"That's how it seemed to me. But the fresh air helped. Now it's much easier to breathe, though I'm completely frozen."

Eddie jumped under the blanket and pulled Anna closer to him. He was so cold! As if he had just taken a dip in the nighttime Thames. Anna wanted answers, but everything Eddie said only raised more questions.

However, she didn't have to wait long for an answer. The wail of sirens echoed outside their windows in the early morning.

"What's going on down there?" Eddie, still half asleep, covered himself with a pillow. "Did they steal another flowerpot from the lobby?"

Despite his nonchalance, Anna sensed something far worse than the theft of a street vase. She tried to stay calm and glanced out of the window. Down below there were at least five police cars; the entrance to the building was cordoned off with yellow tape, and a crowd of onlookers and residents were temporarily unable to enter their homes. She tried to pour coffee into a mug and ignore the slight trembling of her hands. She tried not to connect the events of the night, not to think about the worst possible scenarios, until there was a knock on her door.

"Good morning, ma'am."

"What happened?" Anna skipped the greeting.

"A murder of unprecedented cruelty," the officer stated coldly. "Where were you last night? Did you see anything, hear anything?"

"My friend and I ... We stayed home the entire night. We were asleep—heard nothing."

Anna's heart raced. Of course, she remembered Eddie's midnight disappearance. Of course, she knew how tightly packed this building was with cameras and motion sensors, the mere thought of which made her head spin and her eyes darken.

"All right. Can I talk to your friend?" the policeman asked suspiciously calmly.

"Of course." Anna took a step towards the bedroom but stopped. "Why are you questioning residents? Didn't our security system provide you with surveillance footage?"

"Thank you for asking, ma'am, but for some reason the cameras were out of order at the time of the crime."

It's hard to say whether Anna felt relieved by this information, but her heart noticeably calmed, and the dark pre-dizziness veil lifted. While the sleepy Eddie spoke with the sergeant, Anna pondered whether his disappearance had been accidental. An even more radical thought, causing her palms to sweat, was: was she ready to cover up the deeds of the demon hidden within him?

The rain persisted throughout the day, discouraging any desire to leave the flat. It also seemed like the police had taken up permanent residence in the lobby, and Anna preferred not to see either them or what had happened there.

The day swiftly turned into evening, and evening transitioned rapidly into night. They sipped wine, wrapped in a blanket. Today, Anna looked at Eddie differently, as if she were seeing him for the last time. As if these embraces were temporary and the kisses exchanged this night would soon be remembered with profound yearning. What would become of them? What would become of him? Such simple questions now seemed like an intricate puzzle that no one could decipher.

The movie had ended, but Anna couldn't recall what it was about. She hadn't noticed Eddie falling asleep. She twirled the slender stem of the half-empty wine glass in her hands, scrutinizing his relaxed face—his hair casually strewn on the pillow, the hollow cheeks, and those lips so dear to her. She couldn't part with him. With anyone or anything, but not with him. It was a kind of insane attachment akin to a narcotic—a real madness adorned by the beautiful and enticing phrase "true love." A feeling capable of both killing and resurrecting equally.

And those weren't just words. Perhaps love has a demonic nature and was not bestowed upon humanity by God?

"Talk to me," Anna whispered, looking at Eddie but wishing to see someone else.

He was in a deep sleep. Not a single muscle twitched.

"Why are you doing this? Why? Explain it to me! What? What do you want from us?" Anna implored, wanting an answer, but no one in the entire world could give her one.

She didn't notice when she fell asleep. But upon waking, she once again discovered Eddie's disappearance. Rising in horror, she looked around. The balcony door was open, and behind the billowing curtain in the wicker chair sat her beloved, although now he could only be recognized by his robe and outline. His skin had darkened, his figure lost its sharpness, and his eyes had turned into a pair of burning dots.

The blood in Anna's veins ran cold. None of her nightmares could compare to what she beheld now.

"W-what do you want?" she whispered almost inaudibly.

The demon turned. Two burning points emerged from the dissipating darkness, staring straight into her soul. More precisely into the hidden corners of her soul, effortlessly reading her most terrifying thoughts and undesirable desires.

"How intense his feelings are," the demon uttered from a distance, as if whispering directly into her ear. "He will never be able to hurt you. Even if I want him to."

"Why do you kill?" Anna suddenly felt a surge of courage.

"Didn't they explain it to you at Rathlin? I need to feed." In the black cloud, it was impossible to discern any emotion.

"But killing innocent people ..."

"Do you analyze the behavior of cows before slaughtering them? Look for the most sinful beef to make a steak?"

"But what about the children?" Anna finally mustered the courage.

"Veal is very tender and soft, isn't it?"

Anna swallowed. "I want you to leave Eddie's body," she asserted firmly.

The demon averted the glowing embers of his eyes. "Your Eddie is dead. Only thanks to me is his body still alive. If I leave him, there will be a decaying corpse in that chair—a body that his soul will be forced to abandon."

It became difficult for her to breathe, a dense lump of hurt and incomprehension forming in her throat. She heard everything that this creature said. She understood every word, but she refused to accept the truth.

"And for how long?" She forced the words out with difficulty. "How much time is left for us?"

"Until death do us part!" He laughed a horrific laugh. "I enjoy being in this body. So many emotions. It all stirs up and allows me to feel life, passion, and love again."

"Were you once human?"

He didn't answer.

Anna pressed her temples. How was she going to live with all of this now? She had always sought answers to her questions, but right now, when she could get them, she didn't want to know anything. Now she reproached herself for her excessive curiosity. She despised herself for her slowness, for not protecting Eddie. Her eyes moistened, and soon large salty drops fell onto the blanket. Over the past few days she had come to hate many people, but more than anyone, she hated herself.

"I want to make a deal." Anna suddenly lifted her eyes.

The demon focused its bloody pupils on her.

"You don't care who you devour, do you?" she said disdainfully, wiping her cheeks dry.

THE GULL CRY HOTEL

Chapter 29

"Good evening, Mrs. Farrel." Henry lifted his police officer's hat.

"Good evening." Anna paused on the stairs. "Do you have someone for today?"

"He's in the car." The sergeant nodded. "According to unverified information, a seasoned pedophile. But we don't need evidence, do we?"

"If he's innocent, he'll stay alive. That's the deal, and I trust it."

"As we all do," Henry hastened to confess. "As we all do …"

"Prepare him. My husband is hungry."

"Mrs. Farrel?"

"Yes?" She turned again.

"I was informed that at the Maze Hill Hotel in central Dublin, Vinny Leighton, a rapist and killer who bribed witnesses and evaded justice, was murdered by someone unknown."

"Really?" Anna feigned surprise.

THE GULL CRY HOTEL

"Yes, madam. I was also informed that you and Mr. Farrel stayed at that hotel on that very night."

"What a coincidence! We heard nothing—slept like logs"—she smiled weakly—"and apparently left before the body was discovered."

"No worries." Sergeant Bathurst smiled in response. "You could celebrate Christmas here with us on Rathlin. I have friends in the city police, and they strongly recommend you avoid Dublin in the coming months. They say winter is expected to be stormy."

"Thank you, Henry." Anna nodded appreciatively. "Thank you for everything," she added.

Anna descended to the hallway, lingered by the empty chair, and walked into the dining room. The air was filled with the scent of baked goods and bergamot. She picked up a cup with a floral pattern from the table and filled it with fragrant tea. She walked to one of the round tables and sat by the window.

"Would you like some blueberry pie?" A voice came from the kitchen.

"With great pleasure," Anna replied.

Soon Rosemary appeared, joining Anna for tea and gazing into the mist beyond the window.

"How are you doing?" Anna finally broke the silence.

"We're doing well." Rosemary exhaled.

Anna looked into her eyes.

"We really are doing well. Frank had long ceased to be himself," she confessed with a sigh, "the man whom I married. He fancied himself on a mission, as if he belonged, chosen by gods. He was killing in the name of duty, and frankly, not without pleasure. It seemed to me he sought revenge for the death of our son each time. Yet with all these atrocities, no one can be brought back to life. I lured guests, welcomed them, knowing that the next night held something ominous for them. Frank always remained in the shadows. He conceived plans, tried to systematize his knowledge about his master, delving deeper into the occult. His attitude even changed towards Matthew and me. Sometimes it seemed to me that if the master asked for the sacrifice of our eldest son, he would bring that bloody offering without hesitation. He would spend hours online, purchasing rare books on demonology; from that time, science and rationality held much less interest for him. Father Kaiden, Green, and Jill supported his insane idea of creating a real cult. They were so engrossed in this that they even wanted to involve Casper. I was categorically against it, and thankfully Benedict stood up for my position. Once a month they would go to their rituals. They came back completely changed. Sometimes it seemed to me that upon their return, they ceased to resemble humans altogether."

"But why did the master kill them all?" Anna stammered, her thoughts returning to that dreadful night.

"Because they wanted to control him." Rosemary shrugged. "They understood the system by which they started to make sacrifices."

"Henceforth, they had no desire to heed a master; they yearned to be the ones issuing commands." In the distance, Benedict's voice echoed, causing Anna to start. "Don't be afraid, my dear. It's just me, your old friend." He grinned reassuringly.

"They saw something that could shake the beliefs of everyone living on the planet. They fancied themselves pioneers of a new religion," Rosemary chimed in.

"After that attempt, we stopped hearing our master." Benedict approached the tables and filled his mug with aromatic coffee. "I was unsettled by the new direction—desperately trying to bring our watch post back to its former course."

"Watch post?" Anna frowned.

"That's what we called it—a watch post on the border between worlds." Benedict smirked. "Frank, a doctor by education, devised a system that in the beginning worked flawlessly. He proved that we can hear the otherworldly, but only by wholeheartedly believing in it. He found out that faith is the most powerful source to hear not only the voice of God but also the voice of the Devil. Only when you're ready to believe absolutely everything, knowing that you might seem insane, may you clearly hear *his* voice. It all began with images of the dwarf hidden in video footage. If the image lingered in the subconscious and the patient's consciousness could read it, such an ultra-sensitive person could be turned into an oracle in a matter of days. When you descended to the hall barefoot and in a bathrobe while Matthew Infiltrated your room and tiptoed with a childlike gait, we were all convinced that you were an excellent candidate. And Frank began to prepare you, just as he had prepared me and Jill Amsterham before."

"But why did you stop hearing *his* commands?"

"I suppose it's only because no matter how paranormal everything that happens here may seem, over time a person can adapt to absolutely anything. It's a unique adaptability that has allowed our species to survive for tens of thousands of years. Eventually we became accustomed to this bloody madness, just as we did to communicating with the demon. Rituals of sacrifice became a mundane part of our lives. Our receiver"—he tapped his temple—"broke. Because only a consciousness on the brink is capable of slipping through the crack between our worlds, hearing and seeing what other people are not privy to."

Anna didn't quite understand what Benedict was talking about, but for some reason she didn't want to.

"Tell me, did you really hear *his* message that night?" Rosemary glanced at her with a hidden intensity.

"No." Anna lowered her gaze, deciding to omit the horrifying orders in her head to "kill them all." She saw no point in complicating things; everything was already too complex.

"Then why did *he* spare you?" she continued to ask.

"Perhaps gods are nothing but our own reflection," Anna responded hesitantly, recalling their brief conversation with this creature. "And maybe we'll be able to look into their eyes when there isn't a single drop of evil left in us."

"Or maybe you found that elusive balance between good and evil," Benedict chimed in.

"I hope you have enough love to keep *him* in Eddie's body." Rosemary sighed.

Is love the answer to all questions? That very feeling even the Devil himself desires to experience ... Mrs. Farrel pondered but didn't dare to articulate it.

CATHERINE G.LURID

THE GULL CRY HOTEL

CATHERINE G. LURID

3:13 AM

El sets off with his colleague Marian to Asia. After a twelve-hour flight from London to Bangkok, their journey leads them through Patong to one of the picturesque islands in the Indian Ocean. Their destination is a point that cannot be found on the world map. Only when you zoom in from a satellite image will you see Koh An—a jungle-covered remnant of lava, the sandy beach of which is only fifty leisurely steps long.

It is here that secret agents have been assigned to meet with the mysterious Mr. Lee. By the will of fate, Raymond Lee knows a little more about the world than any of us. And this time his terrible prophecy will make the blood of even the most cold-blooded leaders of the counter-terrorism department run cold. What Mr. Lee saw in his vision is capable of turning life on Earth upside down. But the most terrifying realization is that his predictions have never been wrong.

THE GULL CRY HOTEL

Chapter 1

El ushered Marian Flay to the window. She smiled warmly and began to examine the giant wings of the airplane.

"Is everything all right out there?" El couldn't help but ask.

"Yes, yes." Tension appeared on her face.

"Marian?" She turned around, trying to listen to every word of her superior. "You're not afraid of flying, are you?"

"Me? No, why?" She smiled only with her lips.

***

When El was choosing a new partner, he was given a whole stack of personal files. Each file had a long number instead of a name, and under the number was the standard small print: *Counter-Terrorism Department*. First of all, El divided the agents by gender. He found women more efficient, more methodical, and, most importantly, he knew they were harder to seduce. Thailand was a beautiful country, El thought, but devious, and he would have to fly there often. Besides, female agents always smelled good, ate less, were less likely to be addicted to alcohol, and took up less space.

After quickly scanning the photos of young men, El began to focus on the "agents in skirts." Skirts have long disappeared from the uniforms of special agents, but the sticky nickname remains. Thirteen folders on the right and only three on the left. Carol—hair dark as night, smooth black skin—looked at El from the first folder. Her serious, focused gaze spoke of perfectionism and a tendency towards aggression. Carol would only be efficient until El started working outside the regulations. At the first opportunity—and there would be plenty of those—Carol's settings would immediately falter, and she would resort to hidden, and then possibly quite unhidden, sabotage.

The photo from the second folder stared back with calm gray eyes. Slightly hooded lids and near-perfect facial symmetry spoke of a remarkable inner balance. El loved balance. He loved minimal makeup, unremarkable features, typical height, typical weight. Agents like her were hard to describe verbally and therefore hard to make a composite sketch of. An Asian wouldn't be able to recognize this woman among a selection of similar faces; they would easily mistake the secret agent for one of the numerous tourists from England, Australia, and the USA.

Marian Flay, El read under the photo. *Thirty-two years old, legal education, impeccable service ...* He flipped the page.

Among her special skills were sprinting and swimming. Marian wasn't afraid of fire, water, or heights. She was a good shot, had awards in kung fu, and knew chemistry and poisons. According to the next two paragraphs, the fair-skinned blonde with a moderate scattering of freckles not only had a whole set of particular abilities but also a squeaky-clean reputation.

Just what I need, concluded El and didn't bother opening the third folder.

***

The flight attendant politely asked the passengers to fasten their seat belts and to make sure the folding trays were in an upright position. The airplane was taking off. The heavy Boeing with 360 passenger seats started to move, and Marian flinched visibly.

"Do you have problems with flying in general or just takeoffs and landings?" asked El.

"The last … two," Marian replied through gritted teeth.

"Do you know why we're flying to Thailand?"

"No. I only know what I was told by you."

"Our destination is Bangkok. We'll stay there for the night and take a flight to Phuket the next day."

"Why wait overnight? Why not head straight to Phuket?"

THE GULL CRY HOTEL

"You've never flown to the other side of the planet, have you?" El squinted. Marian pressed her lips together and shook her head. "Even in business class, twelve hours of flight will take its toll, believe me. Especially since we're not just flying on a huge airplane. It's also a time machine, by the way."

"How so?" Marian frowned.

"It's currently 7:45 p.m. in London on a rare Sunday evening without rain, right?" El looked at his expensive watch.

"Yes," confirmed Marian.

"We'll arrive in Bangkok at lunchtime on Monday, which is eighteen hours later, if the numbers are to be believed. But when we fly back, we'll save time thanks to the rotation of the Earth."

Marian finally looked out the window. The plane had reached a sufficient altitude for her to relax and enjoy the flight as much as she could. She closed the window shade and breathed a sigh of relief, leaving her seat belt fastened.

"So why we are going to Thailand?" she remembered to ask.

"Let's prepare for the flight, get comfortable, order a glass of champagne …" Marian gave El a worried look. "Just for a better sleep. Sometimes there's turbulence over the Himalayas, and I don't want you to have a panic attack." El shrugged.

"No, no, I handle it well," Marian protested.

"Don't even object. One glass of light sparkling wine won't hurt you," he insisted.

"Honeymoon?" asked the flight attendant, Penchan, in a simpering tone.

Of course, no one could have guessed that El and Marian were secret agents. The long flight had forced them to dress in comfortable sportswear and sneakers. They wore no badges, and instead of classic black briefcases, they carried two backpacks. Their clothing was in suitcases, the necessary equipment would be provided upon arrival, and the top-secret documents were stored in the most secure place—El's mind.

El grinned but preferred not to answer. Penchan politely handed them embroidered satin pouches containing various flight necessities. El let Marian go ahead, and she disappeared into the restroom.

"This ordinary soap smells like a whole spa in London," she said upon her return.

El noticed that she really did smell very nice. "You ain't seen nothing yet." He smirked. "The smells of Thailand will stay with you for the rest of your life."

THE GULL CRY HOTEL

Marian narrowed her eyes, sensing the irony in El's words. Within moments the flight attendant appeared again with a selection of foil-covered trays and champagne. "I don't …" Marian began, only to falter when El accepted two full glasses.

The beef steak, vegetables in spicy sauce, and shrimp salad were just as delicious as the food in a good restaurant. The sauce proved too hot for Marian, and she quickly reached for the cold drink.

"I suggest you start getting used to spicy food. Besides, not all restaurants in Thailand serve chilled champagne."

Marian laughed. El glanced at her sideways—he enjoyed her laughter as much as he was enjoying their dinner.

"So why are we flying to Thailand?" Marian asked, once again bringing up business.

"There's a man there named Raymond Lee."

"An Asian?" Alcohol had loosened Marian up—now she was trying not only to listen attentively to her boss but also to engage in lively conversation.

"An American."

"Sounds like a Chinese surname."

"Presumably some great-grandfather." El shrugged nonchalantly.

Despite the fact that Lee was the most common Chinese surname, nobody would have thought that Raymond had even a drop of Asian blood. Except maybe for his almond-shaped eyes or his dark hair—darker than the usual North American brunet.

"So, what's our assignment regarding Mr. Lee?" wondered Marian.

"B1," El said succinctly.

"Personal conversation? That's it?" Marian choked on her drink. "Twelve hours of flying just to talk to someone?"

"Fourteen hours of flying, two hours in a Thai taxi, and forty minutes on a motorboat in the Indian Ocean," replied El, taking a sip of champagne and staring at the tiny bubbles clinging to the thin glass.

"Raymond Lee lives without internet or mobile connection?" whispered Marian.

"Why not? Mr. Lee has access to all the luxuries of the modern world. Only for a short time each day—just a couple of hours—but it seems to suit everyone involved."

"So why can't we contact him over the internet? It's just a B1. It doesn't even need a lie detector."

"This man predicts the future." El paused. "And quite often we communicate with him through satellite connection, no worries ... but sometimes he makes predictions", El paused again, leaving Marian breathless, "that we'd rather hear with our own ears."

Marian opened her mouth to ask something but suddenly fell silent. Fueng, Penchan's friend, collected the trays and refilled El's champagne. Marian declined politely, twirling the glass in her pale fingers.

The orange lighting in the cabin changed to a subdued purple. Soon, Penchan appeared with the bedding sets, including a soft blanket and a flimsy pillow. The business-class seats allowed the agents to recline almost completely for sleep, which could not be said for the cramped economy seats.

El couldn't sleep. Marian lay down and turned away from him towards the window, but he knew she wasn't one of those who fell asleep quickly. Especially now, after hearing all that.

***

The first time El met Raymond Lee was on the steps of a typical apartment building located to the north of Greenwich Village in Chelsea. This neighborhood covers a large area to the west of Sixth Avenue between 14th and 34th Streets and is considered one of the most attractive places in New York. The area, almost entirely devoted to residential property, combines various architectural styles, from elegant nineteenth-century townhouses to modern industrial lofts. Narrow rows of three-story apartments with external fire escapes fit snugly into the autumn landscape of one of the picturesque streets of the city. Here, one could easily run into a famous TV presenter rushing to their Porsche or an up-and-coming pop star running errands. Beside them lived the unknown Raymond Lee.

The bright brickwork of one of the apartment buildings seemed to reflect the fiery foliage of the abundant maple trees. The black railings of the high entrance were covered with a thin layer of road dust—the person who lived here seldom left the house.

El unbuttoned his austere black coat and reached for the doorbell. The carved door opened before he could touch it. On the threshold stood a dark-haired man with pale skin and expressive blue eyes. Both froze for a moment, then Mr. Lee slammed the door shut and locked it right in front of El's face.

The agent leaned his ear against it. Mr. Lee's heavy footsteps indicated he was running. *You can only run that fast if you're running downstairs*, El guessed.

He flew up the steps and, after a few yards, leaned against the door of the neighboring apartment. Pressing the doorbell, he pulled his ID from his pocket and, ready to introduce himself on the spot, opened it up. A frightened woman cowered by the open door as El rushed inside. All the flats had the same layout; in these multi-level narrow apartments, it's practically impossible to change anything. In the hallway, the staircase led up, with the basement door underneath. El pulled the handle and ran into the darkness. A tiny ray of light pierced the heavy curtains.

French window, El calculated, and the next moment, he appeared in the inner courtyard. He jumped onto a rickety table, pulled himself up by some metal bars, and, jumping over the low fence, stepped into the road.

"Stop—don't move!" He cocked his gun.

The fugitive stopped dead in his tracks in the alley and raised his hands. El approached him and said, hardly out of breath, "I'll put away my gun, you'll put down your hands, and we'll return to your home for a normal conversation."

***

"What department are you from?" Raymond washed his hands thoroughly with soap and dried them with a disposable towel.

"International Counter-Terrorism Department." El pulled out his identification again, meanwhile inspecting the spacious living room.

The huge cement wall was whimsically decorated with a strange portrait in a grotesque frame. Tall windows without curtains allowed in plenty of daylight, which was reflected by the massive low-hanging crystal chandelier. Between the warm brown leather sofas was a glass coffee table. Everything looked clean. Too clean—not a speck of dust, not a coffee cup ring, perhaps not a single fingerprint.

"What brings you here?" Raymond Lee sat down in an armchair and leaned back.

"Shall we calm down, Raymond? Our conversation might take longer than we anticipate," replied El.

"Have I broken any laws or been seen with terrorists?" Raymond looked to be in his thirties, with well-manicured hands that had never seen hard work. He could have worked in IT. However, there were no computers around—not even a television or a phone.

To live these days without gadgets? There must be some clues. El looked around again.

Instead of a ceiling, there were wooden beams above. Up there was an open space, and if one moved into the kitchen area, one could see a huge bed. So much air and light—such a stark contrast to El's London apartment, where every inch counted as useful living space.

"How do you support yourself?" El knew the answer but couldn't help asking.

"I got lucky."

"How lucky?"

"A horse I bet on won a couple of races. And there's the Mega Millions," Raymond replied modestly. "Everything is documented, my taxes are paid, the amounts in my account match those with the IRS. I don't sponsor anyone, and no one sponsors me. The counter-terrorism department can sleep peacefully."

"Then why run away?"

"I thought you were a burglar."

"Is there anything worth stealing here?"

Raymond put his hands in his jeans pockets, looked down, and smiled. "Steal me, not something from here."

After just two races at the Pegasus World Cup, the embodiment of American extravagance, Raymond had made eighteen million dollars. Amazingly, after such luck, he had stopped betting on the races and switched to the national lottery. Three winning tickets had added another ten million to his savings. But when he returned to the races, the organizers immediately contacted the intelligence services.

After numerous checks, Raymond turned out to be completely clean. He had lived with his mother in New Jersey, graduated from high school, and got a job as a janitor in the psychiatric hospital where his mother had been sent by a medical council decision. After her death, he had disappeared for a while, but within a year he had sold his apartment in New Jersey and moved to New York.

His life in the big city seemed typical—he lived on the outskirts, searched for a job, and went to interviews. And

El would have never learned about Raymond if it weren't for one terrifying scene captured by one of the street cameras that are everywhere in New York City.

"I want to show you a video." El pulled a Sony Vaio P from his spacious coat pocket—a full-fledged laptop almost half the size of a netbook.

"Not bad. Your company is well equipped."

"The department is well funded." El flipped through the files, opened the black-and-white video, and handed the latest gadget of 2010 to Raymond.

It was a recording from the CCTV outside the subway on Greenwich Street. On the left side of the screen was the date, 9/11/01, and on the right, the time was frozen at 8:40 a.m. Raymond tapped a button and the recording began to play. He didn't need to watch it; he remembered that New York morning vividly.

Raymond emerged from the subway and stopped at the gray barricade. He tried to take a step onto the street, but for some reason he couldn't. A young woman stopped beside him, arguing with someone on the phone and clutching her right arm. Raymond glanced at her and tried again to step past the barricade. His foot hovered above the asphalt and then returned to its place. Suddenly he looked up at the sky. The recording cut off at 8:42 and resumed with a close-up of his face. His nostrils flared as if he was inhaling an unknown scent. He closed his eyes, taking deep breaths, then suddenly he flinched as if he

THE GULL CRY HOTEL

had heard a sharp, frightening sound. He looked around in fear and grabbed the chatty woman by the shoulder. He said something quickly. She cursed him and pushed him away. Raymond released her and ran back underground in an unusual hurry. Three minutes and forty seconds later, the first explosion shook the North Tower of the World Trade Center, also known as the Twin Towers. A terrorist-controlled plane had crashed into it.

Chapter 2

Raymond's eyes fluttered open, greeted by the lavender light seeping through the verdant jungle thicket and onto the gossamer mosquito netting above his bed. The roosters crowed incessantly, their clucks and caws echoing around the bungalow like a chorus of chaos. Raymond rolled over and buried his head in the pillow, attempting to drown out the pre-dawn activity that he had never quite grown accustomed to during his three-year stay on Koh An.

It was no secret that Mr. Lee had a fondness for his island, but there were moments when he yearned for the bustling metropolis of New York City, particularly during Christmas time.

Today it was the relentless rain that roused Raymond from his slumber. Glancing at the clock, he saw that it was nearly nine in the morning. He sat up in bed and rubbed the sleep from his eyes. The damp air carried with it the piquant aroma of patchouli, permeating the bungalow with its spicy scent. Raymond clicked on the coffee machine and made his way to the shower, relishing the feel of the lukewarm water cascading down his body. It wasn't long before he spotted a speckled lizard frozen on the ceiling. There were countless such creatures on the island, and they had become Raymond's closest companions, voraciously devouring the insects that plagued the equatorial region. The standard practice in these parts was to leave gaps between the walls and the ceiling to promote ventilation and drying. But in a climate where the humidity reached one hundred percent, mold was an ever-present threat—one that only the natural drafts could mitigate. As a result, crawling, flying, and scurrying beasts could easily find their way into Raymond's bungalow were it not for the ever-hungry lizards that patrolled the premises.

Sometimes he found frogs in his clothes, but only during the rainy season. Furthermore, the wide bed, a sacred place of rest, was meticulously covered by a canopy during the day and night. After checking his slippers for signs of life, Raymond slipped his feet in and picked up a cup of coffee. He walked out onto the veranda, inhaling the smell of rain, and settled into a wicker chair. One night he had left his sneakers right there, and in the morning, someone had placed small yellow eggs in them, thoughtfully covered with slime. Since then, no matter where he left his shoes, he always checked for repulsive contents before putting them on.

"Mr. Lee!" A burly Thai man with an umbrella ran up to the bungalow. "Khidaw?"

"Yes, thank you," Raymond replied. He knew that "khidaw" meant "fried egg" in Thai, but that was about all he understood in the local language.

The jungle was shrouded in a translucent haze. It began beyond Raymond's garden, where the workers had built a high fence. On such a small island, there were no monkeys—the fact had pleased Raymond considerably when he had bought the land—but an incalculable number of snakes lived there. Obviously, the fence only protected against the snakes that swarmed the land at every moment, and no one was surprised by their tracks in the sand, left from night parties, as if hundreds of cyclists had taken a ride at dawn. No one poisoned their burrows or touched the serpents—the Thais knew how to live in a prudent neighborhood, and Raymond learned from their example. Only occasionally the snake-catching service came to clean up the inhabited part of the island, taking the most hectic ones back into the jungle.

In front of the house, parasitizing on the trees, purple orchids bloomed, sapodilla filled with juice, and plumeria shed its flowers into the shallow pool.

The downpour beat mercilessly against the palm leaves and the sprawling reed roof of the cozy villa, occasionally pouring down in heavy streams. In the distance, thunder rumbled.

"It will end soon." Kiet placed the tray on the veranda table and leaned out from under the roof.

"Forget it—we're not in a rush," said Raymond.

THE GULL CRY HOTEL

Kiet laughed. "After lunch, they'll bring the groceries." He bowed politely and, opening his umbrella, ran off again.

The aroma of breakfast permeated Raymond's nostrils like a narcotic potion. He looked at the tray—amidst the cucumbers, crispy bacon, and homemade potato chips, a khidaw dish was beautifully presented.

Raymond loved the morning. He loved the rain. He loved Koh An.

The tropical downpours always ended as abruptly as they had begun, as if someone had opened the faucet and closed it half an hour later. Raymond changed his white shorts for swimming trunks and descended from the high veranda. The best houses were the ones on stilts. Floods couldn't reach them, and it was harder for any wildlife to get to the living space, although as it turned out, for these creatures, nothing was impossible.

The wet paths had taken on a deep gray color, and thin streams of rainwater still dripped from the enormous leaves. Along the beach, the crowns of tall coconut palms were swaying in the wind. Some of them had bent heavily over time, deciding to rest on the white sand.

Raymond had not yet seen the ocean, but he had already heard it. The first half of the day it was always calm, the tide usually coming in. It was pleasant to swim at this time, because by noon the ebb began and the ocean receded hundreds of yards, exposing the sand and sharp corals. By evening the ocean returned, but the timing of these fluctuations constantly changed. At the end of the beach, along the rocky cliff, the depth was greater, making the ebb less noticeable. There lived the varans, and neither Raymond nor Kiet wanted to disturb them.

Raymond walked to the sand, removed his sandals and white shirt, and hung his towel on a bent palm tree. The temperature of the Indian Ocean, which spread out like a turquoise strip at his feet, was always the same 80 degrees Fahrenheit, both in winter and in summer. He waded in waist deep and looked around. The water was crystal clear: Small shoals of tiny transparent fish flickered past, and spiral-shaped shells with thin legs ran along the bottom and buried themselves in a rush.

Raymond lay on the water's surface; the ocean perfectly held his relaxed body. His ear canals filled with water; now he could only hear the sound of the sea and his own breathing. He looked at the rocky cliff and dense jungles covered by low mist. There were cumulus clouds on the horizon, fishermen's boats, and the silhouettes of rounded rocks hovering over the ocean—the constant evaporation turned this world from real to ghostly.

Raymond closed his eyes. His body almost merged with the ocean, became a part of it, swaying in its leisurely rhythm.

***

THE GULL CRY HOTEL

He was lying in a bathtub in a New York rental apartment. After working as a waiter in a busy restaurant, his legs were so sore that the hot bath was the only place where he could recover before the next day.

Suddenly his hands went numb. His body slowly slid down and disappeared under the water. The dim light of a bare bulb penetrated the strangely greenish water. At that moment, Raymond was thrown forward with force and hit something as hard as concrete. He was no longer in his cramped bathtub; his paralyzed body was being thrown back and forth by a powerful mass of water. Sharp glass shards, heavy logs, and dead people crashed into him at tremendous speed.

Raymond didn't feel any pain. Pain is just a signal from the brain that something is wrong with the body. But when you're almost dead, those signals don't make any sense, and the brain simply stops sending them. He had bumped into some metal structure, and something slippery underneath had pushed his torso up to the surface. Now he could see the destroyed buildings of an Asian coastal city. Dirty water had flooded the shore up to the tops of the tall palm trees, sweeping house roofs and broken boats deep into the jungle. Everywhere there was only mud, pain, and death.

Someone grabbed Raymond's leg with a dead grip and dragged him back under the water. He thrashed in convulsions with his last bit of strength and resurfaced in his own bathtub. Everything was just the same except for the screams and inconsolable crying that still echoed in his ears. He knew ... knew for sure that very soon, something terrible was going to happen somewhere on Earth.

Since early morning, New York had been covered with thin snow. The country was getting ready for Christmas, and the restaurant schedule was packed. Raymond left his apartment earlier than usual and got to work only slightly late.

He put on his uniform and entered the kitchen. It was unusually empty for the beginning of the workday. Somewhere at the end of the huge space, people huddled around a small television screen—a terrible tragedy had occurred on the other side of the planet. A nine-point earthquake in the Indian Ocean had caused a deadly tsunami that had hit the shores of Indonesia, Sri Lanka, southern India, and Thailand. The waves were over fifteen meters high, and the ocean had advanced hundreds of miles into the jungle. It had happened at 7:58 a.m. Thai time and 7:58 p.m. New York time—just when Raymond was taking his bath.

The tragedy claimed over 200,000 human lives and became one of the most destructive in modern history. When Raymond bought the island, the coastal service required him to install an evacuation route indicator in case of a tsunami. Such indicators can work in coastal cities, where it becomes entirely unclear where to run if water is literally everywhere, but not on Koh An. If a tsunami ever came there, no one would have a chance of survival.

***

As Raymond opened his eyes, he surveyed the rare low clouds and shifted his gaze to the rocky cliff. There stood a man, and Raymond saw him. Not with his eyes, but he knew for certain there was a man up there. He knew what he was wearing, where he was looking, and what position he was standing in. When he had purchased the uninhabited island, he had sincerely hoped that there were no people and therefore no ghosts. But as it turned out later, one eerily lucky tourist had crashed onto the rocks after a failed jump from a height.

Just one, but always ruining the view, thought Raymond, closing his eyes again.

When he finally decided to stand, the water only came up to his knees—the ocean was retreating. Athit, Kiet's wife, was cooking delicious beef with wood mushrooms in a spicy kiwi sauce, and the aroma of the exotic dish spread all over the beach.

Raymond uncorked a bottle of cold Riesling, grabbed a glass from the kitchen, and walked out onto the wooden veranda that extended onto the sandy shore. Several woven chairs were arranged there for guests, along with a couple of tables.

He wasn't expecting anyone today except for the guy on the motorboat who delivered groceries to the island each week. He filled the polished glass and sipped the wine. The sun warmed his shoulders, and he looked straight out at the ocean. It turned crimson.

Raymond lowered his gaze. His heartbeat quickened. He took a deep breath, drank some more wine, and raised his head. Mangled corpses floated on the brown foamy waves. Not one, not two. They were everywhere—as far as the eye could see.

Athit, wearing Vietnamese flip-flops, approached carrying a tray with a plate full of food.

"Not now." Raymond struggled to swallow his saliva. His neck tensed, his stomach felt unpleasantly tight, and heartburn crept up his throat.

The elderly woman immediately turned around and marched back to the kitchen.

Raymond no longer dared to look at the eerie ocean. He picked up the bottle from the table and walked to his bungalow. He took out his mobile phone from the cabinet, turned it on, and sent a single message to the only number he had saved.

Something terrible is coming. Massive. I've never seen anything like it.

He left his phone on the bed and stepped out of the room. He settled back into the wicker chair on the sprawling veranda and took two large gulps of wine, inhaling the stale midday air. These spontaneous, chillingly realistic visions had plagued him for seven years, ever since he had met El Roberts.

***

"You have to learn how to predict this stuff ahead of time so we have hours, days, months, and years to prevent it, you understand?" El's stern face loomed over him. His sharp, straight nose, strong chin, and intense brown eyes made it seem impossible to resist him.

"But I can't. I don't know how to control it!" Raymond blurted out.

"Correct me if I wrong, but you can somehow predict the lottery and horse racing results …"

"A lottery in a day, horse racing in just a few hours. I don't understand how I can help you by reporting on a tragedy just one hour in advance. And how can I know if it's one hour or one minute, one day or one year?"

"You must come up with something. Develop some sort of system, train your abilities …"

"Easy for you to say." Raymond stroked his hair. "What if I can't?"

"Then we'll have to add a couple of new clues to the case," answered El calmly.

The tension made Raymond's temples ache. "No, you can't pin Christine's death on me. You know I didn't kill her!" he shouted.

"Think, Raymond. What's more important: your life, Christine's life, or the lives of three thousand people? People who died. People whose death you predicted. And that's just what you got caught on. How many more deaths have you foreseen in your life? How many times have you known in advance and stayed silent?"

"This isn't my choice!" He swallowed.

"True. But for some reason, God or the Devil—I don't know who's in charge up there—gave you this ability." El glanced at him fiercely.

A faint line of sweat broke out along the edge of El's graying hair. It wasn't easy to have this conversation. Threatening the poor kid with prison … he was demanding the impossible. However, it was only impossible at that very moment.

"And how much time do I have?" asked Raymond, calming down.

"Three months," El squeezed out.

"You have no idea how hard this is! Just throw me in jail right now. Why drag it out for three long months?" Raymond exploded.

"Six months." El softened slightly.

THE GULL CRY HOTEL

"And if I succeed?"

"You'll be able to participate in any horse race, make any bet. If you want, you can even buy yourself an island and move there. No one will stand in your way."

***

The phone beeped quietly on the bed. Raymond didn't budge. White plumeria flowers circled lazily on the surface of the shady pool. They hypnotically attracted his gaze, and soon he didn't have the strength to tear himself away from their unhurried movement. Four digits were spinning in his head, and he waited patiently for them to arrange themselves in the right order. Another message came through—Raymond didn't even flinch. He took another sip of wine and finally saw the number. It appeared as dark blue veins at the bottom of his pool.

Kiet materialized around the corner in a flurry. "Mr. Lee, your lunch is ready!" The butler lifted a copper tray with a domed lid.

"Bring it over—let's eat." Raymond waved his hand.

"You're thinking too much again," Kiet remarked. "Mr. El might be coming soon?"

"I think he will …" Under the lid was an appetizing dish adorned with miniature corn cobs. "You don't like him, do you?"

Kiet pretended he didn't understand the question. "If you go for a swim, I'll clean the pool, sir." He bowed obligingly.

Raymond nodded. He poured more wine, but it no longer made him drunk. On the contrary, the drink sobered him, relaxed his brain, which had been inflamed with strange visions, allowed him to step back from direct participant to indifferent observer.

In the six months that El had given him, Raymond had visited almost every casino in the country. He tried to guess as far in advance as he could, and gradually he began to succeed. First came a strange vision, then he deciphered it, and then he searched for the date.

Once he had been sitting in a Las Vegas hotel trying to see the numbers of the roulette. Suddenly the building shook. He grabbed his passport and money and rushed out onto the street. He ran through the crowded hall, not understanding why no one else seemed to feel the vibrations. When he was outside, there was another explosion in the southern wing of the tower, leveling the rest of the hotel to the ground.

"There's a bomb! Oh God! There's a bomb somewhere!" he shouted.

Raymond was taken to the police station. It was the shortest detention in Las Vegas—ten minutes later, he was released. Soon El contacted him, and Raymond passed on all the information he had about his terrifying

THE GULL CRY HOTEL

vision. From that day on, the hotel was put under surveillance. For eleven long months, there were no signs of terrorist attacks, explosions, or even ordinary shootouts. But exactly one year later, when El's superiors were getting tired of waiting for a miracle, information was received that an explosive device had been found in the southern wing of the hotel. A window washer working at height had eight kilograms of dynamite on him.

Since then, Raymond had known how the exact date was shown. He tuned this channel like the antenna of a radio receiver and now he also had the channel guide. He often withdrew into himself for whole days, looking for signs everywhere. They added up to digits, which in turn added up to a terrible number—and then he could say precisely how much time the department had left.

Chapter 3

El glanced at the sleeping Marian. He didn't need a partner. He had flown to Asia alone many times before. He was never bored, he didn't suffer from bouts of loneliness, nor did he have a strong need for social interaction. So why had he meticulously chosen her; why did he bring her along? Now he would have to explain to her things that were sometimes inexplicable, convince her that it was all true, and look into eyes full of confusion. Why? Most likely because he wanted an objective witness by his side—someone who would acknowledge that he was not crazy. After all, after years of working with Mr. Lee, El had truly started to doubt his own sanity.

The agent turned over onto his other side, fluffed his pillow, and closed his eyes.

But as his consciousness began to drift into the realm of Morpheus, the plane suddenly plummeted into free fall. Five seconds felt like an eternity. After a warning signal resounded throughout the cabin, the clicking of seat belts added a further layer of anxiety, and the Boeing plunged into an air pocket, lifting El's body from his seat. Marian screamed and clutched the armrest with her right hand

and El's forearm with her left. He just smiled. "Don't worry, we won't crash," he said calmly.

"How do you know?" Marian was losing her composure.

The plane once again gained altitude but soon desperately lost it. A wave of screams swept through the cabin.

"If this plane was destined to crash, Raymond would have said so."

"What if he decided to get rid of you?" Marian pressed herself into her seat. "Would he have told you?"

And if Raymond had decided to get rid of him, El was taking Marian with him—the woman who, despite all her strengths, was damn similar to Christine. He had seen that unfortunate woman in the morgue in photos when he was studying the life of the boy in New Jersey. The young Christine, torn apart by a psychopath, no longer felt any pain. She had suffered through her own hell, but horror was forever frozen on her marble face with its black, ugly bruises. Unlike Raymond, El never confused the living with the dead. But now, in the dim light of the emergency lamps, Marian's face shone with a deathly pallor. Red capillaries spread across the whites of her tired eyes, which were instantly filled with the same fear of death as Christine's.

***

"You promised me!" Raymond yelled. He was beside himself with anger.

"I've kept all the promises I made to you, Raymond." For the first time, El's voice filled with concern.

"In Las Vegas I only asked for one thing—for Clifford to stay in jail till the end of his shameful existence. For Christine and my poor mother!"

Raymond paced back and forth in the bungalow's living room. No one had told him that Clifford, the rapist and murderer, had died in the mountain Alcatraz, the strictest prison in the United States. When the agency had received the news of his death, the death certificate was immediately classified. Not a single word about the strange incident in the prison bathroom, not a single mention of Florence or Colorado in any media outlet. How had Raymond found out? As always! El had never even dreamed that it would remain a secret for long. He was just biding his time.

"He's dead. I have no control over people's lives," El protested, outraged. "You should be happy." The agent reached for the coffee machine, noticing his hand was shaking. "You should be happy," he repeated, stuck in the stuffy air that filled the room. "Now that sadist is burning in hell."

The coffee machine sputtered and splashed hot water on El.

THE GULL CRY HOTEL

"What do you know about hell?" Raymond thundered.

"I'll stop by in a couple of days," El replied without turning around. "Maybe then you'll stop confusing a secret agent with Charon."

He left the bungalow, descended the stairs, crossed the tropical garden, and was on the beach in a minute. He had no intention of leaving the island so soon. As usual, he dined with Raymond under the stars until the night tide. The Thai man who piloted the motorboat slept in a hammock near the palm leaf canopy, unaware that the tenant was about to leave.

"I need to go back to Patong," El shouted, catching up with him.

The man jumped up and ran after him. Two hundred yards of wet sand tested El's patience—the driver had left the engine far from the shore, taking into account the low tide. They had just jumped into the boat when El's neck was pierced by a sharp pain. He lowered his head and massaged his neck, feeling his muscles like stone under his fingers. A second later, something made him turn around. Raymond was standing on the white sand, drowning in the mist of the jungle island. "Damn it," El muttered.

Soon, Koh An turned into a lonely hovering cloud over the water, and El noticeably calmed down. It was forty minutes to Patong from there, but it was dusk already. The fiery water swallowed the sun, forgetting to release the moon into the darkening sky. El strained, trying to see something, but blackness covered everything like a thick curtain. The Thai man turned on a dim flashlight that seemed to only blind the eyes and attract mosquitoes. They raced towards Patong's invisible shores without maps or navigation, relying solely on the sailor's memory and skill.

Suddenly the engine sparked and, with a loud bang, started smoking. The smell of kerosene mixed with fumes, and the deafening roar subsided. The boat drifted a few yards on inertia and stopped.

Damn it! cursed El. *Damn you, Raymond. Did you really set up a meeting with Clifford for me?*

The Thai turned on his flashlight and leaned over the engine, his shadowy figure merging with it, swearing loudly in his own language when the motor suddenly jolted.

"Damn it!" El cautiously looked into the water, standing in the middle of the boat and trying to hold on to the framework of the awnings.

The water below was black. It splashed and crashed against the sides, boiling and foaming. El strained his eyes.

"Holy mother!" The next moment, he fell to the floor.

"Mister, what's going on?" the Thai asked, climbing carefully around to him.

THE GULL CRY HOTEL

El breathed heavily, struggling with a horrifying vision. He stood up again, hunching over, and looked over the starboard side. Hundreds of dead gray hands reached out for the boat, vying to rock it. The nights here were hot all year round, but hallucinations like this sent chills down El's spine. He pressed the emergency signal button of the GPS on his watch, still not believing his eyes. The vessel was hit again on the right side, followed by a strange groan. The sailor fell off the board he was sitting on and crouched in the stern. Cold sweat dripped down El's forehead when he realized that he wasn't hallucinating.

"Phu tay thi mi chiwit," the Thai whispered uncontrollably.

"Who is that?" El tried to compose himself and wiped the sweat off his face.

"The living dead …"

"Well, yes … how did I not figure it out?" El muttered under his breath.

Both fell silent. Someone was quietly scratching the bottom of the boat. In the darkness, El felt as though the dead were already there, that they had broken through the bottom and would sink this damn vessel any minute and then start to tear their flesh to pieces. A bright spotlight appeared from behind one of the dark islands scattered along the Andaman coast. The sound of the boat grew louder, drowning out the eerie scraping beneath them.

The Thai jumped to his feet and started screaming—of course, he didn't know that someone was after them.

***

El took a long shower and collapsed onto the bed. *What was that?* he thought.

He couldn't believe that Raymond Lee was able to do something like this—such an act of blatant wickedness. And if he was, El simply wasn't prepared for this.

***

"It's now 11:15 p.m., and Raymond Lee's interrogation is beginning." The recording given to El for review of the case in New Jersey began to play.

He listened to it four times and then fast-forwarded to the end for the fifth time.

"How did you find out about Christine?"

"She came to me," Raymond replied in a young, subdued voice.

"She came to you … and you killed her?"

"She came to me hours after she was dead." The boy took a hard breath, clearly answering not for the first time.

"I haven't heard anything about the walking dead in my area, but lately there have been too many cases of one fucking rapist and psychopath," the investigator pressed Raymond.

"I see ghosts. They come to me." Raymond's voice was weak, devoid of any persuasiveness. "Christine came so clearly that I thought she was still alive. I wanted to help her sit down and then call the hospital, but when I got closer, she vanished into the doorway. An extremely pale and disfigured face appeared again, but this time behind the mesh screen of the front door."

"And at that moment, you remembered how you killed her?" The investigator slammed his fist on the table, making Raymond's voice tremble.

"I didn't kill her! I just followed her!"

"You followed her when she was alive?"

"I followed her spirit," cried Raymond, completely broken.

With such a testimony, there was no escape from prison. The boy had found Christine's body in the woods while it was still warm. There wasn't even a tiny chance of denying his involvement, and his mother took the blame for him. A childhood friend of hers, a psychiatrist who had always harbored feelings for her, managed to have her declared insane and spared her from the penitentiary. He also arranged for Raymond to work as a orderly at his clinic and allowed young men to spend the occasional night with his mother. Just as Raymond turned nineteen,

Alicia was diagnosed with tuberculosis and passed away suddenly within the clinic's walls, as if she had been holding on until her beloved son matured and was able to live without her.

***

"If he saw dead people in the nineties, he could have easily learned to interact with them or even control them by now," thought El, splashing cold water on his face.

That night he couldn't sleep at all. He couldn't even stay in the stuffy room any longer—the incident at sea had stunned him, possibly even broken him in some way. He stepped out onto the balcony. There was a wicker lounge chair and a low marble table. He ordered coffee and, for the first time in ten years, opened a pack of American Spirit. Only a couple of yards separated his bare feet from the gurgling pool—the balconies on the first floor opened straight onto the water, allowing for round-the-clock swimming. The blue lighting beautifully shaded the tropical mini jungles. Planted in thick clusters, they served as a hedge for adjacent balconies, providing minimal but appreciated privacy. A delicate avocado scent wafted from the massage salon, while the bar, designed to resemble an island in the middle of the blue ocean, gave off a sharp bourbon aroma. El took a sip of coffee and lit his cigarette. The quality tobacco, skillfully blended with fragrances, calmed his brain like a professional psychologist.

THE GULL CRY HOTEL

Could it have been a hallucination? But what about the guy who ran the boat? Nothing matched, and after his second half-smoked cigarette, El decided to swim. The water now filled him with dread, but he couldn't go on like this. He needed to confront his phobias here and now, returning himself to his former idyllic, fearless state once and for all.

He descended the chrome staircase into the warm, transparent water. A plumeria flower brushed against his back as it floated by, and El jumped in fright—he was still far from an idyllic state.

He swam over to the bar and ordered a cold whiskey. It was that sleepless night when he decided to find a partner—someone whose purpose would be not to protect him from an unexpected supernatural attack but to at least be a witness of it.

***

The plane jolted again, and oxygen masks rained down from the ceiling. For a moment El was ready to believe that Raymond, despite everything, had decided to kill him and Marian, but their flight stabilized.

"The plane hit a zone of turbulence. We're through the rough patch," announced the pilot with a slight east Asian accent. "We're gaining altitude again."

Marian stared at the floor, slowly coming to her senses. "Don't worry, we'll definitely make it now," said El, patting her shoulder. He reclined his seat and fluffed up the small pillow once again.

The scent of coffee woke him. The cabin lighting changed to orange, and people in economy class started bustling around. He stretched his back. Marian jumped up as if on command and soon disappeared into the restroom. El could have slept a little longer, but it seemed like pre-landing anxiety had taken hold of all the passengers at once.

He reclined his seat, handed the blanket to Penchan, and received a cup of filter coffee from Fueng.

"Coffee for your wife?" came the unexpected question.

"You better ask her," El replied coldly, suddenly realizing that except for her special skills, he knew nothing about this woman.

"I'll have coffee, thank you."

Marian appeared out of nowhere and took her cup. Once again the scent of spring flowers, patchouli, and orange emanated from her, and El involuntarily turned his head to inhale more of this magical morning blend.

"You seemed much more confident ordering champagne for me than coffee." Marian gave a rather charming smile, but El caught a shade of sarcasm in her tone.

After breakfast, Marian asked for another cup of coffee and decided to open the window shade. Below them the ocean stretched out, an endless blue canvas. Rare clouds hung above it, casting sharp navy shadows. Some of them could easily have been mistaken for the rolling islands scattered along the coast of Phuket.

Marian stood in awe. "How beautiful!" she exclaimed. "It's so different from the Atlantic."

El knew that Marian had only flown across the ocean from London to America and from America to London—once to Canada and once from Philadelphia to Lisbon. And she was absolutely right. Everything was different in the Atlantic: the colors, the horizon, the coastal curves, and the air. Even when a huge iceberg appeared on the almost black water, the view from above did not stir the imagination with the same force as an island overgrown with misty jungles in the middle of crystal-clear turquoise.

The plane flew past the winding white line of the beach and soared over land.

"In forty minutes, Bangkok," whispered El. "A massive city."

Marian turned around and met his eyes unexpectedly close to hers. She blushed and hugged her coffee mug more tightly.

"When I first came here, it was night. Bangkok started shining with lights long before we landed. It seemed to me then like a gigantic living organism. Bangkok breathed, thought, lived, and the plane, like an annoying fly, circled above, trying to find a place to land. This city has lungs that it breathes with, it has a heart that beats. But God forbid you end up in his cloaca, Marian. Heaven forbid!"

She gave him an aghast gaze and set aside her unfinished coffee.

The plane circled the city and began to descend. This time Marian looked calmer and much more relaxed. She didn't grip the seat and didn't grab El's arm, which disappointed her companion slightly.

The plane landed smoothly and, after taxiing for another ten minutes, came to a stop. The agents left the aircraft and walked through the bright corridors of the airport. Stretching their muscles, they waited in a long line at passport control and, after all checks, finally arrived at the giant hall where their identical black suitcases were spinning alone on the conveyor belt.

They crossed the registration hall of Suvarnabhumi Airport, where Marian was fascinated by the twelve-meter demon statues. Under ornate and gilded costumes, creatures with lavender, turquoise, red, and blue skin peered out. Their wild gazes, half revealed by sunken eye sockets, were complemented by fangs and frightening grimaces. Domed hats towered over their elvish ears; they brandished an array of enormous weapons in their hands.

THE GULL CRY HOTEL

"Perhaps more than anything else, Thais believe in spirits, especially the restless ones." El stopped and lifted an indifferent glance to one of the demons, seeing Marian's interest. "There used to be a cemetery here, right under us, and these guardians were installed to calm the souls of the dead. According to legend, they must not let the spirits from the world of the dead get into the world of the living in case they create another mass grave here."

"Isn't there enough space in Bangkok? Why destroy the cemetery?" protested Marian.

"Come and see for yourself." El smirked and strode towards the exit.

Thailand's air greeted them with nearly a hundred percent humidity and 86-degree heat. Marian took a breath and grabbed on to El. Her lungs hadn't expected this, and she suffered from oxygen deficiency, swiftly causing severe dizziness.

"Are you okay?" El supported her.

"I can't breathe here," she replied weakly. "It's like a real steam room. I'm not even kidding."

"You'll get used to it." El took Marian's bags. "And you'll even come to love this air. You'll see!"

Printed in Great Britain
by Amazon